About the Author

Brittany is a former middle grades science teacher, who graduated from UNC Chapel Hill with degrees in Education and Biology. She lives in North Carolina with her seven cats, who are really just small dragons. She spent over ten years committed to cat rescue before stepping back, allowing more time to write.

Emerald

Brittany Leake

Emerald

Vanguard Press

Vanguard Press is an imprint of
Pegasus Elliot Mackenzie Publishers Ltd.
www.pegasuspublishers.com

First Published in 2025

Vanguard Press
Sheraton House Castle Park
Cambridge England

Printed & Bound in Great Britain

Dedication

For the real Evey. May we meet again at the Rainbow Bridge.

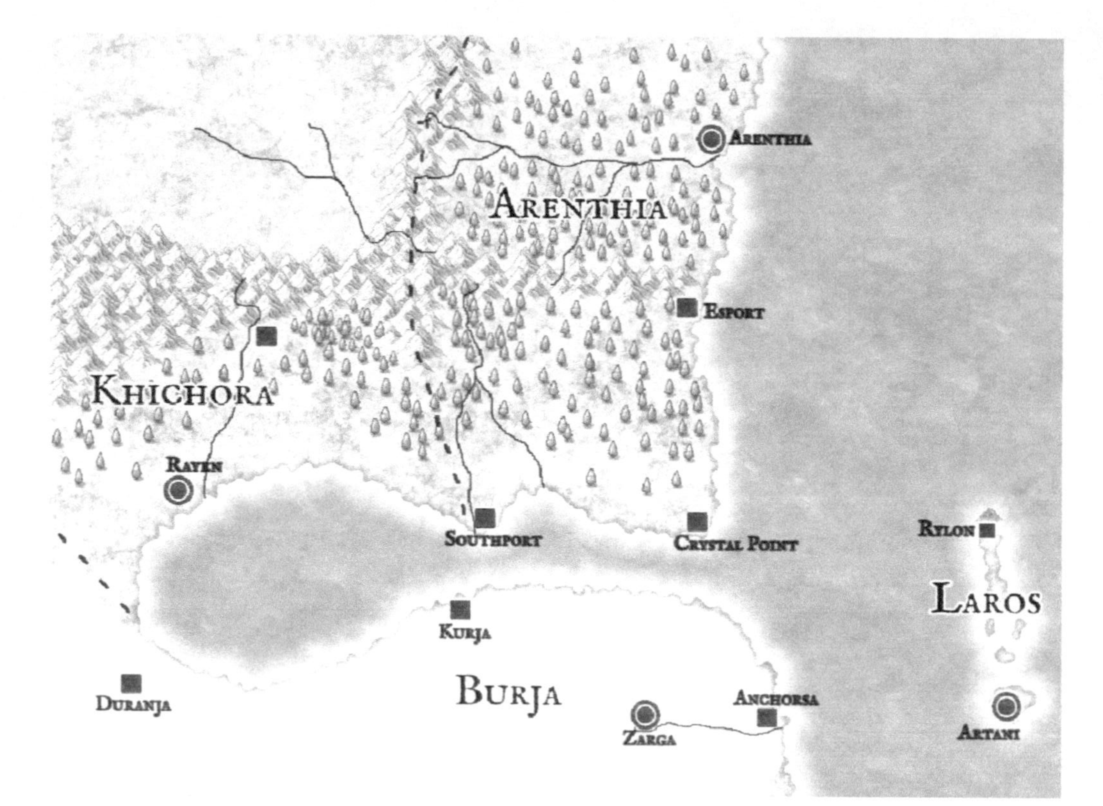

ARENTHIA
ARENTHIA
ESPORT
KHICHORA
RATEN
SOUTHPORT
CRYSTAL POINT
RYLON
LAROS
KURJA
DURANJA
BURJA
ZARGA
ANCHORSA
ARTANI

Prologue

"Breathe, love," Geon whispered gently to his wife, Elyn, as he smoothed the hair back from her hot face. "You're almost there."

Elyn didn't respond, but she inhaled sharply as another pain took her. Geon glanced worriedly at the midwife. She nodded.

Geon's chest tightened. The birth of his first child was thrilling, but completely and utterly terrifying. Watching his wife, the love of his life, in so much pain…it was almost unbearable. He wished he could take the pain away from her, but all he could do was hold her hand and watch. Even then, the midwife didn't seem happy about his presence.

"Elyn, it's almost time," the midwife said calmly, patting his wife gently on the knee. "With your next pain, I want you to push *hard.*"

"We're going to meet our baby very soon," Geon said, squeezing her hand.

She smiled up at him, tired from the last twelve hours of laboring, but she nodded and squeezed back. "It will be a boy," she said firmly. "I know it."

"Always so certain." Geon shook his head. "What if I said I wanted a girl?"

"Well, then you'd be out of luck, because I'm not

doing this again."

Geon kissed her head and smiled. Her grip on his hand tightened, and she gasped.

"That's it," the midwife interrupted. "Now, breathe…and *push.*"

Elyn bore down hard, completely silent, pushing with all her might, her grip on Geon's hand like a vise, until he felt his bones straining.

"Breathe," the midwife called. "I can see the head…relax and wait for the next pain."

She laid back against the pillows of the bed they shared, catching her breath, eyes closed.

"You're doing perfectly," Geon whispered. "It's almost over."

She opened her eyes and looked at him intently. "I love you," she said slowly, smiling slightly. Strands of her hair covered her sweaty red face, but Geon thought she had never looked so beautiful.

"I love you too, Elyn," Geon said, swallowing back emotion. "And this baby will be more loved than any other child in the world."

"Oh!" Elyn gasped, taking another breath and curling forward instinctually.

"That's it," said the midwife. "Yes, here comes the head! Keep going, keep going…"

"Something's wrong," Elyn forced out. "I feel…"

Slowly she relaxed, falling back against the sweat-soaked sheets.

"Elyn?" Geon asked worriedly. He glanced at the midwife, who was frowning.

"Everything is fine, dear," the midwife said, rubbing his wife's leg reassuringly. "You're doing beautifully. One more push like that and your baby's head will be born."

Elyn nodded her head slowly, eyes fluttering closed.

The silence seemed to stretch on forever until Elyn murmured indistinctly and leaned forward.

"That's it, Elyn. One more good push…keep going…almost there…yes! That's the head!" Geon peeked – the midwife held his child's head gently in her hand. His heart leapt.

"Elyn, he's almost here! You're almost done," he said, giving his wife's hand another squeeze.

She squeezed back gently. "Yes, almost done," she whispered.

Geon's head whipped around to look at her face. Her skin looked gray.

"Elyn?" Geon gasped.

She smiled slightly but didn't open her eyes.

"Last push now," the midwife called out.

Elyn frowned and whimpered as her body took over. Within moments, Geon heard a baby's cry. His child. Their child.

"It's a boy," the midwife said quickly. Geon looked away from his wife in time to see her cut the cord and bundle the baby – *his son* – into a clean towel as the baby cried loudly.

"*Hmm*, I told you so," Elyn said, her voice barely more than a whisper.

The midwife practically shoved the newborn into Geon's arms. "Move," she barked abruptly.

Geon watched as she examined Elyn – checking her eyes, taking her pulse, pressing on her still swollen belly. Elyn didn't protest.

"What's happening?" Geon said urgently. Elyn was turning white before his eyes, but he couldn't see much blood.

The midwife glanced at him, her eyes anxious. "I'm not sure," she said quickly. "Something is happening. It's not the birth…she didn't even tear. She's just…fading. Like something is draining the life right out of her." She stood back, shaking her head. "There's nothing I can do."

"What? What do you mean? You have to do SOMETHING!" Geon's heart was pounding, and he gripped his son tightly.

"Sit with her. Hold her hand," the midwife said sadly as she moved aside to make room for Geon.

"Geon…" Elyn whispered.

He leaned close.

"It's…all right." Her eyes fluttered but didn't open. Geon reached out to touch her hand. It was ice cold.

"Our son…" she whispered. "Take care…"

"Everything is fine," Geon choked out. "You're going to be fine. Our son is healthy and beautiful and perfect."

"I know," Elyn breathed. Then she was still.

Geon stopped breathing. The baby stopped crying. The world stopped spinning.

"Elyn?" he finally whispered. Then louder, "Elyn! Elyn, NO!"

The midwife put one hand on his shoulder and the other on Elyn's wrist. She shook her head, and Geon's vision blackened at the edges.

The baby started to squirm and fuss. Geon looked down, staring into the eyes of his son until their vivid blue was the only thing he could see. He took a deep breath.

Another.

In and out.

Reaching up slowly, he offered his child a finger, which the baby gripped tightly. He choked out a sound somewhere between a laugh and a sob.

"Hello, Delan," he whispered.

Chapter 1

"I'm dying," Zhafaera croaked, her head hanging over the railing of the ship.

Delan clamped down on his anxiety and rested a hand on her back, brushing aside her messy hair to better see her face in the thin moonlight. It *was* deathly pale.

"You're not dying, you're just seasick." He tried for a light tone.

Zhafaera looked up at him then, and the glare she gave him could have melted stone. Delan tried not to flinch, but it was a close thing.

"What I meant," he said hurriedly, trying to save himself, "was that you'll be fine once we get there."

Delan tried to sound confident, but quite frankly, he wasn't at all sure that what he said was true. Zhafaera had been sick non-stop since they'd found this ship nearly two weeks ago and hopped aboard with the other refugees from the dragon attack – those few that had lived. It seemed that everyone in the north of Arenthia suddenly wanted to be in the south, and Delan couldn't blame them. He still had nightmares of the pack of dragons – was pack the right word? What did you call a group of dragons? – flying over the capital city, blasting and burning everything in their paths. In the course of a night, the whole city had been practically demolished. It wasn't something Delan ever wanted to see again, but he didn't really have much hope for that. Dragons weren't exactly easy to stop.

Their best chance was currently heaving her guts out over the side of the ship.

Delan held her hair back and moved his other hand to grip her upper arm, steadying her against the wind battering them. The weather had been incredibly rough, and their little ship was definitely looking a bit worse for wear. Traveling in the winter had never been ideal, but now it was downright dangerous. Storm after storm had rolled in, giving them no break from the enormous waves and strong winds whipping the ship around. Zhafaera said it had to do with the fact that her uncle Velexar had tried to extend the summer in the north. He had caused winter to come early in the south, but that apparently hadn't been enough to maintain balance – this weather was the world's way of coping as the north suddenly went from balmy to frozen.

It was no wonder Zhafaera was sick. She certainly wasn't the only one, but she was the worst. He suspected it had to do with what had happened to her while she was Velexar's captive. She'd been half starved already when he found her, weak and drugged. She'd only had a few days to recover before they boarded this ship, and those few days hadn't contained much food either. Rubbing his hand in small circles on her back as she relaxed again and rested her head on the railing, he could feel her spine prominently. As sick as she was, she'd barely been able to eat or drink anything, and the weight she'd lost was truly alarming. Her flaming red hair, usually glossy and long, was now a dull orange and cut to her shoulders, another courtesy of her time in captivity.

We just have to get home, he thought. He'd convinced the captain to head for Crystal Point, his home, assuming it was still standing. They'd had their own dragon attack, but it was just one dragon, and Zhafaera had been able to stop it. Still, it had done quite enough damage in just a bare few minutes. He could only hope a dragon hadn't made a return visit to finish the job.

Thinking of the attack reminded him of Alec, and he quickly pushed the thought away. That didn't stop the guilt or the black hole of grief from opening up in his chest and threatening to burst out. His brother. He'd killed his brother.

It had been instinct, a desperate attempt to stop them all from being burned alive when Alec had transformed into a dragon, but it didn't change the facts or stop the nightmares. Delan's throat burned at the memory, and he could feel the panic rising. Blinking rapidly, he clamped down on his emotions, trying to think of something else. Anything else.

Thankfully, Zhafaera chose that moment to pull back from the railing. Her hands shook as she wiped her eyes and mouth with a dirty handkerchief.

"Better?" Delan asked gently, reaching out to pull her into a hug.

"For now," she said thickly against his chest. Looking up, she met his eyes. "Please, Delan," she whispered, so softly he barely heard it over the wind and waves. "Please, get me off this ship."

"I will," he said. She opened her mouth to speak again, but he beat her to it. "We'll be home soon."

She shook her head. "Delan, I can't make it much longer. We have to get off. Please, we can walk the rest of the way; I don't care, please." She sounded close to tears. She'd asked to get off before, but Delan had never heard her beg like this. Not to anyone, for anything.

He wavered but willed himself to reason with her. "Zhafaera, we can't. We have no supplies, no horses—" his voice caught at that, remembering his horse, Shadow. He cleared his throat. "We could freeze to death before we got anywhere close to Crystal Point, or the dragons could catch up with us." He stroked her hair and pulled her head back to rest on his chest. "We'll be there soon. A couple of days, I promise."

"That's what you said last week," Zhafaera murmured as she shivered against him.

With a sigh, he kissed the top of her head and took her hand, turning and to lead her back below deck. She stumbled, and he quickly wrapped an arm around her waist, ready to catch her if she fell. She'd fainted more than once already during their trip.

Slowly, they moved to the small door that led to the interior of the ship. Bypassing the ladder that would take them down to the hold with the rest of the passengers, they made their way down a short hallway to the captain's quarters. He'd insisted they take it after Delan had told them who they were in order to convince him to change his course to Crystal Point. Originally the ship had been planning to head east to Laros, the country made up of a chain of volcanic islands, but Delan had needed a different direction, and telling him he was the lord's son and Zhafaera the new queen had been the only way to get him to stay a course down the eastern border of Arenthia.

Delan wasn't sure the captain would believe him at first, seeing as how Velexar had claimed that Zhafaera was dead. But growing up, she and her mother, Queen Karaena, had been visible enough that apparently she was more recognizable than he had expected now that Velexar's spell to make the country all but forget them was broken. Before long, the entire ship knew who they were carrying.

It probably helped that even in her weakened state, she exuded a feeling of raw power. Every now and then, Delan could see the Sapphire that was bonded to the flesh over her heart, giving off a faint glow. He wasn't sure if it was supposed to do that – it was supposed to be a secret after all, and he couldn't remember her mother ever glowing – but he had a sinking feeling it was helping to keep her alive at this point. The longer they were on the ship, the more often it seemed to glow. Deep down, he was afraid that she was right – that being on this ship much longer might actually kill her. The thought made him feel incredibly guilty, but he knew this was their least risky option. No way could she walk the rest of the way in her current condition.

Entering the captain's quarters quietly, Delan could just see the outline of a cat on the foot of the bed. Evamoria, the young dragon they'd become responsible for a few months before, had stayed in her black cat form while on the ship. People were terrified by what they'd seen or even heard about that night, and even a "small" dragon was likely to cause a panic. No one paid any attention to a cat on the ship, and Evey had taken up the disguise fully, hunting the rodents she found on the ship. But Delan knew she needed a good meal too. Probably a whole deer by this point.

As Delan helped Zhafaera into bed, one golden yellow eye opened, glowing faintly in the dark room.

How is she? Evey asked in his mind.

Delan gave a tiny shrug in response, not wanting to alert Zhafaera to the fact they were talking about her. They were able to communicate mind-to-mind because he was a Black mage, meaning he couldn't pull magic from the elements like most mages, but he *could* draw through other mages. Delan had only found out about his power a few months ago, so he wasn't exactly missing magic, but he *had* found it useful. Zhafaera was a White mage, able to draw magic from all elements, but she was far too weak to try to pull magic from, and it wouldn't be considered polite to try to pull from either of the other two mages on board. Not to mention it would be dangerous. He was fairly used to pulling from Zhafaera at this point, used to her power; the others were nowhere near as powerful, and he wasn't at all confident that he wouldn't hurt them.

He was somewhat surprised that he could even identify the other mages they were traveling with. Neither of them had openly used magic; Delan could just *feel* it around them and feel what element they had an affinity for. It was a new skill that he hadn't expected but that he filed away in his brain under "useful." Now if only one of them had been a healer.

Climbing into bed next to Zhafaera, he wrapped her into his arms. She was shivering slightly, and he pulled the thin blanket up over them and held her close. Soon her shivering stopped, and her breathing became slow and even. Delan lay awake a long time, just praying that they'd make it home soon.

***

Three days. It took another three days to reach Crystal Point, and if Zhafaera hadn't been so weak by the time they anchored offshore, she would have throttled Delan.

To be fair, she knew it wasn't his fault. The storms had slowed them down to the point where a journey that normally took a week took over two. The two worst weeks of her life, and possibly her last. She felt like death.

She'd never experienced seasickness before, and she now knew why some people avoided sailing by any means necessary. Unable to get away from the heavy rocking motion of the ship, made worse by the storms buffeting them, her nausea just got worse and worse, until her brain felt like it was sloshing in her skull. It was torture.

Then again, she wasn't entirely sure that what she was experiencing was seasickness. She suspected her pregnancy had more than a little to do with how sick she was. She couldn't remember her mother ever talking about it being like this, but perhaps that's why she'd only had one child.

Two children, Zhafaera corrected herself. If Velexar

20

was right, Alec had been her brother. Or at least, her half-brother. Knowing her mother, Zhafaera thought it unlikely that they had the same father. *I won't be like that,* she reminded herself.

Standing on the deck with a blanket around her shoulders as the crew (and a number of refugees who had gotten a crash course in sailing over the last couple of weeks) readied the boats that would take them to shore, Zhafaera glanced at Delan. She hadn't told him yet. She wanted to, but she was nervous. Not because she thought he would leave her, or tell her to get rid of it, or curse her for letting this happen. All of those scenarios had gone through her mind, but they weren't what held her back.

It was more her own feelings about the pregnancy. She knew it took two people, but she still felt guilty, and silly, and stupid about letting it happen. And yet…she was thankful. This baby had saved her from Velexar, had undoubtedly saved her life, and despite everything, she wanted it more than anything. She loved it. And she was afraid of losing it.

She knew her body was starting to give out. The last two days, she'd given up on food entirely and stuck only to water; not ideal, but it meant she vomited less. She'd been too ill for too long, and every day she waited for the bleeding to start. Before they'd gotten on this *gods forsaken* ship, she'd been able to draw enough magic to examine herself. She'd felt it there, a tiny pulse of energy low in her abdomen, and the thrill she felt made her almost giddy. But once they'd set sail, she'd been too sick to use magic at all, and she couldn't tell if that tiny pulse was still there.

All she could feel lately was the pulse of the Sapphire. As her own energy waned, the energy of the Sapphire filled its place, giving her what little strength she had left. It hadn't tried to overwhelm her – once she mastered and bonded it, it seemed content to rest as a comfortable, soothing presence in one corner of her mind.

When the boats were finally ready, she was on the first one, Delan gripping her arm tightly and helping her in. Once the boat was full, Zhafaera held Evey in her lap for warmth and tried to focus on the shore as Delan took up an oar and helped row.

The second she felt the boat touch the sandy bottom, Zhafaera breathed a sigh of relief that nearly became full-blown tears. Several men hopped out and began dragging the boat further up onto the beach, but Zhafaera couldn't wait. She stood, disturbing Evey, and clambered over the side, her feet splashing in the ankle-deep water, hardly caring how cold it was. Stumbling forward out of the water, ignoring the cries behind her, she barely made it to dry sand before she fell to her hands and knees. Lowering her forehead to the cold sand, she took long, deep breaths, trying to stop the sloshing in her brain and stomach.

For the first time in weeks, she reached out magically, spreading her senses out to feel the solid ground beneath her and the energy humming through it. She was too tired to draw more than a trickle to her, but that trickle was enough to ground her. The nausea was still there, but at least she was finally still.

"Zhafaera!" Delan thudded to the ground next to her.

"Are you all right? Can you walk?"

Zhafaera didn't lift her head, enjoying the feel of solid ground too much to move. "Just give me a minute," she murmured.

Delan hesitated, putting a warm hand on her back. "Go on ahead," he said to someone above her. "We'll catch up."

"But, my lord—"

"Don't worry, they'll let you in," Delan said firmly.

Zhafaera had no doubt of that. Their ship wasn't the only one anchored in the deep waters outside the small cove. At the southernmost tip of the continent, it looked as though Crystal Point had become a refugee camp. From the ship, Zhafaera had seen a city of tents outside the walls, and she could imagine it was much the same inside. Lord Geon would never turn anyone away.

By the time Zhafaera lifted her head, their boat was already moving back towards the ship for the next load of passengers. It was already late afternoon, and they would need to get everyone off before it got dark. She supposed some might stay on the ship, but it certainly wouldn't be her.

Delan was still kneeling next to her, looking at her worriedly, and Evey sat next to him, her head tilted to one side.

"I'm okay," she said to them both, taking a deep breath and reaching out to Delan. He helped her stand, and she clung to his arm as dizziness swept through her.

"Do you want me to carry you?" Delan asked carefully. He'd gotten snapped at more than once on the ship for asking that question.

"No, no, I can walk," Zhafaera said, shaking her head to clear the last of the dizziness. They moved slowly across the beach, taking care with each step, until they finally reached the fissure in the cliff that hid the path up to the Keep. Zhafaera was panting slightly.

She looked up the path. It was a long, long way up. And steep. And treacherous. No one else was on the path; they must have already reached the top. She sighed and made to step forward when Delan stopped her.

She looked at him. "Please?" he asked. "I swear, I'll put you down at the top."

Zhafaera looked back to the path. There was no way she'd make it all the way up. Better to save her strength and walk when people could see her.

Looking back at Delan, she nodded, reaching for her to wrap her arms around his neck as he bent and lifted her into his arms.

Resting her head against his warm chest, she drifted.

***

Delan hadn't even broken a sweat by the time he reached the top of the cliff. Zhafaera weighed next to nothing. He wasn't sure if she had fallen asleep or passed out, but he was anxious to get her inside and resting. Hopefully, now that they were off the ship, she'd be able to recover.

Entering through a side door in the wall, Delan paused as he took in the commotion in the courtyard in front of the Keep as the new refugees were welcomed and, presumably, found places to stay. Children clung close to their parents, their eyes wide with both fear and excitement. Delan looked away. Some of them weren't much younger than Alec.

"Delan!"

Delan's head snapped toward the voice. As the crowd parted, he could suddenly see his father sprinting towards them. He'd never been so happy to see him in his life.

Skidding to a stop in front of them, Lord Geon gripped Delan's head between both of his hands. "We thought you—"

"We're okay," Delan said.

His father let go and looked down at Zhafaera, still asleep. His eyes shot back to Delan's. "What happened to her?"

"Velexar captured her. And she's been sick as a dog the whole way back."

Geon frowned. "So you made it to the capital?"

"Yes."

His father looked around. "Alec?"

Delan couldn't speak, and when his father met his eyes again, he just shook his head and looked away.

"I see." The crack in his voice was nearly enough to break Delan. But he focused on what he could do.

"She needs a healer. Do we have any?" He jerked his head to indicate the crowd behind them and the full camp of refugees.

He could feel his father physically shaking himself to pull himself together. "Yes, we do, actually. Several." He waved someone over, but Delan was hardly paying attention. Did Zhafaera look paler?

"Come," Geon said. "We can set her in the library until the healer gets here."

They skirted around the thick crowd until he reached the front door and was surprised to see two guards. One he didn't recognize, but the other was Ban, a big, dark man somewhere in his fifties, and Delan's friend. Originally a guard at the Royal Palace in Arenthia, he'd retired here because the warm, moist air was easier on his joints. Or so he always said. Delan's brain tripped up seeing him again – another puzzle piece fitting into place. What if Ban had *really* been left here to guard Alec?

He didn't have time to think it through before Ban clapped a hand on his shoulder and ruffled his hair. "Delan! You made it!" He looked down as if noticing Delan's arms were full for the first time. "And the Princess. We thought—" he cut off abruptly, meeting Geon's gaze before looking out over the growing crowd of people milling through the courtyard. "Come, come inside."

Zhafaera didn't stir when Delan eased her onto the sofa in front of the library fire and took a seat on the floor next to her, leaning his head back against the armrest. Evey curled up next to Zhafaera, and his father took a seat in an armchair across from them, looking at the cat curiously. They were silent for a long time.

"So Velexar is…"

"Dead."

"And the Sapphire?"

Delan tapped his own chest to indicate where

Zhafaera had bonded it. "She has it."

"That's good."

Please don't ask what happened to Alec. Delan thought.

As if he'd heard the thought, Geon said, "You picked up a stray cat along the way?"

Delan hesitated and looked at Evey. She gave a slight twitch of her tail. *Go ahead,* she said.

"Dad," Delan said slowly, "she's a—" Delan was cut off by a small knock and the sound of the door opening. A man dressed in plain clothes with a silver collar around the base of his throat stood in the doorway. The healer.

"I was told to come here…" He trailed off as he saw Zhafaera on the couch. He hurried forward, moving around the sofa to get a better look at her.

"What happened?" He shot a look at Delan, as if he'd done something, then turned back to Zhafaera. His eyes widened. "Is this…?"

As soon as his hand touched her forehead, there was a bright flash of blue, and the healer jerked back as if burned. Zhafaera sat bolt upright, gasping for breath as she stared wildly around. When her gaze landed on the mage, she pushed herself as far back into the couch as she could, throwing one hand across her belly and the other out in front of her, warding him off.

"Don't touch me," she hissed venomously. "Don't you dare touch me."

Delan was shocked at her reaction. "Zhafaera, he's a healer, let him look at you…" But she was already shaking her head.

"No."

"Zhafaera—"

"I said *no.*"

The healer had stepped back and was shaking out his hand. "That was a good shock you gave me," he said, his voice light but laced with pain. He met Zhafaera's gaze. "I can't force you, but I strongly suggest you let someone look at you." He paused, frowning. "It doesn't have to be me."

Zhafaera took a breath, visibly trying to calm herself. She glanced at Delan, and he reached out and took her hand. "Please?" he asked. "For me? I'm worried about you," he whispered.

She bit her lip. Looking back to the healer, she shuddered. "Fine," she said roughly. "But it has to be a woman."

As the healer rushed out of the room, ice settled in Delan's belly. He'd tried not to think about it, but now, her reaction to a strange man touching her…the ice turned to heat as anger flooded his body, thinking about what Velexar must have done to her. He clenched his free hand to keep it from shaking with rage.

"Can I go to my room?" Zhafaera asked abruptly. "I'd rather see a healer there."

"Yes, of course—" Delan began.

His father interrupted. "Actually, your room is occupied at the moment." Delan frowned but said nothing. Who could possibly be here that would be given Zhafaera's room? It was one of only three with its own washroom and therefore reserved for special guests.

"Come on," he said. "We can go to my room." He glanced at his father. "Unless that one is occupied too?"

He shook his head. "Of course not. But if she's taking your room, do you want—" he stopped and looked from Delan to Zhafaera and back again, smiling slightly. "Nevermind."

Delan flushed, embarrassed but not arguing, and stood. He bent to lift Zhafaera, but she stopped him with a hand on his chest.

"I can walk," she said tiredly.

Chapter 2

By the time they reached the second-floor landing, Zhafaera was regretting her decision to walk. But by then she was committed. By sheer force of will, she made it to the third floor, ready to collapse on the bed – *Delan's bed* – and almost walked smack into someone.

"Sorry," she mumbled, stepping back and nearly falling back down the stairs. Delan's arm was around her waist and holding her safely to him before she could blink.

Looking up, she saw a very attractive woman with long, blond hair and green eyes. She was tall, much taller than Zhafaera, nearly Delan's height. She was dressed in a long woolen gown in a blue that contrasted nicely with her eyes. Standing in front of them, her mouth hung slightly open, ruining her overall polished appearance. She quickly recovered herself and broke into a huge smile, showing off perfectly straight, white teeth. Zhafaera had a feeling they'd found who was staying in "her" room.

"Delan!" she cried, leaning past Zhafaera to place a kiss on each of his cheeks. Zhafaera saw red. "It's so good to see you; it's been *ages*!"

To his credit, Delan was beet red, his eyes darting around like he was looking for an exit, and Zhafaera felt slightly mollified. She turned her attention to figuring out who this woman was. She was clearly a noble; therefore,

Zhafaera should know her. It had been over four years since her last Tour with her mother, but…

"Esla Cordon, is that you?" Zhafaera said as cheerfully as she could manage.

Esla blinked at her. Then went dead white. "Princess," she said, inclining her head. "I hardly recognized you."

"Queen, now, actually," she said coolly. "In fact, I believe I have a crown here somewhere…" She patted at her dress. With effort, she reached out to Delan's mind. *Your ex-lover, am I right?*

"I have it," Delan whipped the crown they'd found in her mother's room out of an inner pocket and placed it delicately on her head, his eyes wide. Not *my lover*. His voice was faint in her mind, but she heard it.

Zhafaera winked at him, her jealousy fading at his vehemence, and looked back to Esla. "I hear you supported my uncle's *illegitimate* claim to the throne."

Esla gasped and dropped her gaze. "We thought you were dead," she said to the floor.

"Not yet," Zhafaera said. "But not for a lack of effort from my enemies."

She let the silence stretch, somewhat enjoying watching the other woman squirm. Delan was the one to break the silence.

"What are you doing here, Esla?"

"Our manor burned months ago, along with most of the rest of the town." She met Zhafaera's gaze and didn't look away. "A dragon. I believe it was looking for someone."

Guilt burned in Zhafaera's belly. The inn. The *one*

time they'd stayed at an inn had been only days after leaving Crystal Point. When assassins had shown up in the middle of the night to capture Zhafaera, they'd barely made it out in time. They'd heard the dragon and the fire from the woods as they'd left and put as much distance between them and the town as possible. They hadn't gone back to help.

"Anyway," Esla said, looking back to Delan and recovering her smile somewhat, "we've been here ever since! Our people helped rebuild the village here, and just in time too, what with all these refugees after the…" She stopped. No one liked to talk about the dragon attack, it seemed.

"Right, well, thank you," Delan said awkwardly. "But Zhafaera really needs to lie down." His hand still firmly around her waist, he moved her around Esla, and they headed down the hall. Zhafaera forced herself not to look back, and she soon heard the sound of footsteps moving down the stairs.

When they reached his room, Delan opened the door and moved quickly inside, pulling Zhafaera with him. Closing the door, he spun to face her, his face anxious.

"She wasn't my lover," he said hurriedly. "A couple of years ago, she got it in her head that she wanted to marry me, and she *wouldn't leave me alone.* I got piles of letters. She and her brother would show up here and—"

"Delan," Zhafaera held up a hand to stop the flow of words. "It's okay. I don't care what you had with her." It was almost the truth. Or at least, it *should* have been the truth.

He reached up to cup her face with one hand. "I just want to be sure you know that I was never interested in her." He leaned forward and kissed her gently on the lips. "Just you."

Zhafaera smiled, the last traces of her jealousy fading away. "Good," she whispered.

He kissed her again on the forehead. "Come on, come lay down on the bed."

"I'm so tired I can't even make a joke out of that," Zhafaera said as she sat and eased herself back against the pillows.

Evey hopped up next to her. *I like beds.*

"Me too, Evey. Me too." Zhafaera sighed, relaxing into the comfort and closing her eyes.

A knock at the door broke her moment, and her eyes snapped open.

"Come in," Delan called.

Zhafaera tensed as the door opened but relaxed somewhat when two women walked in. The first was an older woman with steel gray hair wrapped in a bun and a plump figure. She didn't wear the silver collar of a healer, but Zhafaera could feel her power just the same. When her brown eyes fell on Zhafaera, they instantly narrowed, and her mouth thinned into a hard line. *Gods, just how bad do I look?*

The other woman was really only a girl. Her long black hair was braided tightly behind her head. She had the same roundness to her face as the older woman, the same brown eyes, and Zhafaera thought she might be her daughter. *Granddaughter,* Zhafaera thought, reassessing the difference in age. The girl carried an enormous black leather bag, following her grandmother to Zhafaera's bedside and setting it down next to her as the older woman sat next to Zhafaera on the bed. Zhafaera had never known a healer to carry a bag like that; usually they relied only on their magic. She was curious now.

"I'm Aroha," the healer said, offering her hand to Zhafaera. Zhafaera took it; she wasn't sure she'd ever shaken hands with anyone before. Usually they just bowed. Then she realized the woman had two fingers over her wrist, taking her pulse. "And this is my granddaughter and apprentice, Darcia," she said, indicating the young woman with her free hand. She curtsied.

"I'm Zhafaera."

Aroha smiled. "Yes, I know who you are," she said, inclining her head slightly. She released Zhafaera's hand. "And your pulse is racing out of control." She eyed her appraisingly. "Are you nervous?"

"A little." Zhafaera glanced at Delan, who was leaning against the wall, watching the healers work, but looking ready to step in if Zhafaera freaked out again.

"Don't be," Aroha said gently. "We're here to help you. You, boy," she barked suddenly, startling everyone. Delan stood up straight as she turned to face him.

"Yes?"

"Make yourself useful. We need a pitcher of water, a pot of tea with honey, and something for her to eat." Delan looked to Zhafaera in surprise.

"I couldn't possibly eat," Zhafaera said, her stomach roiling at the thought.

"By the time I'm finished with you, you will," Aroha said firmly. "Now hurry," she said to Delan.

Delan waited until Zhafaera gave the tiniest nod of her head, and then disappeared from the room at speed. Evey darted out the door behind him, no doubt hoping to find a meal of her own.

As soon as the door closed, the healer turned to Zhafaera. "First things first – is there anything you want to tell me?"

Zhafaera hesitated only a moment. "I'm pregnant," she blurted out.

Aroha nodded. "I figured as much when I heard you asked for a woman. Nausea? Dizziness? Any fainting?"

"Yes," Zhafaera said. "The nausea is the worst. I was sick the whole way down from the capital. I–I fainted a couple of times on the ship, but I thought that was just because I'd been so ill."

"Darcia," Aroha started. But the girl was already pulling out a large amber vial of liquid and a small cup from the black bag. "Good girl," Aroha started.

Pouring a small amount of the liquid – which turned out to be a dirty-looking green – into the cup, she handed it to Zhafaera and said, "Drink."

Zhafaera's stomach squirmed – the color didn't make it look very appealing. "I've never known a healer to use herbs," she said.

"You're stalling," Aroha said flatly. "Drink."

Zhafaera drank the liquid in one gulp. Surprisingly, it didn't taste as bad as it looked. As soon as she felt it hit her stomach, her nausea vanished. She melted into the pillows in relief.

"Better?"

"Much." Zhafaera eyed the bottle of the miracle liquid. "Can I keep that?"

"Yes, at least for now. I want to make sure we keep the nausea under control. You need to eat. You're incredibly underweight."

"I know."

There was a pause. "You were held captive?" Aroha asked.

"Yes."

"How long?"

"Ultimately, about four weeks."

Another, longer pause as Aroha held her gaze. "Were you raped?" Her voice was gentle.

Zhafaera's throat tightened at the memory of Velexar's hands on her. "No," she said, but her voice shook slightly.

Aroha noticed. "Do you want to talk about it?"

"I—" Zhafaera shook her head. "I wasn't raped. But he–he would have. But I was already pregnant."

Aroha's face was grim. Darcia looked shocked. "Do you know how far along you are?"

"The healer that Velexar had examine me said—"

"A male healer?" Aroha interrupted.

"Yes."

She tutted. "They have no business with pregnant women."

Zhafaera didn't know what to say. She felt validated, and that in itself was a relief.

"Now," Aroha said briskly. "How far along?"

Zhafaera cleared her throat and shook her head back, shaking off the memories. "About ten weeks, as near as I can figure."

Aroha met her gaze and held it. "I will ask this once. Do you want to keep it?"

"Yes," Zhafaera answered immediately. She looked away, crossing her arms over her belly. "I–I know we're in a war, and it's not the right time, and I really shouldn't—"

The healer cut her off. "It has nothing to do with should or shouldn't. It is only about what *you* want."

"I want it," Zhafaera whispered.

Aroha simply nodded and moved on. "Lord Delan is the father?"

Zhafaera blushed. "Yes."

"Have you told him?"

She shook her head.

"You should. You need the support."

"I know," Zhafaera said, somewhat irritated. "I just haven't been able to find the right time."

"If you wait for the perfect moment, you'll have delivered by the time he figures it out, and that will be quite a shock."

Zhafaera actually laughed. "I'll tell him soon."

"Good. Now, may I examine you?" She waited patiently as Zhafaera fought her anxiety.

Zhafaera took a breath. "Yes, I'm ready."

"All right then. Try to relax." She placed one hand on Zhafaera's forehead and the other over her belly, and they both closed their eyes.

Zhafaera could feel the magic flowing through her, questing, moving through every inch of her body looking for injuries. Zhafaera felt the Sapphire's energy rise up through her, investigating this new magic. Aroha paused.

"What is—"

Zhafaera pulled down the neck of her dress just enough to reveal the Sapphire nestled between her breasts.

Aroha inhaled sharply. "So it is real."

"Yes. Is it fighting you?"

"Not exactly. It's just…odd. Like it's following me." Aroha sounded mildly disconcerted.

Zhafaera reached out with her mind and followed the tendrils of the Sapphire's energy through her body, soothing it and bringing it under her control. "Try now," she said.

Aroha continued her examination, and Zhafaera felt her relax. After a while, Zhafaera could feel the bulk of her magic hovering around her belly. She reached out with a tiny tendril of the Sapphire's energy. There. The tiny pulse. It was still there. She breathed a sigh of relief just as Aroha pulled away.

Zhafaera opened her eyes, grinning.

Aroha smiled back at her. "Yes, you're still pregnant. But you're severely weakened." Her mouth pressed into a thin line. "I have to warn you – you're still pregnant now, and things seem stable enough, but in your condition…I can't guarantee that you won't miscarry."

Zhafaera swallowed the lump in her throat. It was what she was afraid of, but it wasn't unexpected.

She nodded. "What can I do?" she asked hoarsely.

"You need to rest and eat," the healer ordered. "Beyond that, there's not much I can do. It's up to your body to recover from this." She indicated the vial of anti-nausea liquid. "And I want you to drink one cupful of this every twelve hours to control the nausea. We can try weaning you off of it in a few days and see if the nausea has eased now that you're off the ship, but for now, I want you to take it regularly."

A tentative knock on the door interrupted them. Darcia scurried to open it.

Delan stood in the doorway, carrying a tray laden with food. Suddenly Zhafaera was starving.

"Start slowly," Aroha said as Delan set the tray on the bedside table. She poured Zhafaera some tea. "Start with this and let it settle. Then move on to the rest." She indicated the bowl of stew and hunk of bread. "It's all right if you don't eat all of it. Just eat what you can."

Zhafaera was already sipping her tea. It was wonderful, and she could already feel the energy slipping into her veins. Real energy, not the magical energy that had been sustaining her for weeks. She sighed happily.

"I want you on bed rest," Aroha continued. "That means you do not get out of this bed for anything except to relieve yourself."

Zhafaera blanched. Stay in bed? "But I have to—"

"You don't have to do anything but rest right now, if you want to live." She gave her a pointed look. Then she turned her intense gaze on Delan, who wilted just slightly. "Lord Delan, see that she stays in that bed until I return to check on her in the morning. Anything she needs, have someone fetch it." Delan nodded, a determined look on his face.

Zhafaera refused to pout. She knew it was probably for the best, but dammit, she didn't like being confined. "Can I at least bathe?" she asked, more sharply than she intended. She liked Aroha.

The healer eyed her appraisingly. "I would like to say no, but I know you'll just do it anyway. And truth be told, you'll probably feel better for it." She pointed a finger at Zhafaera. "You may bathe, but then straight back into this bed. Understood?"

"I promise."

"Good." She moved towards the door, closely followed by Darcia.

As soon as the door closed behind them, Delan was at her side. "What did she say?" he asked worriedly.

"She said I'm fine," Zhafaera said soothingly. "I'm just weak and malnourished." *And pregnant,* she thought. But the words stuck in her throat. "I just need rest and food." She tried for a reassuring smile.

Delan reached out and smoothed her hair. "You eat, and I'll draw you a bath."

Those were quite possibly the best words Zhafaera had ever heard.

Chapter 3

Delan was halfway through pumping water into the tub in the washroom when there was another timid knock on the door. He stopped pumping and moved to open it. A young servant girl stood there, holding a stack of towels.

"Um, Mistress Aroha sent me to help, um, the Queen?" She was so nervous she couldn't meet Delan's gaze.

"Come in," he said gently. "I've almost finished drawing her bath. I'm sure she'd appreciate the help." He could feel the disgruntled look Zhafaera was giving to his back.

The girl set down her towels and moved like a whirlwind around the room – first getting a fire started in the small stone fireplace, then lighting candles around the room to ward off the darkness that was now falling outside, and finally scurrying to the washroom and taking over pumping the water. Delan moved over to the bed, where Zhafaera was now sitting on the edge.

"Will you be OK if I leave you here with her? I need to find my father," he said quietly.

Zhafaera scoffed. "Of course I will. There's no need to hover, I'm fine." She took his hand and squeezed it. "Truly, I'm feeling better already."

Delan didn't want to leave her, but she *did* look

brighter. And his father deserved an explanation.

"Your Highness – I mean – Your Majesty?" The girl was peeking out from behind the door to the washroom. "Your bath is ready."

Zhafaera stood, Delan ready to catch her if she stumbled, but she seemed steady on her feet. As she entered the washroom, she called over her shoulder, "Out! Go find your father."

Delan left, making his way towards the stairs and heading down. He assumed that at this time of the evening, his father would be in the library. Dinner had finished some time ago; Delan had managed to grab something for Zhafaera just as the cooks and servants were finishing clearing away the meal. Apparently, there were enough important people in the castle to warrant using the formal dining room, something they hadn't done in *years*. Not since the last time the royal entourage had visited. Delan wondered about their provisions with all the refugees.

When Delan reached the library, the door was open a crack, and he could hear voices. One voice in particular. Peeking through the crack, he could see Esla and her brother Elden sitting on the sofa, their backs to him, talking with his father.

Geon made eye contact with him, but before he could acknowledge his presence, Delan jerked away from the door and backed away slowly. He wanted to avoid those two at any cost, and besides, he couldn't talk with his father in front of them. Not for what he needed to say.

Moving back towards the stairs, he decided to go back to his room. He wasn't *hiding* per say, he just…wanted to check on Zhafaera. He knew his father would be up late – he could speak to him later. Delan tried not to feel relieved that he didn't have to talk about it yet. What would his father think of him when he learned what happened?

The minute he opened the door to his room, he knew something was wrong. Crying – no *sobbing* – was coming from the washroom. Delan darted across the room and burst into the washroom to see Zhafaera in the tub, her arms wrapped around her knees and her frail body wracked with sobs. The servant girl sent to help her looked petrified.

"What happened?" he asked, rushing forward and dropping to his knees next to the tub.

"I don't know, my Lord. As soon as she got in the tub, she just started—"

But Delan wasn't listening. He'd barely been gone five minutes, and this happened. "Zhafaera, what's wrong?" He placed a hand on her shoulder, and she jerked, startled. Her head shot up, her tear-streaked face turning to him. With another loud sob, she released her knees and threw her arms around his neck, sloshing water over the side of the tub. Wrapping his arms around her, he held her as she continued to cry.

"Let me fetch the healer back," he began.

"Nooo," Zhafaera moaned. "I don't…need…"

"What's wrong?"

"I…I don't…know…"

Delan caught the eye of the servant. "It's okay, you can go," he said quietly.

"Do you want me to get Mistress Aroha?"

Delan looked back at Zhafaera. She didn't seem to be hurt. "No, not yet. I'll send for her if we need her."

The girl nodded and vanished through the door.

Delan held Zhafaera while she cried, stroking her hair soothingly, but not speaking. By the time her sobs began to change into slow, shaky breaths, the bathwater was lukewarm. Finally, she released him, wiping her face with her hands.

"I'm sorry," she said thickly, not meeting his eyes.

He kept a hand on her thin shoulder. "Don't be. What happened? What was that about?"

She took another shaky breath but still wouldn't look at him. "I don't know." She held her breath, as if waiting for the right words to come. "I just…you left, and I had this – this overwhelming feeling that you wouldn't be back. And then everything just sort of hit me at once, and I–I just – I fell apart, I guess." She shrugged.

Delan reached out and took her chin in his free hand, turning her to face him. Her face was red, and not just from crying. "It's okay, Zhafaera, you don't have anything to be embarrassed about. After what you've been through—"

"That girl must think I'm a mess," Zhafaera interrupted, grimacing.

Delan shook his head. "It doesn't matter what she thinks. And by the way, I think she was too terrified that she'd done something to cause it to think much beyond that. She practically ran out of here." He brushed her wet hair off of her face. "But Zhafaera, you know I'm not going anywhere."

"I know," she whispered. "It was stupid. I just – I

don't know. I panicked."

Delan's heart squeezed. She rarely admitted any vulnerability, even to him. "Come on, lie back," he said gently, releasing her chin and easing her back into the water. "Let's get you washed and into bed."

She nodded and didn't protest as he rolled up his sleeves and picked up the soap. He worked on her hair first, working up a lather and kneading his fingers down to the scalp. He could feel her relaxing with each gentle motion. When he'd finished, he leaned her forward and used a pitcher by the side of the tub to rinse her hair, then picked up a sponge and worked soap into it. Running it quickly over her back, he tried to ignore her spine and ribs visible under her skin.

Finished with her back, he let her lean back against the tub again. "Can you do the rest?" he asked quietly. She may have been naked in front of him, but it wasn't sexual, and he didn't want to make her uncomfortable.

She nodded and took the sponge from him. She finished the job quickly, the water rapidly cooling and turning a dark shade of gray as she scrubbed off the grime.

"Can you hand me—" Before she could finish her sentence, Delan was already helping her stand, holding out a towel for her and wrapping it around her. She was shivering slightly.

Delan steadied her as she dried herself off and offered her a second towel for her hair and unplugged the bathtub, letting the water drain through another pipe in the floor. It was full dark outside now, and the only light came from a handful of candles in the room. Leading her back out to the bedroom, he sat her in the armchair close to the fire so she could warm up while he found her something to wear. They hadn't yet had a chance to fetch her any clothes, so some of his would have to do. Pulling out a loose shirt, he helped her dress quickly. The shirt swamped her, but it would work for now.

"Come on, let's get you back in bed," he said, trying to help her up.

"Not just yet," Zhafaera protested. She shivered. "I'm just warming up." She pulled her legs under her on the chair and snuggled closer to the fire.

Delan sighed and pulled a blanket from the basket near the fire, wrapping it over her. "How about this? I'm going to take my own bath, and when I'm done, you'll get in bed? Deal?"

"Yes," Zhafaera said, giving him a weak smile before turning back to the fire.

Delan washed as quickly as he could, listening for Zhafaera the whole time. She didn't make a sound. Her outburst had scared him, but he really couldn't blame her. Hells, half the time, he wanted to do the same thing.

By the time he climbed out of the tub, it felt like he'd lost half his weight in grime. It was wonderful. After cleaning his teeth, he hurried into the bedroom to dress. Zhafaera hadn't moved from her position in front of the fire, and her eyes were closed. He dressed quickly and moved over to her, torn between waking her and getting her into bed as the healer had instructed.

"I'm not asleep," she murmured, opening her eyes.

Delan leaned down and kissed the top of her head.

"You were peeking, weren't you?" he said teasingly.

She grinned up at him. "Maybe just a little. I had a good view." There. There was that familiar spark in her eyes that he'd been missing. The light that made her Zhafaera.

He stole a kiss on the lips, then reached under her and lifted her into his arms. She squeaked.

"Put me down, I can walk!"

"You keep saying that. But since you've been breaking the rules by being out of bed, which Mistress Aroha specifically tasked *me* with keeping you in, meaning I'm likely the one to get wholloped if she finds out, I think the least you could do is let me carry you back to bed. Besides, we're already here." Delan was grinning as he set her on the bed.

Zhafaera masked a smile and scurried under the covers. Delan went around to the other side and climbed in next to her, pulling her close with her back to him. Breathing in the scent of her, he finally started to relax.

"Did you find your father?" she asked. "You weren't gone very long."

"He was busy," Delan said. "I'll talk to him later."

"Oh," Zhafaera said quietly.

"Gods, it's good to be in a real bed again." Delan knew he was changing the subject, but he didn't want to think about that conversation.

Zhafaera sighed. "Especially one that's not rocking."

"Feeling better?"

"Much."

"Good. For a while there, I really thought you were

trying to die on me." Delan tried to keep his tone light, but really, he wasn't joking.

Zhafaera tensed slightly. "I told you, we're hard to kill once we bond the Sapphire. It doesn't give us up without a fight." She paused. "Unless it kills us itself."

"That's not likely, is it?" Delan felt a flash of concern. Not that he could do anything about it.

"No, it likes me." He could hear Zhafaera's smile. "We've bonded well."

It was still odd for Delan to think of the Sapphire as something relatively sentient. It was a gem after all. But the way Zhafaera spoke of it, as if it were another person, almost…he was trying to wrap his brain around it.

"Can I ask you something?" Delan said tentatively.

"You just did." There was amusement in her voice, but she sounded tired.

"The Sapphire shocked the first healer earlier. The man."

"That wasn't a question." She no longer sounded amused.

"Why?"

***

Zhafaera froze, fully awake now. Here it was – the question she'd been dreading. The one that would lead to a *very* difficult conversation.

"Zhafaera, are you all right?" Delan asked, his voice laced with concern.

"I…I'm not sure what to tell you. It didn't like him."

"Why not?"

"Because *I* didn't like him."

Delan was quiet for a time. "I know something happened to you while Velexar held you captive," he finally said quietly. Zhafaera stopped breathing. "Do you want to tell me about it?"

"Not really," she whispered, closing her eyes against the memories.

"That's okay," he said softly. "It's just – I want to be here for you."

Zhafaera stayed silent, struggling to keep her breathing even. She wanted to just let it go. Go to sleep and let the moment pass. But she couldn't. Delan deserved to know the truth.

"He didn't rape me," she finally managed to get out. The next words were harder. "But he wanted to. He would have."

She felt Delan stiffen next to her and could feel the anger rolling off of him in waves. "That bastard. You're his niece."

"And my mother was his sister," she said coldly. "That didn't stop him from raping and bonding her."

Delan made a choking sound. "What do you mean, he 'bonded' her? Like you bonded the Sapphire?"

"Similar, but more difficult to do with another human being. We have a stronger sense of self, and ultimately, bonding is about merging the core of who you are with that of another."

"But why?" She could tell Delan was working hard to control his tone, but his voice was tight with anger.

"It's about control. When you bond another person, you can control them completely. At least if the ritual is done properly." Now that she'd started, she couldn't stop. "It's forbidden magic, for obvious reasons. It involves an intimate blood ritual. Four years ago, Velexar tried to bond my mother. And he mostly succeeded but couldn't complete the ritual. Not enough to give him total control. She fought him, and it's why, four years ago, she withdrew from the world." Zhafaera paused for a breath. "It was only when he told her he intended to bond me that she almost broke free. And he killed her."

Delan was quiet, processing what she'd said. "Why did he want to bond you?"

"He couldn't bond the Sapphire himself," she said. "It didn't like him, so it was too dangerous. It would have destroyed him. So he needed to be able to control someone who *could* bond the Sapphire. Me."

"Why couldn't he complete the ritual with your mother?" Delan asked. "Why didn't he bond *you*?"

Zhafaera had to give it to him; he was persistent. She rolled over to face him, meeting his eyes in the light from the fire. "Are you sure you want to know?"

"Yes," he said without hesitation.

She braced herself. "My mother couldn't get pregnant." The words tumbled out in a rush. "One way to seal the ritual, the one that gives the strongest bond, involves a child between the…the participants. And ultimately, the sacrifice of that child."

Delan's eyes closed, and his mouth twisted. "That's—"

"Disgusting, I know. There's a reason it's forbidden."

"And he was going to—"

"Yes." Zhafaera laid a hand on Delan's chest and felt his heart pounding. "He touched me, but he didn't rape me. He couldn't."

They were both silent for a long time. Zhafaera waited. He was close – so close to the truth.

"Because you were more powerful than him?" Delan finally asked. He sounded like the words were pulled from him by force.

"No," Zhafaera shook her head, her pulse quickening. "My mother was more powerful than he ever was. It has nothing to do with that."

"Then what?" He paused. "What don't you want to tell me?"

"I'm pregnant," she blurted, almost before he'd finished his sentence.

Silence.

"What?"

"You heard me," Zhafaera whispered, looking down at her hand on his chest, avoiding his gaze.

"But you said…you just said he didn't—"

"He didn't, it's not his." She spoke quickly, still not looking at him. "Delan, I was *already* pregnant when I was captured."

Delan went dead still, the only sound in the room the crackling of the fire, unnaturally loud in the complete and utter silence. Her hand was still on his chest, and she could feel his heart rate ticking up…and up, and up, until it was flat out racing. The silence stretched until she couldn't stand it anymore. Pulling away, she made to roll over, away from him, before the tears she could feel building could start to fall.

"Don't," he whispered, tightening his grip and pulling her hard to him. His breathing was ragged in her ear.

"Delan, I—"

"I love you," he breathed.

Zhafaera let out the breath she hadn't realized she'd been holding. With it came the tears, though thankfully silent this time. Throwing one arm around him, she burrowed closer, her forehead pressed into his chest.

"I love you, too," she choked out.

Pulling back just enough to slip his arm between them, he lifted her chin, drawing her up to face him. She didn't have a chance to decipher the emotions she saw there before he was kissing her hard. His hand moved into her hair, brushing away a tear as it went, his other arm underneath her, and gripping her tightly. Relaxing into him, she opened her mind and let his emotions flood in. It was happiness and relief and a deep warmth that could only be love. There was also fear, tightly controlled, and traces of anger, but not at her. Suddenly, he pulled back, breathing hard.

"What?" Zhafaera said, breathless.

"Stop that." He loosened his grip but didn't let her go. "I could feel you poking around."

She gave a small shrug, defensive. "I wanted to know what you were feeling."

"That's cheating." But he was grinning.

"It was less poking around and more like opening a

door you were trying to beat down."

"That's fair," he said. He bent his head and kissed her again, much more gently this time, but no less passionately.

"Why didn't you tell me before?" he asked softly when they broke apart again.

Zhafaera shrugged and tried to roll away again, but Delan wouldn't let her. "I don't know, I just – I couldn't find the right time."

"We were stuck on a ship for over two weeks with nothing to do but talk, and you couldn't find the right time?"

She shoved him slightly. "There were either people around, or I was hurling my guts up over the side. Didn't quite seem like the right moment."

Zhafaera saw the exact moment that realization dawned on him, and she suppressed a giggle. "You weren't seasick."

"Well, it certainly didn't help."

"Gods, will it be like that the whole time?" He looked worried.

"No," Zhafaera said quickly. She didn't even want to entertain the idea. "Thankfully the medicine the healer gave me stopped the nausea right away, and she left the bottle." Delan looked briefly over his shoulder at the bedside table, where the large vial sat. "Besides, it should stop on its own as I progress."

"How far along are you?" She could see Delan's mind trying to count backwards.

"About ten weeks."

His eyes widened. "First time lucky then, I guess," he said with a grin.

She rolled her eyes, then looked at him seriously. "Listen, there's something else—"

"You're having twins?" he joked.

"No! Stop, be serious," she scolded. Her giddiness fell away. "Look, I'm not in the best shape here." Delan's face grew somber. "The healer said everything is okay for now, but, well, I could still miscarry. It's why she wants me on bedrest."

Delan's face was worried. "But *you'll* be okay?"

Her face must have shown the hurt she felt at his lack of concern for the baby. "No, I didn't mean – I mean, I *want* this baby, but *you* are the priority. You have to be," he said softly.

Zhafaera hesitated. "The healer asked…she asked if I wanted to get rid of it."

Delan went still again. "What did you say?"

"I know we're just at the start of this war. I know it's not the right time. I feel silly for letting it happen." She wrapped an arm around her waist and held up a hand as Delan opened his mouth. "But I *want* it. It's mine."

"It's *ours*," Delan whispered into her ear, pulling her close again.

Chapter 4

Delan wasn't sure how long he'd been lying next to Zhafaera. Her breathing had become slow and steady some time ago, and he knew she was asleep. Delan couldn't sleep. His mind was racing, and aside from that, he still needed to talk to his father.

Zhafaera shifted in his arms, and Delan reluctantly let her go as she rolled over away from him. Getting up quietly, he dug out a heavy robe and a pair of slippers and crept out of the room.

Evey was sitting in the hallway. *Where are you going?*

To find my father, Delan told her, glancing down the hall towards Geon's room. There was no firelight flickering under the door, so he was either already asleep or still in the library. *How long were you waiting there?* He asked Evey.

Not long. I was trying to figure out how to open the door without drawing attention.

Sorry. Delan frowned. *I would say we could leave it open a crack for you, but Zhafaera needs –* he looked back at his door. *Actually, she needs a door that locks.* They'd never really had a need for locks in the castle before. They had a handful of guards, but Crystal Point was a *safe* place. Now, with this many people…it just made him nervous.

He looked at Evey, meeting her green eyes that

weren't *quite* that of a cat. *Do you want to go in with her or come with me?* He wasn't sure which option he preferred. He'd feel better with Evey guarding Zhafaera, but there were things that would be easier to show his father than tell.

I'll come with you, Evey said, trotting off down the hallway like a shadow.

Delan followed Evey, and together they made their way silently down the stairs. The library was just across the hall, and Delan could see light coming from under the door. He took a deep breath and knocked lightly.

"Come in," Lord Geon called.

Delan hesitated before gritting his teeth and pushing open the heavy wooden door. His father was already on his feet and moving towards him before Delan had fully entered the room. Not slowing, he threw out his arms and wrapped Delan in a tight hug. Delan returned it just as fiercely; he'd missed his father. Emotions swirled and rose in him, cracking the tight lid he had on his grief and letting it spew forth. Before he knew it, tears were falling, his chest felt as if it were caving in, and he was clinging to his father as he hadn't since…since he was Alec's age. His father just held him tighter.

It was some time before Delan was able to get a hold of himself. Clapping his father on the back and letting go, he turned quickly and wiped his face on his sleeve. A handkerchief came into his field of view, and he took it, embarrassed. Until he heard his father blowing his own nose.

Turning, he watched his father move back to his desk

and pull out his bottle of brandy. Pouring two glasses, he gestured to the chairs by the fire. Delan closed and locked the library door, then moved to take a chair and a glass. His hand shook slightly as he tossed back the drink in one gulp, feeling it burn its way down his throat. Without a word, his father refilled his glass. This time, Delan only took a small sip.

They sat in silence for a while as Delan's racing thoughts began to calm. Finally, Geon spoke.

"From the look on your face, I take it she told you?"

Delan jumped. "Told me what?" he said unconvincingly. Zhafaera hadn't given him permission to tell anyone else about the pregnancy, but if his father guessed…

"That she's pregnant," he said with a wave of his hand.

"How did you know?" Delan asked, slightly accusing.

He thought his father might roll his eyes. "Delan, please, have you ever known Zhafaera to be seasick? Ever?" He paused. "Then she asked for a female healer." He was ticking off items on his fingers now. "And you two are sharing a room. It wasn't a difficult leap."

Delan set his glass down and put his head in his hands. "I was with her for nearly three weeks after the attack, watching her heave her guts up over the side of that ship. I can't believe I didn't think of that." He looked up at his father. "To be fair, we had *extremely* rough weather."

That explains it, Evey chimed in in his mind. She had taken up a spot next to the fire and was following the conversation intently. His father didn't seem to have noticed. *Her energy has been...odd. I thought it was the Sapphire, but that fluttering...it must be the child.* Delan ignored her.

"You must have if the trip took you this long," his father was saying. Delan refocused on him.

"It was miserable. I really thought she was going to die on me."

"Has she bonded the Sapphire?" Delan nodded. "Then it's going to take more than nausea and malnourishment to kill her." He paused. "Is it yours?" he asked quietly.

"Yes," Delan said. Anxiety spiked at the thought of being a father.

"It's not...?"

"No. I asked her. She says Velexar didn't – didn't—" Delan stopped, unable to say the word out loud for the anger cutting off his throat. He bit out the next words. "He wanted to bond her, like he did her mother, but he couldn't – she was already pregnant." He glanced at his father and saw his own rage reflected there.

"Well, that certainly explains a lot," he spat out. "If he bonded Karaena..." There was sweat on his brow, and he looked faintly ill. "And you're sure he didn't—"

"Yes." The anger was churning through Delan's body.

"Good," his father said, relaxing marginally. "In that case, congratulations!" he said with forced cheerfulness, leaning forward and clapping Delan on the shoulder. "Traditionally, a man goes out and gets blind drunk with his friends after news like this, but as your friends are currently busy, I suppose this will have to do." He grinned at Delan and lifted his glass. Delan clinked his glass against his father's, and they both took a sip. "I'm going to be a grandfather," he said with real joy. "But how do you feel?"

"Like I might have a heart attack," Delan said, taking another sip of his brandy.

"That's normal," his father said sagely. "It doesn't mean you don't love her, or want the child."

Delan let out a breath. "I *do* love her, and I *do* want the baby. It's just…terrifying." The brandy was loosening his tongue, but talking with his father *was* helping.

"It *is* terrifying," Geon said. "But trust me, you'll figure it out. You'll be a great father. The way you take care of Alec—" he cut off abruptly.

Delan's heart sank, and grief squeezed his chest tight. There was silence except for the crackling of the fire.

"Delan, can you tell me…"

Delan didn't want to. He didn't want to say it. Saying it would make it real, and his father would hate him. But he had to. He dropped his head into his hands, pressing the heels of his hands against his eyes to block out the memory.

"I killed him," he whispered.

Silence. "I'm sure it wasn't your fault," his father finally said softly.

Delan's head jerked up, and he looked at his father. "You don't understand. *I killed him.*"

He watched as his father's face crumpled. He was shaking his head, as if in denial. "I – what happened?"

"Dad, he had been turned. Zhafaera killed Velexar, but Alec didn't come back. He said his true master was coming. And then," Delan swallowed at the nightmare memory. "He shifted into a dragon." Geon's eyes widened, shocked. "He was powerful. So powerful. We watched as he became this – this thing. Red and black. Not full grown, but bigger—" he stopped. He hadn't yet told his father about Evey. Glancing at the black cat by the fireplace, he saw her head tilt. Not the time yet. He continued in broken words, still staring at Evey instead of his father. "Alec, the dragon, he breathed fire at us. Zhafaera was too weak. She couldn't stop him. And I–I pushed the fire back into him. He burned alive from the inside out."

There was shocked silence. He chanced a look at his father, expecting to see hatred there. Instead, all he saw was shock, grief, and confusion. "I think I'm missing some parts of this story," he finally said.

Delan nodded. "There are other things you should know."

"Clearly."

Delan took a deep breath and stared into the fire. "Number one: I'm a Black mage. We figured *that* out when I exploded a whole camp full of soldiers that were holding me captive. Fire is easiest for me. Zhafaera thinks I'd been drawing from Alec for years, helping him control his own powers."

"Number two," he pointed to Evey in her black cat form. "That is not a cat. Evey," he said, raising an eyebrow.

Evey backed up into the clear space behind the chairs. He watched as the cat began to grow. The whole body expanded…and kept expanding. The neck and snout elongated, ridges appearing above those bright green eyes and huge white teeth growing from the muzzle. Her toes grew into three-inch-long claws; the tail lengthened, and spikes appeared along the spine, going from the back of the head to the tip of the tail. As the body continued to swell, the fur retreated, as if it were being sucked into the body and was replaced by iridescent, multi-hued scales. Delicate black wings unfolded from the body, spreading slightly to fill the space before Evey folded them tightly against her body.

Delan's eyes widened. It had been a while since he'd seen her in her true form, but he swore she was bigger. Taller and broader. She barely fit in the space. If she stretched her neck fully, she would be touching the ceiling. She was still much, much smaller than a full grown dragon, but certainly bigger than when they had first met her, when she had been about the size of their horses.

He glanced at his father. His eyes were as big as saucers, and he seemed frozen in his chair. Delan stood and walked over to Evey, laying a hand on her warm neck and stroking her smooth scales lightly.

"It's okay," he said soothingly. "She's a friend. We found her in the mountains after her mother was killed. She's very young." Evey gave a small snort. "But not a baby," he added quickly. "All of the remaining dragons sided with Velexar. But we think they were just using him, getting close to the center of our power, and biding their time to take over. When he was killed…we think they were coming for the Sapphire. But we got out."

Evey gave a shake of her head and shrunk back into

her cat form. She tilted her head, staring intently at Geon, who looked utterly shaken. *Tell him I won't hurt him,* she said to Delan.

"She says she won't hurt you."

His father opened his mouth. Closed it. Opened it again. Paused. "She speaks to you?"

"Yes," Delan nodded. "We can speak mind-to-mind. Because I'm a mage." He resumed his seat by the fire, and this time, Evey jumped up on the arm of his chair, fully joining the conversation now.

"I–I just – I'm sorry," his father said, looking at Evey. "I've just never met a dragon before." He inclined his head slightly. Evey tilted hers, confused.

It's a sign of respect, Delan told her.

Oh. I'm sorry I scare him.

He'll get over it.

Geon cleared his throat. "Anything else I should know?"

Delan shrugged. "Probably a lot."

"Just start from the beginning."

***

Zhafaera woke to bright winter sunlight streaming through the windows. Delan was asleep next to her, still dead to the world. Rolling over, she gently wrapped one arm around his middle, snuggling closer to him and inhaling his scent. Which was mixed with the scent of alcohol. She frowned. He must have gotten up; he *had* needed to talk with his father after all. She wondered what time he'd come back to bed. She'd been out cold.

At her movement, Delan stirred. He gave a tiny moan and buried his face in the pillow. Zhafaera grinned. "A little hungover, are we?" she said quietly.

Delan rolled over to face her, his eyes still closed. Throwing an arm over her, he pulled her close. "No," he murmured. He cracked one eye open and winced. "Maybe a little."

"Did you talk with your father?" Zhafaera asked anxiously. She knew that couldn't have been an easy conversation.

"Yes."

"How did it go?"

"I think he might have been a little traumatized by seeing Evey in her dragon form, because that's when he *really* started drinking."

That's not my fault, Evey chimed in. *You told me to change.* Zhafaera could feel a warm ball near her feet that she assumed must be Evey. There were definitely perks to sharing a bed with a dragon. Her body heat kept Zhafaera's toes warm even in winter.

Delan opened both eyes and groaned, squinting. "I should never have tried to keep up with him."

"How did he take...you know...Alec?" Zhafaera asked carefully.

Delan's face went blank, and he looked at her seriously. "Well, I don't think he hates me."

"Of course he doesn't," she said. "Is that what you were worried about?"

"Zhafaera...I killed my brother." She could hear the

waver in his voice.

"Did you ask him about Alec being your brother?"

Delan brought a hand to his forehead. "No, we got sidetracked. By the time I got to the part where we confronted Velexar, it was three in the morning, and we were both more than a little drunk."

"What time do you think it is now?"

"Hells if I know. Are you hungry?"

Zhafaera realized she was. It was still an odd feeling. "Actually, yes," she said, putting a hand on her belly. She made to get up, but Delan held tight.

"Oh no, you don't. Bed rest means you stay *in the bed*. I'll get you something to eat." He kissed her on the forehead and climbed out of bed. He was dressed and out the door before Zhafaera could form any kind of protest. She felt guilty being waited on, but he was right – she *wasn't* supposed to leave the bed. Except for using the washroom.

Gingerly, she climbed out of bed and took care of her needs as quickly as possible. She was just happy to be able to brush her teeth properly again. When she was done, she got back in bed and waited. She felt a twinge of nausea in her hunger pangs, and took a dose of the anti-nausea liquid. It was gone instantly.

After a few minutes, she sighed. "Now I'm bored," she said to Evey.

I think you're going to have to get used to it for now.

"I know, but still. I don't like it." She felt better, and she was antsy. And anxious for some reason. She had a sudden feeling of claustrophobia. A flashback to being locked in another room, waiting for someone far less pleasant than Delan to come in. Her heart rate ticked up, and she had a sudden urge to open the door, just to make sure she could get out.

She jumped out of bed and dashed to the door, flinging it open. And there stood Delan and Geon.

Delan was carrying a tray laden with food. Zhafaera's mouth watered at the sight, and her anxiety over the closed door vanished.

"Zhafaera!" Delan scolded. "You're supposed to be in bed!" He nudged her backward with the tray, herding her back to bed.

She scurried back into the bed, sitting up and eagerly taking the tray.

"Where were you going anyway?" Delan asked, still reproachful. He handed Evey a sizeable chunk of ham, which she immediately began to devour. Geon was staring warily at the dragon-cat.

"Nowhere. I just…I didn't like the door being closed."

"Oh. Ohhh," Delan said. Zhafaera could almost hear the click as his mind made the connection. "I'm sorry. But it's probably safer that way." He hesitated. "I was even thinking we should put a lock on the door."

Zhafaera paused with a spoonful of oatmeal slathered in honey halfway to her mouth, her heart beating quickly. "I don't know about that." She bit her lip.

"Do you want me to leave the door cracked now?" Geon asked from where he still stood by the door.

"N-no, it's fine." Zhafaera took a deep breath, pushing the memories away, and continued eating. "And come in," she called to him with her mouth full.

He made his way over to the bed. "You're looking better this morning," Geon said.

"I'm feeling better," Zhafaera couldn't believe the difference a day made.

"You gave us a bit of a fright yesterday."

"Did I look that bad?" Zhafaera asked.

"Yes," Delan said without hesitation. He was now sitting on the bed, picking food off of her tray for himself.

"Thanks," Zhafaera said dryly. She looked to Delan's father. "Thank you for hosting me again, Lord Geon. And taking in the refugees."

"It's the least I can do. They all needed somewhere to go. To get away." His face clouded.

"We're going to have to find a better solution. The dragons will eventually make their way south," Zhafaera said worriedly.

"That's a problem for another day, when you're stronger," Geon said. "For now, we're okay here. We have a handful of mages here that can help defend us should anything happen."

"It won't be enough."

"Long term, no. But hopefully enough for now." Geon smiled brightly. "On another note, I hear congratulations are in order."

Zhafaera flashed a look at Delan, who blushed. "You told him?" She tried to stifle her irritation. It had been hard enough telling *Delan* that she was pregnant, let alone anyone else.

"He guessed," Delan said with a shrug, but he looked

uncomfortable. "Actually, he made me feel like a complete idiot for not realizing it myself."

Zhafaera softened. "You had other things on your mind. And it's not like I was exactly forthcoming." She looked to Geon. "And…thank you. It's–it's a bit tricky right now. It's why I'm on bed rest."

"That's what I assumed," he said, nodding. "You've been through quite an ordeal, from what Delan told me last night."

Zhafaera took a breath. "I'm sorry about Alec," she said quietly.

"Me too." Both Delan and Geon had identical looks of pain on their faces.

"I'm sorry I couldn't save him."

Geon shook his head. "It's not your fault, anymore than it is Delan's," he said, putting a hand on Delan's shoulder. "You both did what you could. What you had to do."

Zhafaera bit her lip. "About Alec…Velexar – he told us…" *Just spit it out,* she thought to herself. "Was Alec my brother?"

Geon looked away. "How did he…?" He took a breath. "I guess that doesn't matter." He met Zhafaera's eyes. "Yes, he was your brother. Half-brother, anyway. You had different fathers."

Delan was quiet. Zhafaera asked the question for him. "Was he also Delan's brother?"

"Yes."

Delan let out a breath but stayed silent.

"So you and my mother…?"

"Yes, we had an affair. It didn't last long. She quickly realized she didn't need to use her body to get my cooperation, and after that we settled down into a friendship. But, well, not before Alec." He looked distinctly uncomfortable.

"Why would my mother hide him?" Zhafaera pressed.

Geon took a moment to answer. "I know she suspected Velexar's intent to make a grab for power for some time. I suppose she worried that her pregnancy could be used against her, much as Velexar wanted to do to you, from what Delan has told me."

"So she hid it. And made everyone believe that Alec was your wife's…"

"Yes. I didn't like the idea, but Karaena was not one to argue with." His eyes took on a far-away look. "She said it wasn't difficult. It was so close to the truth anyway. He was my son – she just had to hide her pregnancy. She used the Sapphire's power to make it so that no one thought too much about who his mother was. And it worked. At least until Velexar had him, I suppose."

Zhafaera was quiet, digesting the information. She had a brother. And he was dead.

Geon cleared his throat. "On another note, you're officially Queen now that Velexar is dead. I think we should have a formal coronation."

"Why? It seems so silly. There's hardly a country left to rule."

"There's a lot of the country left to rule. Just because the capital is lost doesn't mean all of these people aren't Arenthian." He gestured towards the window to indicate the swarm of refugees currently living in Crystal Point. "Besides, we're going to have to work with our allies, and I think it will be better if you've been formally crowned."

Zhafaera sighed. "But the resources—"

"It doesn't have to be anything ostentatious," Geon interrupted. "I'm thinking we could perform the ceremony on the steps of the Keep – people can gather in the courtyard. I believe we have a mage of each element here now. They can perform the official coronation. And I'm sure we can manage some kind of feast afterwards, even as limited as we are."

Zhafaera sighed. He was probably right. It was something that needed to be done, but she didn't have to like it. She had vague memories of her mother's coronation after her grandmother died – she'd only been four. She remembered having to sit still in the Cathedral for hours, the bright colors of gowns and robes, the loud music at the feast that she fell asleep at halfway through. But Geon was right; this could be a small affair, short and to the point, and it *would* be advantageous when dealing with the leaders of other nations.

"Can you arrange it?" she finally asked.

"Of course, Your Majesty."

Zhafaera pointed at him. "Don't get formal. We'll be related by blood soon. It's Zhafaera."

"Certainly," Geon said with a smile. "Except in public."

Zhafaera suppressed another sigh. "I suppose."

There was a knock on the door, and Geon moved to answer it. Aroha and her granddaughter stood in the doorway. Upon seeing Geon, Aroha inclined her head. "Lord Geon," she said. "I've come to check on the Queen."

"Of course," he said, stepping aside to let them in. Turning, he said to Zhafaera, "I'll take my leave now. And I'll make the arrangements." Aroha gave him a look. "And of course we won't do anything until you've been cleared to leave your bed."

Zhafaera glared at his back as he left.

Chapter 5

Delan stood next to his father at the foot of the steps of the Keep, a little apart from the large crowd that had gathered in the courtyard and stretched far back into the village to watch the coronation. Zhafaera was kneeling in front of four mages – Water, Earth, Fire, and Air – as they took turns speaking. One of them, the Air mage, was younger than Zhafaera, maybe only fourteen. She looked petrified to be standing in front of a crowd of people, crowning the next queen.

The ceremony didn't last long. Before he knew it, his father was stepping forward, kneeling, and holding out the crown on a deep blue velvet pillow. The air around it began to glow, and it slowly lifted off the cushion and moved towards the group on the steps, the small sapphires set in the silver waves glinting in the winter sunlight.

As the crown reached Zhafaera, the sapphires seemed to glow with an inner light that grew brighter the closer it got. Delan glanced around quickly but couldn't tell if anyone else could see it. He turned his attention back to the steps just as the crown touched her head and settled into her flaming red hair.

"By the power vested in us by the land, the sea, the air, and the sun," the four mages spoke together, "we crown you Zhafaera, Queen of Arenthia." With that, they clasped their hands in front of them and knelt, and Zhafaera rose to her feet.

Delan joined in the cheering, letting out a loud whistle as she turned to face the crowd. His father elbowed him in the ribs, but Zhafaera caught his eye and flashed him a smile. She was stunning in a long blue gown that sparkled with silver embroidery, and her short red hair that brushed her shoulders in loose curls had regained its shine. The crown on her head sat steady like it was a part of her, which Delan supposed it was now. But her face was still pale, and her body was just this side of skeletal. She'd spent a week in bed, and even then she'd only been allowed up because she insisted. Aroha had conceded on the condition that the ceremony be as short as possible, which Delan now thought was for the best. Zhafaera looked strained, and he glanced back to where Aroha and her granddaughter stood at the front of the crowd with the half dozen or so other mages, both wearing identical frowns. They looked ready to deliver an "I told you so" speech at any moment.

When the cheering showed no sign of winding down, Zhafaera raised a hand, palm out. Silence fell immediately.

"Thank you *all* for your support," Zhafaera began, smiling as she addressed the crowd. "I know what a difficult time this is. Many of us, myself included, have lost our homes, and we are grateful for the hospitality of Lord Geon," she inclined her head, and Geon bowed. Zhafaera continued. "I can't promise that this will be over quickly or that our lives will go back to what they were. But I *can* promise you that I will do everything in my power to keep you safe and to *fight back* for as long as I draw breath." The crowd cheered again, and Zhafaera waited.

"Thank you," Zhafaera called over the crowd. "Bless you all."

Zhafaera inclined her head, and the entire congregation dropped to its knees. Delan's heart swelled with pride, love, and sheer admiration for the woman that stood before them, speaking with a ferocity that made him believe that maybe, just maybe, they stood a chance at surviving. From the looks of hope on the faces of the crowd, he could see that they believed it too. His father had been right – this coronation was essential.

After a few moments, Zhafaera broke the silence.

"Rise," she called out, lifting her arms. Delan thought they shook slightly and felt anxiety spike in his belly. "Now everyone, go and enjoy the feast!" With that, she turned and walked away into the Keep, the four mages falling into step behind her.

"Perhaps we need to work on her closing remarks," his father murmured.

***

Zhafaera was just glad she hadn't fainted when she stood. Even in the cool winter air, she'd been sweating from the exertion of just being out of bed. She hardly even remembered what she'd said, but everyone seemed pleased with her, and she supposed that's what mattered. *Almost everyone,* she thought, catching Aroha's eye across the Great Hall, where they had gathered as many people as would fit for the feast – everyone else had places in the village. But Zhafaera could tell Aroha had noticed her weakness, even if no one else had.

Who was she kidding? Delan had definitely noticed if the way he was hovering was any indication. Sitting at the head table in front of the hearth, Zhafaera had Delan on one side and Geon on the other. They *were* the hosts after all.

"If you try to cut my meat for me, I will not be held accountable for my actions," she whispered out of the corner of her mouth as she caught Delan staring at her again.

"Trust me, I know better than that," he said wryly. "I'm staring because you're beautiful, not because I'm worried."

Zhafaera blushed. "Don't think flattery will help you." She'd seen herself in the mirror. She looked nothing like her old self – the pale waif in the mirror was not her. Although she had to admit, the short hair was much easier to take care of, and without the added weight, her curls were much more pronounced.

Delan took her hand and gave it a gentle squeeze. "Better me watching out for you than Aroha."

"Fair enough." The healer was looking like she might force her back into bed at any moment.

Zhafaera was just wondering how early she could leave the feast when two people detached themselves from the crowd and made their way towards the high table. The woman, Zhafaera recognized as Esla, whom she'd managed to avoid since their first encounter. Her companion could only be her brother, though Zhafaera hadn't met him yet and she only had a vague memory of him from their Tours. They were a matched set. Twins, if Zhafaera remembered correctly, and they looked it. The only difference was his hair was shorter, only just brushing his shoulders, while her long, blonde hair was twisted up in an elegant knot for the occasion.

When they reached her, they each bowed and curtsied low. She felt Delan stiffen beside her, and his grip on her hand tightened just a bit.

"My Queen," they murmured in unison. Zhafaera suppressed a sigh. She may be queen now, but that didn't mean she suddenly appreciated the bowing and scraping.

"Lady Esla," she said, inclining her head. "It's good to see you again."

"I trust you're feeling better?" Esla inquired politely.

"Yes, much, thank you." Zhafaera nodded at her twin. "Lord Elden, correct?"

Zhafaera extended the hand, not holding Delan's, and Elden stepped forward and took it, placing a kiss on the back that lingered entirely too much for her taste.

"Your Majesty, you're even more beautiful in person," he said smoothly, not releasing her hand. "I can't tell you how happy we all are that you survived the attack on the capital. We were all so worried."

Zhafaera tugged her hand back with a little more force than was absolutely necessary. She didn't like the brother any more than she liked Esla, but for different reasons. Or perhaps not so different, she thought, catching Esla eyeing Delan hungrily. She squashed her irritation and refocused on Elden.

"Yes, it was a near thing," she said, trying to block the memories that rose up at the thought of that night. "But Lord Delan got me out." She looked to Delan and smiled. His answering smile was tight.

"You give me too much credit," he said, shaking his head.

Elden turned his attention to Delan as if only now realizing he was there.

"Lord Delan, it's good to see you," Elden said, reaching out to shake Delan's hand. Delan was forced to release Zhafaera, shaking hands briefly, before quickly taking Zhafaera's hand again. Zhafaera had a feeling she knew why he was so reluctant to let go. "My sister and I have missed your company lately."

"Yes, well, I've been quite busy, even before Zhafaera arrived," Delan said tensely.

"No doubt," Elden said.

"Your father says you're quite the hero," Esla cut in silkily. "You're so lucky to have been able to protect our queen."

"Our queen is quite capable of protecting herself," Delan said. "I only helped as she required."

Good answer, Zhafaera thought, though she knew it wasn't true. She would have died, or worse, if Delan and Evey hadn't rescued her.

"It's a pity your brother wasn't so lucky," Elden said, and Zhafaera went cold. Did he really just…? She tightened her hold on Delan's hand; whether to hold him or herself back, she wasn't sure.

"We did all we could, but we couldn't save him," Zhafaera interjected. "His loss is a great tragedy felt by us all."

"Of course, of course it is," Elden's attention snapped back to Zhafaera, his face now a mask of concern. "It must have been terribly traumatic for you."

"Yes, it was," Delan said simply. Silence hung over the group for a moment.

Elden was the first to recover. "Well, thank the gods you're both safe. I don't think my sister could do without you, Delan." Delan turned red and made a slight choking noise, but Elden ignored him, focusing on Zhafaera. "And you, my queen…do you intend to take a Consort now that you have been crowned?"

Zhafaera met his green eyes and blinked. "I imagine I will," she said lightly.

The slow smile that spread across Elden's face made her slightly queasy. She was sitting here, holding hands with another man, and he thought…

"Your Majesty," Lord Geon interrupted. "You remember Lady Greina," he said cheerfully, indicating the older woman that had come up to speak with him. He started and looked at Elden. "Oh, Lord Elden, Lady Esla, I apologize, I didn't see you there. I hope I'm not interrupting."

"Not at all," Elden said sharply. He turned back to Zhafaera. "I apologize, Your Majesty. We've been monopolizing your attention when you have other guests to attend to. Perhaps we'll speak again soon in a more private setting." Zhafaera fought an eye roll as the two took their leave and returned to their seats. She'd never been so grateful for an interruption in her life.

"Lady Greina," she said, flashing Geon a smile and turning to the newcomer. "How lovely to see you again; it's been too long…"

***

"Now you see why I try to avoid them at all costs," Delan said, closing the door behind him. Zhafaera had taken her leave from the feast fairly early, saying she needed to rest, Aroha following close behind her as she exited the room.

Delan had stayed a little longer, but he made his escape not long after Zhafaera. Or he'd tried to anyway. Once Zhafaera left, it seemed everyone wanted to talk to him. It took him almost a full hour to get out of the Great Hall, and he was more than relieved as he entered the quiet room. Zhafaera was sitting in one of the chairs by the fire, deep in thought.

"Yes, they are quite something." Zhafaera turned to him, making a face. "I think the brother thinks I'm going to take him as Consort."

"Over my dead body," Delan said, slipping out of his dress coat and heading to the other chair next to her.

"I think you're intended to marry his sister," she said lightly.

Delan cringed as he sat, leaning back and stretching his feet to the fire. "I refer to my first point."

"That bad?"

"Yes."

78

Zhafaera stared into the fire. Delan reached out and touched her hand, and she jumped. "You're not jealous, are you?" he asked incredulously.

"What? No, no, I was just thinking," she said, taking his hand and blushing slightly. She was silent for a few moments, and Delan waited. "Delan, have you – have you given any thought to being my Consort?"

He froze, his grip tightening on her hand. Thought about it? Hell, he'd dreamt of it for more years than he cared to admit. Now that she was pregnant, his dreams were far more intense.

"Zhafaera, I'd marry you if I thought you'd agree to it," he said, meeting her gaze. Her eyes widened, and he held up a hand. "No, I'm not asking. I know the answer. Arenthian Queens never marry. That's okay. I just mean, I'll be here no matter what my title is. For as long as you'll have me."

Zhafaera blinked at him for a moment, then broke into a grin. "So you *have* given it some thought."

Delan grinned back. "Obviously. But I don't want you to ask me because you're jealous—"

"I'm not jealous!"

"…or because you want to, I don't know, stake a claim on me."

Zhafaera looked at him with a puzzled expression. "I'm pretty sure that most of the point of a Consort *is* to stake a claim."

"Really?"

"For the most part. Otherwise, it would just be the same as we are now."

"Well, what do *I* get then?" Delan asked jokingly.

"*You* get a certain amount of power and respect. It puts you closer to equal footing with me, as far as rank is concerned."

"Your mother never took a Consort," Delan stated.

"No, but my grandmother did. My grandfather was with her for some time, even before she was Queen."

"How long?"

"Ten years or so. Mother was only around six when he was released from his position."

"'Released' sounds like he was being held prisoner."

Zhafaera rolled her eyes. "Hardly. It just sounds better than 'kicked out.'"

"What did he do to get 'released?'" Delan wanted to be around longer than ten years.

"I'm not sure. We didn't talk about him much, and I was very young when my grandmother died."

They fell silent. Delan vaguely remembered when her mother, Karaena had been crowned, but he couldn't really remember the queen before her. "How did your grandmother die?" he asked quietly.

Zhafaera hesitated, her hand drifting up to touch the Sapphire nestled between her breasts. "She wasn't Queen for very long. It takes a toll, you know. The Sapphire. The less powerful you are, the harder it is to maintain control."

"Are you saying the *Sapphire* killed her?" Delan asked, alarmed.

Zhafaera looked uncomfortable. "Mother said she never bonded with it properly."

Delan sat back, absorbing the information. He'd

known the Sapphire could be dangerous, but he thought that once Zhafaera had bonded it, she'd be safe. "So it could kill you at any time?" he asked nervously.

Zhafaera shook her head, but she was biting her lip. "It's unlikely. It's not fighting me, and we've bonded securely. My grandmother wasn't as strong as my mother and I." She flashed him a reassuring smile. "If it went through the trouble of keeping me alive on that gods-forsaken ship, it probably won't kill me now."

"I'm not sure I feel better." Delan could feel the anxiety rising, and he clamped it down. She was fine. Zhafaera squeezed his hand.

"Don't worry. I'm doing much better," she said soothingly.

Delan nodded, squeezing her hand back. "I'm glad," he said.

Zhafaera smiled. "Now about being Consort…"

"What about it?"

"Well, will you?"

"Will I, what?" Delan asked, grinning. For some reason, he wanted to hear her say it.

Zhafaera rolled her eyes. "Will you be my Consort?"

Delan leaned over the small table between them and kissed her. "Yes," he whispered against her lips. Her hands came up and cupped his face, bringing him closer, and he deepened the kiss. Abruptly, he stood, unable to stand the distance their seats put between them, and pulled her out of her chair, crushing her to him.

"We should go to bed," she murmured.

Delan nodded as he ran his fingers up into her hair.

He'd been so afraid he'd lost her, that he'd never see her again, that he'd failed in protecting her. Then once he had her back, he'd been terrified that he would lose her again, that she would die. It was only now that he truly began to relax, accepting that she was here, safe, and on her way to being healthy.

On impulse, he spun her around, walking forward a few steps and pressing her against the wall next to the fireplace. Suddenly, Zhafaera froze. Then she wrenched her mouth away from his, turning her face to the side as her hands came up, pressing against his chest and trying to push him away.

"Stop, stop," she gasped. "Don't, please, stop." The words tumbled out in a rush as Delan felt the electric shock jolt through his body before he could let go.

"Ouch!" he cried involuntarily, shuddering as the shock rolled through him.

"I'm sorry, I'm sorry," Zhafaera whispered, covering her mouth with her hands. Delan could see tears forming in her eyes, reflecting the firelight.

"No, Zhafaera, *I'm* sorry," he said quickly, holding up his hands in a placating gesture. "I'm sorry, it was too soon, I shouldn't have pushed you." She was trembling, and his heart clenched. *I'm such an ass,* he thought. "Are you all right?" He was trying to sound soothing, but his heart was still racing from the shock from the Sapphire, and his chest was on fire.

"You don't understand, I—" She slid slowly down the wall until she was seated, her knees drawn up against her chest and her face in her hands. Delan slowly knelt in front of her, keeping his distance.

"I'm sorry," he whispered again.

Zhafaera shook her head, still hiding her face. "It's not your fault." She paused. "It's *his*."

Delan felt instant rage. Velexar had done this to her. Threatened her. Touched her. *Traumatized* her. "Do you want to talk about it?" he asked, his voice sounding too calm even to his own ears.

Zhafaera looked up, her face streaked with tears. "No," she whispered. She bit her lip. "Just don't – don't pin me." She let out a shaky breath. "I'm sorry," she said, reaching out tentatively. Her hand was shaking. "Did I hurt you?"

"No, I'm fine," he said, offering her a reassuring smile. "The Sapphire just gave me a shock, that's all."

"Sorry," she said again.

"It's okay," he said. "Do you want to get into bed? I can sleep somewhere else."

"No! I mean, yes, I want to get in bed. No, I don't want you to leave."

"Are you sure?" he asked, reaching out a hand.

She took it, gripping it tightly. "I'm sure."

He stood and gently pulled her up after him. Going slowly, they moved over to the bed, where Delan pulled back the covers and let Zhafaera get in first, then climbed in behind her. He maintained a careful distance, not touching her.

As they settled under the covers, Zhafaera rolled over to face him, placing a hand on his chest. Immediately a cool sensation washed over him, erasing the last of the sting from the Sapphire's shock.

"You didn't need to heal me," he whispered. "I'm fine."

Zhafaera blinked. "That wasn't me," she said, surprised. "I–I think the Sapphire just said sorry."

Delan wasn't sure what to do with that. She'd told him the Sapphire was somewhat sentient, but this…this was weird. "Uh, thanks. Apology accepted."

Zhafaera drew closer, and Delan draped an arm gingerly over her, relaxing a little as he felt her trembling ease.

"If Velexar weren't already dead, I'd kill him," Delan whispered.

"But he *is* dead," Zhafaera said fiercely. "And you did *help* kill him."

Chapter 6

"I'll see if I can have breakfast brought to the library," Delan said, moving towards the door. "Unless you need me…"

"Delan, *go*." Zhafaera's voice was muffled as she pulled a dress over her head. "I can get dressed by myself."

Delan shrugged. She'd woken up prickly this morning. "If you're sure. I didn't think Queens really dressed themselves."

"*Delan.*"

"Going, going," he called behind him, slipping out of the door before he really got in trouble. But sometimes he just couldn't help himself.

Heading down to the kitchen, he asked for a breakfast tray he could take to the library, but they shooed him off, promising they'd bring breakfast to them. It seemed the serving staff had increased since he'd been gone, and there were a number of them whose names he didn't know. The influx of people into the village was being felt everywhere. Whereas before the Keep had felt almost empty, now it was full to bursting. On top of the handful of nobles staying with them, the half dozen or so mages that had come were also staying in the Keep. Most of them had chosen rooms on the top floor, where the energy was best, they said.

The servants' quarters and the Great Hall – now that it wasn't in use for a feast – were filled with refugees, most of whom slept on the floor. They'd crammed people into every corner of the keep and beyond. They had to figure out a long-term plan, and fast.

Poking his head in the library, he looked around.

"Good morning," his father called from his place behind the desk. Evey sat at his feet. She seemed to like him, and Delan had caught her following his father more than once.

"Zhafaera's not here yet?" Delan asked.

"No, didn't she come down with you?"

"No, she was still getting ready when I went to the kitchens. Maybe I should go check on her…"

Lord Geon said something, but Delan couldn't make it out, already back out the door and heading towards the stairs. What if she'd gotten tired? Or fallen? Or –

"Delan!"

Delan's head snapped up at the voice, and he groaned internally. Not her.

Esla came bounding down the steps towards him, and he instinctively backed up.

"Delan, how *are* you?" she asked, throwing her arms around his neck and kissing him on both cheeks. "We haven't had *any* time to ourselves; you've been so busy with Princess, I mean, *Queen* Zhafaera, I've hardly seen you since you got here!" She didn't release her hold on him.

Delan tried to move away, but she simply followed, stepping onto the stair he was on.

"It's been *ages* since you came to visit us, and then when we heard you'd gone to the capital, we—" She gasped, and Delan could see tears welling in her eyes. Real or fake, he wasn't sure. "I was so afraid!"

She released her hold to raise one hand to her face and wipe at her eyes, and Delan took the opportunity to duck to the side.

"Oh Delan, I've missed you so much!" she cried, stepping closer and placing her hand on his chest. He took another step back and hit the wall.

"Esla, stop," he said firmly, taking her hands by the wrists and removing them. Holding her steady in front of him, he tried to move her back. She didn't budge.

"Don't be silly, there's no one here to see," Esla whispered, leaning closer. "She's probably still sleeping."

"*She* is standing right here," an icy voice echoed down the stone stairwell. Esla jumped back as if burned, Delan releasing her wrists quickly as his gaze shot up to see Zhafaera on the landing.

"Zhafaera, I—" he started.

She held up a hand to stop him, not looking at him as her eyes locked on Esla. Slowly, she made her way down the stairs, her gaze never wavering. Esla wilted under her stare, and it was all Delan could do not to flinch.

"Enough," Zhafaera said, coming to a stop a few steps up from them. "Hands off of him."

"We were only—" Esla began breathily.

"No," Zhafaera's eyes flashed. "He is my Consort, and you will not touch him. Am I clear?"

Esla looked from Zhafaera to Delan, surprise

overtaking fear for a moment. "Yes, Your Majesty, of course," she curtsied deeply and stayed there as Zhafaera rolled her eyes and pushed past them.

Delan stood frozen for another moment before dashing after her. He almost felt sorry for Esla. Almost. *He* certainly didn't want to be on the receiving end of that stare.

Zhafaera flung open the library door and breezed inside, nodding tightly to a surprised Geon as Delan closed the door softly behind him. Zhafaera stalked to the fire and sat in one of the armchairs, frowning at the flames. Delan swore they burned brighter.

"Everything all right?" His father asked into the silence.

Delan shook his head slightly, hopefully conveying that it was best not to ask. His father must have gotten the idea, because he moved quietly over to the chair opposite Zhafaera as Delan took a seat on the couch.

"Sorry," Zhafaera finally said to no one in particular. She took a deep breath and let it out. "Geon, you should know I've named Delan Consort. We can make a formal announcement, but I suspect *Lady Esla* will spread the word after I've just told her to keep her hands off him."

His father made a sound very much like a choked snort.

"It's not funny," Delan protested. "She won't leave me alone!"

"She will now," Zhafaera said coldly.

"Hopefully."

"I *dare* her to try anything."

Delan suppressed a shiver at the danger in her voice. She really was in a mood this morning.

Just then, there was a knock on the door, and three servants entered with breakfast. They laid out everything on the large wooden table in the center of their three seats and made a quick exit. Evey moved to sit next to Lord Geon, and he immediately tossed her some ham, which she caught deftly in jaws that seemed just slightly too big for a cat.

"All right," Zhafaera said, cutting into an apple. "Tell me: what's our status?"

"For now, we're stable," his father answered smoothly. "The number of refugees has leveled off – some have gone on to Southport, and the numbers coming in have dwindled. Many of them brought at least some food, and we should have enough to last the winter, especially if we can keep the fishing boats in the water. It's usually not ideal in the winter, but there are a couple of water mages that have been helping. Not too much," he added quickly. "Just enough to smooth out the rough waters a bit."

"Good," Zhafaera said briskly. "But I don't plan on staying here all winter. What have you heard from the other nations? I assume those in Southport are ultimately fleeing to Khichora?"

"For the most part, yes. And Khichora is accepting them. They seem to be withdrawing into the mountains, although many are trying to cross into Burja. That's where there's been a slight…problem."

"Burja isn't letting them in?"

"Not willingly, no. There have been a few skirmishes

at the border from what I've heard. And there have been a few ships that have been turned away from Anchorsa that have ended up here."

"Unacceptable in a time like this," Zhafaera said simply. "We need to get as far away as possible. Khichora isn't enough, it's still the same landmass. Laros is too small to hold many refugees, and Gods help me, I'm not getting on a boat for that long." She shuddered. "Burja is our best option. It's not as far as Laros, but the desert isolates it."

Even dragons need water, Evey chimed in. *We should have some time there before they move on from Arenthia.*

Delan waited as Zhafaera translated what Evey said for his father. "How do we convince them?" Delan finally asked.

"It's all about diplomacy," Zhafaera said, eating her third roll. "It's not like any of us have a real military. Arenthia had the most – a few hundred soldiers if you don't count the guards in the capital – and that's gone now. There are no wars amongst ourselves."

"What if they refuse?"

"They won't," Zhafaera stood, dusting off her hands. She looked to Lord Geon. "You have a message mirror, correct?"

"Yes, it's in the East Tower. Some of the mages have used it to find surviving mages."

"Then let's go now. I need to speak with Queen Oraesa."

***

90

Zhafaera was fully winded by the time they reached the East Tower. *Pathetic,* she thought. But at least she'd made it.

Message mirrors were made by mages infusing molten glass with magic as the mirror was made. Any mirror could be used for scrying if you just wanted to look. But if you wanted to talk or interact, it had to be a Message mirror. Most large households had one, and the leaders of each nation typically had enormous ones in their throne rooms, the better for long-distance meetings. When she'd been in the capital, Zhafaera had used hers quite frequently. The one here was full length and set in a simple silver frame. Perfect.

Reaching into the mirror with her magic, Zhafaera focused on her target. Colors swirled through the mirror in a dizzying rainbow display as the mirror searched for the right connection. Abruptly the image cleared, showing a long room flanked with yellow stone columns with gaps open to the air and a wide terrace visible beyond.

"Zhafaera!" a voice called through the mirror almost immediately.

Zhafaera smiled. She knew that voice. Sure enough, a young girl came into view from the side of the mirror. Only fifteen, Princess Liara was tall and thin, her blonde hair cropped close to her head and curling around her ears. She was dressed in colorful, flowing silk pants and a long-sleeved white blouse that billowed out around her. Her large blue eyes peered at Zhafaera in surprise.

"Liara, how are you?" she asked.

"We're fine here. But Zhafaera, we heard you were

dead!"

"Well, I'm not, though just barely," Zhafaera said, grinning at the young girl.

"I'm so glad," Liara said sincerely. "I've missed you. What's happening there? Our mages have been scrying, and Zhafaera, the dragons—"

"I know," Zhafaera cut in. "That's what I need to talk about. Is your mother there?"

"She's in her rooms, I think," Liara said. "Wait here, I'll go fetch her."

"I'll be here." Zhafaera hid a smile. Where was she going to go?

As Liara disappeared, Zhafaera admired the view. Outside their throne room, the sun was shining, and Zhafaera could practically feel its rays warming her. It wasn't freezing in Crystal Point, but Zarga, Burja's capital city, was much warmer, even now, just after the new year, when it was at its coolest.

"Would you prefer that we leave you?" Lord Geon murmured.

"No, stay. She'll bring her advisors. I'd like to have mine." Zhafaera shifted her weight, thinking on what she wanted to say. She knew she had to try and be diplomatic, but she really wanted to scream at Queen Oraesa. How could she pull a stunt like this in the middle of a crisis that would affect them all? They had to band together, or they would all end up decimated by the dragons. Now was not the time for squabbling. But then, Queen Oraesa had never liked Zhafaera or her mother, so really, she shouldn't have been surprised. To be fair, Zhafaera was fairly certain her mother had had an affair with Oraesa's husband, so she supposed she couldn't blame her.

It was some time before the Queen appeared, looking much like her daughter despite the fact that she was covered in jewelry. Pearls and Emeralds hung around her neck, and more Emeralds adorned her fingers. Gold rings made their way up the sides of both ears, and matching bangles hung from each wrist. Her blonde hair was wound into intricate braids around her head, with more Emeralds dotting the cross points. She wasn't wearing her crown, but she didn't need it. She looked every inch a queen. Princess Liara stood behind her, looking anxious.

"Princess Zhafaera," she called as she came into the mirror's sight. "I see your uncle was mistaken when he told us you'd perished with your mother."

Sorry to disappoint, Zhafaera thought. "It's Queen Zhafaera now, actually. I've been formally crowned after the death of my uncle. It's good to see you, Queen Oraesa."

"Likewise," Oraesa said coolly. "I was sorry to hear about your mother. It must have been hard for you, as close as you were."

"Thank you, yes, it's been very difficult." Zhafaera waved behind her to indicate Delan and Geon. "This is Lord Geon, of Crystal Point, and Lord Delan, my Consort." They both bowed.

Oraesa's eyebrows shot up. "You're in Crystal Point – that's not far. And you've taken a Consort." It wasn't a question. "Your mother never took one."

"Yes, well, I'm not my mother." Hopefully Oraesa would believe her in this. "I hear there's been some trouble along your border."

"Ah, I thought this might be the reason for your call." Oraesa shook her head. "I'm sorry, *Queen* Zhafaera, but we simply do not have the resources to take in all of Arenthia."

"I can sympathize," Zhafaera said calmly. Very calmly. "But my people need somewhere to go, as far from the dragons as possible. Burja is our best hope of putting distance between us and them."

"It is my understanding that Arenthia has a responsibility to guard against such incursions from dragons."

"It is *everyone's* responsibility," Zhafaera snapped. "The dragons will not stop with conquering Arenthia. Eventually they will come for you too."

"But as you said, we are further away, and it will take them longer to reach us. We're isolated here in the desert, and we still have our most powerful mages. I understand you lost most of yours in the attack on your capital?" Zhafaera nodded tightly. "So you see," Oraesa continued, "I'm unclear on what exactly Arenthia can bring to the table now, other than thousands of refugees."

"Those refugees need your help," Zhafaera said, gesturing out to indicate all the refugees at Crystal Point. "Many of them have brought food with them, and we're relatively well supplied. We just need somewhere safe to settle for the time being."

"Running and hiding is not a solution to the dragon problem," Oraesa said, and Zhafaera fought hard to control her temper. "Besides, food is not the issue. Our most precious resource is water, and it hasn't rained for months here. Our supply is low, and even the oases are shrinking."

"So water is the main issue?" Zhafaera asked. "We can bring that with us."

"You couldn't possibly bring enough," Oraesa scoffed. "Of course, you and your entourage may join us here, but I'm afraid otherwise our borders will remain closed."

"You can't expect me to leave my people here to die." Zhafaera wasn't really paying attention. Focusing on the Sapphire, she dove into its power, reveling in the deep well of magic waiting for her there.

"That is all I can offer," Oraesa was saying.

Zhafaera released her power outward, shooting her awareness across the sea between Crystal Point and Burja, then in a straight line over the desert to Zarga. She reached the city in seconds, watching it rise up out of the sand, the spires of the palace reaching high above the rest of the city below. The palace itself sat practically on top of the large jungle oasis that the city was founded around, much of it left untouched by royal decree. The Azor River flowed outward from the center, through the bowels of the palace itself. Outside the oasis, the entire city was the color of sand, dry and parched, with low square buildings and tented markets crammed tighter and tighter together the farther they got from the oasis, crowding as close as possible to the water sources.

Hovering directly above the oasis, Zhafaera stopped, gathering power. Reaching down into the oasis, she burrowed deep, drawing water up from the depths of the aquifer and filling the pools at the heart of the oasis. Spreading her awareness out, she drew deep from the power of the Sapphire and *pulled* moisture towards her.

The crack of thunder made Oraesa and Liara jump, looking around, and Zhafaera refocused on them. The sky outside the throne room was almost as dark as night, the storm clouds low and thick. As Zhafaera watched, the sky opened, and rain began to pour from the dark clouds, whipping sideways in the wind. Oraesa turned back to Zhafaera, her eyes wide.

"You have the Sapphire," she said.

"Yes."

"This is cheating," Oraesa said angrily.

"You said you needed water," Zhafaera countered. "Here's your water."

"This much rain after such a drought will drown us."

"Then I suggest you stop complaining about resources and open your borders."

"You can't do this. You can't threaten me and take over my country." Oraesa was nearly shouting now.

"I'm not taking over your country, I'm bringing something to the table." Zhafaera was strangely calm; her attention split between what she was saying and holding the rain clouds in place. The Sapphire's power flowed through her, spiking her adrenaline and giving her a rush. Ultimate power – that's what she held in her hand. Or on her chest. It was intoxicating.

"Can I trust that there will be no further issues at the border?" Zhafaera asked, her voice sounding very far away.

Oraesa glanced over her shoulder at the storm raging outside. "Fine," she spat, turning back to Zhafaera.

"Lovely." Zhafaera clapped her hands together, startling Geon and Delan, who'd watched the display silently. "You can expect me and my *entourage* within the next two weeks."

"I suppose I can send an envoy to Anchorsa to meet you."

"We would very much appreciate that."

Oraesa glanced over her shoulder again. "Now would you please end this? I think this is quite enough rain for the time being."

Zhafaera released her hold on the storm, and immediately the rain slowed to a drizzle. The rest would dissipate on its own. Pulling back fully into herself, Zhafaera released a breath. "We'll see you soon," she said, and disconnected the mirror.

Turning abruptly to Lord Geon, the rush she'd felt with the power of the Sapphire faded and her anger returned. "Please begin preparations. Start dispersing the refugees – try to get as many as you can on ships and the rest on the road to Khichora. Divide them however you see fit."

Geon inclined his head. "At once, my Queen."

Nodding, she stalked to the door and flung it open, still feeling irrationally angry despite her win. She heard footsteps behind her and knew Delan was following. "I'd like to be alone," she snapped.

"Of course," Delan said quietly.

She managed not to slam the door behind her.

"I'm not sure how diplomatic that was," she heard Lord Geon's muffled voice through the door. "But it was effective."

***

Delan waited an hour before he started looking for Zhafaera. She wasn't in their room, or the library, or the Great Hall. He even went down to the beach since it was low tide. The only people there were the fishermen bringing in their boats and preparing their anchors to hold them in place when high tide came up to the cliff face. He chatted with them for a time, trying to take his mind off of Zhafaera, but he was starting to worry. He found he didn't like it when he didn't know where she was. It reminded him too much of when she'd been taken, and his anxiety grew.

Heading back up to the Keep, he found his father in the Great Hall, speaking with the leaders of refugees from various towns as Evey sat close by. He'd spoken to the nobles first, and their quarters were already a flurry of movement as they prepared to be among the first to leave.

When his father had finished and the refugees had scurried off to begin preparations, Delan went up to him.

"I can't find Zhafaera."

"She doesn't want to be found. Give her some space," his father said gently.

"I just want to make sure she's okay."

"She's fine. You need to find something to do. If you'll excuse me, I have to speak with the kitchens. We have a lot of stores that need to be packed up."

Delan ended up in the practice yard with a bow and arrows, firing at targets mechanically as the rhythmic motions helped to relax him. Around him, the village was in motion, everyone scrambling to pack everything they owned as quickly as they could. The decision had been made that families with children would be first on the boats, along with the elderly and the ill or injured. The rest had the option of waiting for the boats to come back or making for Khichora; it appeared about half of them were choosing the latter. Everyone was anxious to get far away as fast as they could. Delan couldn't blame them. He felt like every day was just waiting for dragons to appear on the horizon.

"Delan!" A voice called out across the yard. Delan spun, lowering his bow as he recognized the man.

"Colin!" He called back, surprised. Colin was young, only a year or so older than Delan. His dark hair had grown since the last time Delan saw him, before Zhafaera had arrived, and it now brushed the tops of his shoulders. Holding a hammer in one hand, the blacksmith's apprentice waved. Striding over quickly, Delan hopped the fence surrounding the stables and practice yard, reaching out and clasping his friend's hand. Colin gripped tightly and yanked him forward, pulling him into a hug. Slapping each other on the back, Delan laughed.

"It's good to see you," he said as they broke apart.

"We thought you were dead for sure when we heard about the dragons," Colin said seriously. "And when you hadn't returned by Midwinter…"

"Not quite," Delan said.

Colin hesitated. "I'm sorry about Alec. He was a good kid."

"Yeah, well…" Delan trailed off, unsure what to say. Everyone had offered their condolences about Alec, and the more he heard it, the less Delan knew how to deal with it. He certainly didn't want to talk about what had happened, despite Colin being his best friend. He didn't want to ever talk about it again.

"How's Sara?" he asked Colin, deflecting.

"Oh, she's great," he said. "She had the baby not long after you left."

"Seriously? I feel like you were just telling me she was pregnant!"

"It flies by," Colin said, waving his hand. Delan felt a slight panic rise. Nine months had seemed like a long time from where he was standing, but suddenly it looked a lot closer. *Not even nine months,* he thought.

"So you're a husband *and* a father now. Who would have thought?" Delan joked.

"I know, right? And with Sara." Colin had a stupid grin on his face.

"*Especially* with Sara." Delan laughed as Colin punched him in the shoulder good-naturedly. "Sorry," Delan said. "It's just that she's so beautiful, and you're so…"

"Watch it!" Colin warned.

Delan held up his hands in a placating gesture.

"Hey, look," Colin said. "Why don't you come home with me and have dinner with us? Sara would want to see you, and you can meet the baby."

"If you're sure she wouldn't mind," he said, thinking it would probably be good to meet a baby. Any baby. Before his own was born. *Gods, what do you do with a baby?* He thought.

"She'd certainly mind if I *didn't* bring you home," Colin replied, picking up his hammer and turning. Waving over his shoulder, he gestured for Delan to follow him. Delan had been to his and Sara's new home together a few times before he left, but with all the ruckus, it was probably best to stay close.

"So how's the princess, I mean queen?" Colin asked as they walked.

"She's great. Healing." Delan hesitated. "She's pregnant," he blurted out.

"For real?" Colin asked, looking over at Delan with a huge grin. "How did *you* manage that?"

Delan shot him a look. "Don't tell anyone."

"My lips are sealed."

"Not even Sara."

Colin frowned. "Now, that could get me in trouble. But I won't say anything." He laughed. "Now you *have* to meet the baby. Gotta practice."

"Do you know, I don't think I've held a baby since Alec was little. And that was a *long* time ago," Delan said nervously.

"Don't worry, you have instincts."

"That's what my dad said."

"Well, he's right," Colin nodded firmly to accent his point.

"She's named me Consort," Delan said slowly.

"I thought I heard something about that a little while ago," Colin said with a grin. "Congratulations. Should I bow?" He inclined his head.

"Gods, no."

"You'll have to get used to it. You're moving in high circles now."

"I'm not sure how," Delan said, shaking his head.

"Please, you always had a thing for her," Colin said. "I'm just surprised she went along. Although I suppose being alone in the woods for months wears you down." He grinned as Delan gave him a shove. "Where is she now?" he asked. "Should I have invited her for dinner too?"

Delan's stomach clenched. "I'm not sure. She wanted to be alone, and now I can't find her."

"Ahh, in a mood, is she?"

"What do you mean?" Delan asked.

"Gods, when Sara was pregnant, it's a miracle she didn't kill me. Some days she was ready to fight with anyone who crossed her path. And whatever you do, don't hover. You're as likely to get a smack as you are a kiss."

"So that's normal?" Delan felt some relief. Hopefully this meant she wasn't just getting tired of him.

"Oh yeah, definitely normal. And it only gets worse." Delan groaned.

"But it's worth it in the end," Colin said as they reached the door to his house. Throwing the door wide, he called out quietly, "Sara! Look who I found!"

Delan entered the small house and looked around. It was as he remembered it – the kitchen and sitting room all in one, with a bedroom at the back. There was one addition though – a bassinet that held a tiny, pink baby.

"Delan!" Sara cried, moving forward to hug him. Delan returned the hug tightly, happy to see her. "I'm glad you're not dead," she said with a laugh.

"Me too."

"Delan here has been made Consort," Colin told his wife as he moved towards the bassinet.

"Have you?" she asked, holding him at arm's length and inspecting him critically. "Well, I should think you'd have to start dressing better."

"What's wrong with the way I'm dressed?" Delan said defensively.

Sara raised an eyebrow. So his pants were old and dusty. They were still good.

"Nevermind that," Colin interrupted, walking over with a bundle of blankets in his arms. "Meet Amee," he said, and carefully placed the blankets in Delan's arms.

Delan froze. The baby peeked up at him from its nest of blankets and blinked large blue eyes at him. The shock of dark hair he could see was exactly like her father's. *Don't drop the baby, don't drop the baby,* he thought.

Sara laughed. "You won't drop her," she said easily.

"Did I say that out loud?" Delan was afraid to breathe.

"Yes, and I have complete faith in you," Colin said with a chuckle.

"At least someone does," Delan mumbled.

The baby made a noise, drawing Delan's full attention back to her. "Hi there," he said quietly, smiling at her. She smiled back and cooed, and he relaxed a little. "She's cute.”

“Obviously, with a mother and father like us.”

Delan glanced up at Colin and made a face. “I think the credit goes to the mother.”

“Of course it does,” Sara said. “I worked hard making her. Come, sit.” She indicated the kitchen table. “Dinner is ready, and there’s plenty of it.”

Delan looked back at Amee. “Uhhh,” he said.

“Afraid to move?” Colin asked.

“Exactly.”

“You get over that,” he said, reaching forward to take the baby. He cradled his arms under Delan’s.

“I’m also afraid to let go,” Delan said, hesitating.

“Don’t worry, I’ve got her. Just go easy. There you go.” Amee was safely back in her father’s arms, and Delan could breathe again.

“That is quite possibly the most terrifying thing I’ve ever done.” Delan said as they sat at the table. Sara sat a dish on the table and served her husband, who began eating with one hand with the baby in the other. Just the sight of it made Delan nervous.

“Now,” Sara said as she took her seat. Delan’s gaze snapped to her. “Tell us everything.”

***

Zhafaera awoke from her nap on the library couch feeling refreshed and much less grumpy. And also a little guilty for hiding.

The light outside was dim, almost dark, and most of

104

the light came from the fire, still crackling in the fireplace.
Her feet were warm, and she looked down to see a black
cat laying on her. A *heavy* black cat.

You're awake, Evey said. *Delan was looking for you.*

"I'm sure he was."

He didn't find you here.

Zhafaera blushed. "I used an invisibility spell."

Oh. Evey paused. *Is it okay that I'm here?*

"Yes, of course. I'm feeling better now. Besides, I feel
like I've hardly seen you since we got here. Where have
you been?"

*Mostly I follow Lord Geon. He seems to be less afraid
of me now.*

"That's good."

He's very interesting. He talks with a lot of people.

"What does he say?"

*Mostly it's about the dragons. I wish he could hear
me.*

"Can't you make yourself heard?" Zhafaera asked.

*Maybe, but I'm afraid of hurting him. Communicating
with you doesn't* really *use magic. Communicating with*
him *is different – since he's not a mage, I have to do all
the work, and dragon magic is not meant for humans.*

"You did fine healing, Delan."

Evey tilted her head. *I only just barely didn't kill him.*

Zhafaera shrugged. "I think you should try talking to
Geon. I'm sure he'd like to hear from you. You'd be a big
help."

Do you think so?

"Absolutely."

I suppose I can try.

At that moment, there was a soft knock on the door. Zhafaera peeked over the couch just as Lord Geon opened the door a crack.

"Is it all right to come in?" he asked.

"Yes, of course," Zhafaera said, sitting up straighter. "I'm sorry I commandeered your library all afternoon."

"Not at all. My home is your home." He came fully into the room, and she saw that he carried a tray. She sniffed the air, and her stomach grumbled. "I thought we could eat in here again."

"Thank you." She took the tray from him and placed it on the table. "Evey and I were talking," she said, waving a hand at the black cat now investigating the tray. "Evey?"

Now? The dragon asked.

Zhafaera nodded, and Evey sighed.

HELLO? The voice boomed through Zhafaera's head, and she winced. She wasn't the only one – Geon nearly jumped out of his skin. He blinked, focusing on Evey.

Did I hurt him? Evey asked in her normal tone.

"I don't think so," Zhafaera said. "But I think you can speak quieter."

Less magic. Okay. Hello?

Lord Geon sat up straight. "I heard that."

This is Evey, Evey said.

Zhafaera covered a smile. "I thought so," Geon said.

We can speak now, but you must tell me if I hurt you. Dragon magic can be dangerous for humans.

"Thank you, I promise I'll tell you." Geon smiled at Evey. "This will be much better than the one-sided conversations we've been having."

I agree.

"So, Zhafaera," he asked. "Are you feeling better?"

She blushed. "Yes. I'm sorry I was so irritable earlier. I didn't sleep well."

"That's quite all right," he hesitated. "But I'm afraid you might have made an enemy today."

"Oraesa was already my enemy," she said quietly.

"She wasn't your friend, but she wasn't your enemy," Geon said gently.

Zhafaera sighed. "I wasn't a very good diplomat today."

"I didn't say that."

"You didn't have to."

Geon started eating, and Zhafaera picked at her food. "You did what was best for your people," he said firmly. "But you, personally, will need to be careful with her."

"You think she'll try something?" Zhafaera asked, not really surprised.

Geon shook his head. "Not at first. Your display today might have been dangerous, but it *was* useful. They need the water, and if that means accepting you into the fold, then that's what Queen Oraesa will do. For now."

"I should have done better."

"It's done, and your people will be safer for it." He smiled. "Just maybe in the future, be careful doing anything that requires you to use the Sapphire."

"Fair enough," Zhafaera said. She looked around. "Do you know where Delan is?"

"No, I kicked him out after he spent two hours

wandering around like a lost puppy."

Guilt twisted her belly. "I know I should be grateful to have someone who cares about me so much, but sometimes I just need to be by myself. I'm not made of glass."

Geon nodded sympathetically. "I imagine it's hard for him to leave you after having seen you taken and not knowing where you were or if you were all right. And that's only made worse by the pregnancy. Something in a man's brain tends to just break a little, and we get this primal protection instinct that kicks in. But don't be afraid to tell him when you need space."

"Thanks," Zhafaera said. "I wonder where he went."

Delan? She probed for him in her mind, spreading out her awareness.

His response was immediate. *Zhafaera, are you all right?*

Of course, I'm fine, she said gently. *I'm sorry about earlier. Where are you?*

I'm with my friends and their baby, he said, and an image flashed in her mind of a baby with dark hair and bright blue eyes. *I didn't drop her.* He sounded proud.

Zhafaera smiled, the idea of Delan holding a baby filling her with emotion.

Zhafaera? Do you need me back?

No, sorry, I just wondered where you were.

I probably won't stay much longer, he said.

Stay as long as you like. You could use the practice.

She felt his grin and relaxed.

"So where is he?" Geon asked.

"He's playing with a baby," Zhafaera said, still smiling.

***

Delan climbed the stairs to their rooms, trying to keep a measured pace and not run. So he walked. Quickly.

As he rounded the corner to their hallway, he could see the door to their room slightly ajar. He sighed slightly but smiled – an open door meant that Zhafaera was back in their room. It may not be the safest option, but he knew that she could barely stand a closed door now.

Peeking his head into the room, he found Zhafaera lounging on the couch facing the fire, reading a book. Delan knocked lightly on the door, trying not to startle her, but her head jerked up anyway. She relaxed when she saw it was him and smiled.

"Hi," she said quietly, marking her place in her book with her finger.

Delan opened the door fully, crossed the room in a few strides, and stopped directly in front of Zhafaera. Bending down, he placed a light kiss on her forehead. She tilted her head up and grabbed a kiss of her own from his lips.

"I love you," Delan whispered, bringing his hand up and running his fingers gently through her shorter hair.

"I love you too, Delan." Zhafaera grinned and stole another kiss.

Delan took a step to the side and sat down on the couch next to her, resting his arm across her shoulders. She relaxed into him.

"Sorry for disappearing earlier," she said quietly. "I just haven't been feeling myself. I needed some space."

"That's all right," Delan said as he rubbed small circles on her arm. "You're under a lot of pressure. You did incredible magic today. You're entitled to a break."

Zhafaera sighed. "I'm not sure that was my best work today. I got the point across, but I made Oraesa angry. That might come back to haunt me."

"But your people will be safe in Burja, and that's what matters."

"For now."

Delan didn't have a good response to that. They both knew that nowhere would be safe once the dragons moved outward from Arenthia. It was only a matter of time until they came for Burja too.

Delan squeezed Zhafaera's shoulder. "We have time to figure out our next steps once we get to Zarga."

Zhafaera sat up straight and looked Delan in the eye. "One part of the plan is that we need to continue your lessons." Delan opened his mouth to protest, but she continued. "You're powerful, Delan. As powerful as any White mage—"

"But I'm *not* a White mage, Zhafaera," Delan interrupted. "I'm a Black mage, and I'm dangerous. I killed—" he choked on his words and closed his eyes. Took a breath.

"You don't have to say it," Zhafaera said quietly.

Delan took another breath, sniffed, and opened his eyes. "I killed Alec. I could hurt you too."

Zhafaera took his hand and held his gaze firmly. "You had to, Delan. No, listen. You. Had. To. He killed himself by transforming. Humans can't make the change to dragon and survive. And he would have taken us with him."

Delan gave a slight nod. "Logically, I know that's true," he whispered. "But knowing and feeling are not the same thing."

Zhafaera took Delan's hand and placed it on her belly. Delan's heart skipped a beat. "You saved *us,* Delan. All of us. Our little family is all I have left," Zhafaera finished in a whisper.

Delan gave a slight smile and kissed the top of her head. "Of course you're right," he said. "Swords and knives are not always enough to protect my Queen, I know. And it's not fair to expect you to do *all* the magical work." He shook his head. "And we lost most of the Arenthian mages in the capital. I guess that does leave me to learn."

"Excellent." Zhafaera stood and began to pace. "I want to work as often as we can. We're going to Burja, so we'll need to be careful that you're not detected there. We may not be able to train as often once we arrive, but in the meantime, we're going to focus on earth magic. Burja has a disproportionate number of Earth mages, you know. Probably should do a little water work too. Oh gods, you really ought to learn how to heal. Then again, there may not be another mage you're able to pull from in a critical healing situation. Oh, but warding is going to be important in Zarga..."

Delan leaned back and stretched. Zhafaera stopped abruptly and looked at him. "So where do we start?" he asked.

Chapter 7

"I still say I'm not a guard. Or a manservant," Colin said as he and Delan stood on the deck of the barge, taking them up the Azor river towards Zarga. The delegation that had met them in Anchorsa had been larger than they expected, and the combined parties filled the barge. Luckily, the trip from Anchorsa to Zarga was only two days.

"Zhafaera asked me for people I could trust. That's you and Sara. And Ban," Delan added. His other friend was below decks, where Zhafaera was resting. Since being appointed as one of their guards on this trip, Ban had rarely let Zhafaera out of his sight. Exactly how Delan wanted it – her personal bodyguard.

"You work for me," Delan continued. "Sara serves Zhafaera. We're surrounded by people we trust, and you three get out safely with us. It's a win-win."

"You put a lot of faith in me." Colin sounded unsure.

"Look, if someone comes at us, just whack them in the head with your hammer." Delan nodded to the blacksmith's hammer hanging from Colin's belt in place of a sword.

"That I can do," Colin said.

Delan stared at the city of Zarga as it came into view over the horizon. It shimmered in the heat like a mirage, rising up out of the scrubland surrounding the river. The twisting spirals of the royal palace came into view first, reaching for the sky as the gilded tops reflected the bright sunlight streaming down. Delan was glad he had packed his cooler clothes – the heat was stifling.

A horn sounded from somewhere above them, announcing their approach and startling Delan enough that his hand jerked automatically towards his sword. Not that he was jumpy or anything.

As the sound faded, an answering horn came from one of the sphinx statues flanking the river at the entrance to the city. The city had no walls, but the two statues served as guard posts to warn of any incoming ships from the river. They typically didn't have to worry about incursions from the other sides – the desert served as its own barrier.

Zhafaera appeared at the tented opening that led to the sleeping quarters, and Delan's eyes snapped to her. She looked lovely in a thin gown that billowed around her ankles, her crown sparkling from its place on her head. She didn't wear it often, but today it was necessary. Coming fully out onto the deck, she moved to the railing of the barge and turned her face up to the sun, smiling as she absorbed its energy, her curls floating around her face in the faint breeze off the river. Ban followed her at a distance.

"You're a lucky man," Colin murmured quietly.

"You have no idea," Delan replied, leaving Colin and walking over to Zhafaera.

"Hi," he said quietly, placing an arm around her shoulders. She immediately tilted her head to rest on his shoulder. "How are you feeling?"

"I feel fine," she said, and he could feel her smile. "I had an excellent nap, I'm not nauseous, and I'm with my favorite person."

"I'm your favorite person?" Delan leaned down and placed a kiss on her hair.

"For now," Zhafaera said with a laugh.

Delan gave her shoulders a squeeze. "Are you nervous about meeting with Queen Oraesa?"

Zhafaera sighed. "Not nervous, per say. More like still annoyed with her."

"You do tend to hold a grudge."

"It's a personal flaw." She looked up at Delan. "Are *you* nervous?"

"About meeting the Queen?" Zhafaera nodded. "Of course not. I'm a noble in my own right, even without being Consort. Besides, no way is she scarier than you," he teased.

Zhafaera elbowed him in the ribs as he dodged, releasing her and leaning back against the railing to study her. She looked brighter and healthier, and she'd regained much of her strength over the last two weeks, even if she was still too thin. She looked like a queen.

They fell silent as they passed through the city, listening to the merchants hawking their wares in the markets on either side of the river. Small docks and boats lined the narrow river on both sides, and the barge stuck carefully to the center to avoid them.

The city itself was a mix of low stone buildings and colorful tents stretched between them to provide as much shade as possible. Delan could see rain barrels at the corner of each, still mostly full after Zhafaera's storm.

The palace itself was built straddling the river, with large stone columns holding it up as the water rushed underneath. At the front was a large slatted gate blocking passage, which opened as they came close, swirling the river around in small whirlpools as the metal cut through the water. Through the gate, Delan could see a large set of docks and a large stone staircase rising up in the middle, leading to the main entrance of the palace. Framing it all was the jungle surrounding the oasis rising up behind the towers. The effect was impressive.

As their barge began to turn so the side would come right up to the dock, Delan eyed the delegation sitting under a large red and gold tent, just in front of the staircase. It was difficult to make out faces from this distance, but he thought he could see Queen Oraesa seated in a throne-like chair, with her daughter Liara hovering behind her. Three people stood on either side of her, flanking her chair, and a line of guards stood behind them, everyone waiting and watching silently as the boat docked. Overall, it didn't look like the most welcoming welcome party, but really, what had he expected?

As soon as the barge stopped moving, crew members hopped off, tying it tightly to several moorings spaced out along the side and extending a ramp down from the deck to the dock. Zhafaera straightened her shoulders as the rest of their party gathered on the deck, preparing to disembark. His father stood in the center of a knot of guards; having been named Zhafaera's chief advisor, he led the way down the ramp, taking his time as the handful of guards followed him. Reaching the bottom, they fanned out to either side, leaving a gap in the middle.

Zhafaera looked to Delan as they moved over to the ramp. He gave her an encouraging smile and she shrugged.

"Here we go," she said under her breath.

Zhafaera stepped onto the ramp first, with Delan following a few steps behind and Ban and Colin bringing up the rear. They had determined that Evey would stay on the boat and come in with the servants to avoid drawing attention to her.

As they reached the bottom of the ramp, all eyes turned to Zhafaera. The members of their own party inclined their heads respectfully, but the Burjans didn't move.

Zhafaera took her place in the center, and just in front of the line, Delan standing just behind and to the side of her in a stance they had practiced. There was silence for a moment.

Finally, Queen Oraesa stood. "Queen Zhafaera!" She called, stepping forward out of the shade of the tent. "How lovely to finally see you again in person." She reached out and placed her hands on her shoulders, causing all of Zhafaera's guards to stiffen, and placed a kiss on each of Zhafaera's cheeks. Zhafaera returned the gesture, although Delan thought it seemed forced.

"It's good to finally be here, Oraesa," Zhafaera said smoothly, pulling away. "Thank you for hosting us so graciously."

"Of course, it is nothing you wouldn't do for us," Oraesa said, waving a hand as if she hadn't had to be threatened to accept them. She turned to Delan and his father. "Lord Geon, Consort Delan, welcome. We're pleased to have you." Her voice was carefully neutral, but Delan thought he could see a slight smirk trying to break free.

Delan bowed as his father did the same. "It's a pleasure to meet you, Your Majesty," Delan said.

"Come, come, we must get out of this heat." Turning, Oraesa walked back under the tented pavilion, and Zhafaera followed. As they passed into the pavilion, Zhafaera turned her head and beckoned subtly for Delan and his father to follow.

Moving through the pavilion, Oraesa continued to the steps. As they passed Princess Liara, she reached out and grabbed Zhafaera's hand, falling into step beside them.

"It's so good to see you," the girl whispered.

"You too, Liara," Zhafaera said, flashing her a genuine smile.

As they climbed the steps, Delan followed behind the chatting women; Oraesa's advisors fell into step behind them followed by the Arenthian guards, the Burjan guards flanking them. It felt like an escort, and not an especially friendly one. The Burjans were mostly blonde-haired and blue-eyed with tanned skin, making them difficult to tell apart, looking like drones following their queen bee.

By the time they reached the top of the steps, Zhafaera had fallen silent, letting Liara do all the talking. Delan could tell she was winded and trying to hide it, not wanting to show any weakness in front of the others. He moved slightly closer to her.

"You'll want to get settled into your rooms before dinner, of course," Queen Oraesa was saying brightly as they entered the cool interior of the palace. The difference between the inside and blistering heat outside was remarkable. It had to be magic, Delan thought. "We haven't planned anything too formal for tonight, as we assumed you'd want to rest after your journey," Oraesa continued. "But at the end of the week, we'll have a ball to officially welcome you to our home."

"That sounds lovely," Zhafaera said. "But I hope you didn't go through too much trouble for us."

"Nonsense," Oraesa said quickly. "This is a most excellent reason to have a ball, particularly in such a trying time as this."

Zhafaera smiled blandly. "It's been quite some time since I've been to a ball."

"Of course, what with the challenges your mother faced and then that awful business with your uncle?" Oraesa shuddered. "If only we'd known what had truly happened, we never would have dealt with him."

"Of course," Zhafaera said smoothly. "He could be very convincing."

"Yes, well," Oraesa said, moving on. "While Prince Tristain is here from Khichora, the delegation from Laros has only just landed in Anchorsa, so they should arrive in the next two days, in plenty of time for the ball." She smiled at the surprised look on Zhafaera's face. "Yes, I know it's not a Gathering year, but I thought under the circumstances, it would be best to get us all together, no?"

"Yes," Zhafaera said, recovering quickly. "Yes, that's

for the best. We all need to figure out our next moves." Zhafaera emphasized *all,* no doubt remembering Oraesa's suggestion that the dragons were Arenthia's responsibility.

"Lovely," Oraesa clapped her hands together, and servants that Delan hadn't noticed stepped forward from the sides of the large hall, their heads bowed low. "Please show our guests to their quarters," she said brightly. "Then help the rest of their party unload their things." She turned back to Zhafaera. "Dinner will be served in two hours, at sunset. I trust that will give you enough time to get settled?" Zhafaera nodded. "Wonderful. Our servants will show you the way when it's time. Just let them know if you need anything, and we will be able to provide, I'm sure."

Oraesa and Zhafaera inclined their heads at each other, and Oraesa turned. "Come, Liara," she called behind her as he made her way down the hallway. Liara smiled and shrugged at Zhafaera and scurried after her mother. A servant stepped forward, likely the head of the household from his more formal dress.

"If you would follow me," he said, sweeping his hand towards the grand spiral staircase off to the side. "I'll show you to your rooms."

***

Zhafaera flopped on a long couch the moment the door was closed. Her and Delan's quarters consisted of a large living area, a balcony that overlooked the city, two bedrooms, two washrooms, and closets that were as big as

119

some rooms she'd seen and fully stocked with clothes appropriate for the climate. Which was good, because her current dress was the only thing she owned that was light enough to be comfortable. Lord Geon's room was next door to theirs, and they shared the floor with Prince Tristain and his advisors. Eventually the delegation from Laros would have the rooms across from theirs. Their servants and guards would be in the servants quarters on the same floor, down at the end of their hallway. Out of the way, but close enough should they need anything.

"Are you all right?" Delan asked, taking a seat across from her.

Zhafaera sighed. "Have I mentioned I hate politics?" she asked.

Delan smiled. "Once or twice, I believe."

"It's bad enough that I had to deal with Oraesa, but Tristain...ugh." She threw up her hands in frustration. "I broke his hand once. It was an accident, really. He touched me...well, in a way he shouldn't have, and I twisted his fingers back just a bit too far to make him let go." She sighed. "We used to be friends."

"Let him try something," Delan growled, and Zhafaera grinned.

"Males are all the same. Protecting their territory," she teased.

"Exactly."

She rolled her eyes.

Delan slid off of his chair to kneel in front of her, picking up her hand and kissing it. "If he lays a hand on my pregnant Queen..."

"I'm perfectly capable of taking care of us," Zhafaera said, placing her free hand over her belly.

"Oh, I'm well aware of that," Delan said. "But that doesn't mean I won't defend your honor if given half a chance."

Zhafaera laughed. "Fair enough."

"What about the delegation from Laros?" Delan asked.

"That's an unknown factor," Zhafaera said with a sigh. "They've changed leadership since the last Gathering, so I'm not entirely sure who they'll send. I've spoken to their new leader a few times, but I'm not sure he'd be the one to come. Even Khichora only sent their prince."

Delan leaned up and planted a quick kiss on her lips. "It'll be fine," he said soothingly. "Shall we start getting ready for dinner?"

"It won't take me *two hours* to get ready, Delan." Zhafaera laughed again. "I'm not *that* bad."

Just then, there was a small knock on the door. At Zhafaera's call to come in, Sara and Colin entered along with several other servants carrying their trunks.

"Sorry to disturb you," Sara said with a brief curtsy, made difficult by the basket with a baby on her hip. "We thought it would be best to go ahead and unpack your things."

"Yes, of course," Zhafaera said, standing. "Everything can go in the closets, assuming there's room. I'll show you."

Zhafaera led Sara to her room, while Delan guided

Colin to his. Once they deposited the trunk in the closet, the Burjan servants bowed and left, leaving Zhafaera and Sara alone to unpack. Opening the trunk, Zhafaera eyed the contents.

"I'm not really sure there's anything here that will be much use here," she said with a sigh. She dug through to the bottom of the trunk. "Except these." She pulled out a set of knives and held them up to show Sara.

Sara grinned. "Delan said you were usually armed to the teeth."

"It's true," she said. "I just didn't think it would be polite to wear knives around the palace." She sighed. "Though I'd feel much better with them."

"I can understand that," Sara said. "It's better to be able to protect yourself than rely on someone else."

"Exactly," Zhafaera said. Setting the knives aside, she reached out to Sara, indicating the basket with Amee in it. "May I?" she asked.

"Of course," Sara said, handing her over. Zhafaera took the basket and sat on the bench in the center of the room as Sara began to unpack.

"Aren't you just lovely?" Zhafaera cooed at the sleeping baby.

"She's lovely now," Sara said. "But not so much when she's screaming at three in the morning. Although she's generally a very good baby."

"It seems like it," Zhafaera said.

"When are you due?"

Zhafaera froze. "Excuse me?"

"Your baby. When are you due?"

Zhafaera closed her mouth with a snap. "Is Delan telling *everyone?*" she said, exasperated.

"No, he didn't tell me." Sara smiled. "But the look on his face when he first held Amee – I just knew."

Zhafaera sighed. "Please don't tell anyone."

Sara shrugged and went back to work hanging clothes. "I won't, I promise." She hesitated. "But you'll have to start telling people eventually."

Zhafaera bit her lip. An idea had been bouncing around in her head for a little while now, but she wasn't sure if she could do it. Or if she should. "I'm about three months along, so I expect she'll be born in late summer," she said, deflecting.

"She?"

"Just a feeling," Zhafaera said with a smile. "It feels better than saying 'it.'"

"Gods, Colin called Amee 'it' for the longest time," Sara laughed. "It just doesn't sound right." She paused. "By the way, thank you for taking me on, even with the baby and all," she stopped and looked at Zhafaera. "I know I have no experience with this sort of thing, but I'll do my best."

Zhafaera waved her off. "I hate all the bowing and scraping anyway. I'd do it all myself if it wasn't frowned upon. Besides, I wanted people I could trust, and if Delan trusts you, then I trust you. That's what matters to me."

"I hope I'll prove worthy," Sara said, closing the trunk and straightening. "Now, can I draw you a bath? I can help you get ready for dinner."

Zhafaera suppressed a sigh. "Yes, please," she said

instead, standing and picking up Amee's basket. "I suppose I need to at least *look* like a queen."

***

Two hours later, bathed and dressed, Zhafaera and Delan followed a servant through the palace to dinner. Zhafaera had been here several times before, but Delan was wide-eyed as he took in the incredible opulence around them. Most of the halls were made of yellow sandstone, with evenly spaced columns carved into intricate designs and often inlaid with gold filigree, making them sparkle even in the low light. Works of art sat in recesses set every so often along the walls, ranging from expertly carved precious and semi-precious stones to delicate blown glass statues that seemed to defy gravity to paintings so lifelike, Zhafaera expected them to walk right off the canvas. Oraesa was nothing if not ostentatious, but the amount of art surrounding them was just incredible.

Surprisingly, the servant did not lead them to the main dining room, where Zhafaera had been before, but to a small, intimate patio overlooking a well-groomed garden, with trimmed hedges and flowerbeds surrounding various burbling fountains and small ponds. As the sun had now mostly set, the heat of the day was dissipating, leaving behind a distinct chill in the air. Small fires burned in stone ovens on either side of the veranda, illuminating and warming the space.

As Delan and Zafaera entered, she noted that the only ones present were royalty – Queen Oraesa, Princess Liara, and Prince Tristain were the only ones seated at the table. Zhafaera glanced at Delan, who looked slightly uncomfortable, and shrugged. Oraesa had invited them both, and Delan had enough stature as Consort to join this gathering. If just barely.

"Zhafaera!" Tristain stood, coming around the table to greet her, smiling wide under his head of curly blond hair. Opening his arms wide, he asked, "May I?"

Zhafaera gave a small smile. "Oh, all right." He stepped forward and embraced her in a quick hug, squeezing tight for a moment.

I'm so sorry, I can't believe I was such an ass, his voice whispered in her mind. He was an Air mage.

Zhafaera kept her face smooth, hiding her relief. *I'm sorry too,* she thought back, returning his squeeze. Tristain quickly released her and turned to Delan.

"And you must be the Consort," Tristain said warmly, extending his hand. Delan took it, and the two shook hands.

"Tristain, this is Lord Delan," Zhafaera said, keeping her discomfort out of her voice. Their handshake was just a little too long and a little too tense. "Delan, Prince Tristain."

"It's a pleasure to meet you, your Highness," Delan said, finally letting go of Tristain's hand and inclining his head politely.

"Please, call me Tristain, no need to stand on ceremony when it's just us."

Taking their seats at the round table, Zhafaera put Delan between her and Tristain, sitting with Liara on her other side. Her friend smiled at her happily, and Zhafaera couldn't help but return the gesture. Liara was a genuinely nice person, despite her mother.

"We're so glad you could join us," Oraesa began. "I thought this evening could be just an intimate gathering. A catching up of old friends, you know." She smiled at Delan in a way that didn't quite reach her eyes. "And new friends, of course. Consort Delan, have you been introduced to my daughter, Princess Liara? These three"—she indicated Zhafaera, Liara, and Tristain—"used to be inseparable at Gatherings, you know."

Zhafaera ground her teeth at the attempt to make Delan uncomfortable.

"It's a pleasure to officially meet you, Princess Liara," Delan said easily, inclining his head. "Zhafaera and I have been friends for quite some time as well, and any friend of hers is a friend of mine." He bared his teeth at Tristain in what Zhafaera surmised was supposed to be a smile. Close enough. She would have to let him know that the prince had apologized, although she wasn't sure how much difference that would make to Delan. But it made a difference to her.

The evening progressed with more small talk, and as Delan proved able to hold his own against the powerful people in front of him, Zhafaera began to relax. It wasn't until dessert had been brought out and the servants retreated back inside that the conversation took a serious turn.

"Zhafaera," Liara asked nervously. "Tell us, what *really* happened with the dragons? Why did they invade

Arenthia? And *how*? We only know what our mages have been able to scry – how bad is it really?"

Zhafaera's heart sank, though she'd been expecting the question. They had to make some kind of plan, and they could only do that if they knew the full extent of the crisis.

"Well," Zhafaera began slowly. "It started with my uncle, Velexar, as you know. He was somehow able to ally himself with a faction of dragons and used them to help stage a coup. He killed my mother and took the Sapphire." Oraesa's eyes jerked to Delan, but Zhafaera ignored it and continued. "I made it out of the city, and made my way to Crystal Point, where I knew I had people I could trust." She paused. "Lord Geon and Lord Delan were kind enough to help me. Delan accompanied me back to the city to try to regain the Sapphire and my throne. I was..." Zhafaera swallowed nervously at the memory. "I was captured, but mostly unharmed, and eventually Delan managed to rescue me. Together, we were able to overpower Velexar, and I killed him," Zhafaera finished simply. Glancing around, she realized everyone was rapt with attention.

"The dragons showed up after that," she continued. "They completely razed the city of Arenthia, and we only just escaped with our lives. We think it was their plan all along to use Velexar to destabilize us and then step in and strike when the moment was right."

There was silence around the table. Finally, Tristain spoke up. "How many dragons are we talking about?" he asked quietly.

"We only saw four or five that night in the city, but our best intelligence tells us that there could be nearly a hundred that have now taken over Arenthia." *Thank you, Evey,* Zhafaera thought.

"A *hundred*?" Liara asked, her face pale.

"Yes, that's our best estimate," Zhafaera said. "Although for now, they don't seem to have crossed the Angonite mountains. They seem to be establishing control one region at a time."

"Thank the Gods for that," Oraesa chimed in, sipping her wine. "Hopefully it will give us some time." She raised an eyebrow at Zhafaera. "Do you have any sort of plan to fight them?"

Zhafaera took a deep breath. "I've had one idea," she said carefully.

"Well, let's hear it," Tristain said impatiently when Zhafaera didn't continue immediately.

Zhafaera flashed him a look. "It's the four Gems," she bit out. "I think if we can use all four, we might stand a chance at holding our ground and hopefully pushing them back. I have the Sapphire, and we all know that Laros very likely still has the Ruby," she said quickly. "It's the Emerald and the Diamond that are…unaccounted for." She looked at Oraesa and Tristain. "Do either of you have *any* idea whatsoever where they might be?"

Tristain was shaking her head before she'd even finished. "The Diamond disappeared more than five hundred years ago, Zhafaera. There's no way to find it now."

She looked to Oraesa, whose lips were pursed in a thin

line. "You know we don't have the Emerald," she said tightly. "If we did, do you think I would have allowed you to pull your…little stunt?"

Zhafaera wasn't sure Oraesa would have been able to stop Zhafaera even if she had had the Emerald. Not only was she not a mage, but even if she had been able to find someone she trusted, the Emerald's power wasn't attuned to water. Zhafaera let the comment pass.

"I'm just saying, if we could find them, that would likely give us our best chance," she said with a shrug.

"It's something to consider at least," Delan said, and she smiled at him, grateful for the support.

"Not if it's completely unrealistic," Oraesa snapped. "If *this* is your plan, we might as well give up now."

"Well, if you have a better idea, I'd be more than happy to listen," Zhafaera said calmly. She would not lose her temper again.

"As we speak, my mages are fortifying this city against any enemy incursion, from the ground or the air. Right now, defense is our best offense."

"Khichora is doing the same," Tristain said. "We don't have as many mages – most of them were training in the Cathedral in Arenthia, but we have numerous strongholds in the mountains. Many of our people are retreating there."

"That's an excellent place to start," Zhafaera said. "But eventually we *will* need an offensive strategy. We have to be able to stand and fight."

"Agreed," Tristain said. "We just have to figure out exactly how we're going to do that."

"I think we should wait until the delegation from Laros arrives," Liara piped up. All eyes turned to her, and she wilted slightly. "They may have additional information, and they might be able to tell us about the Ruby, at least."

Zhafaera nodded. "That's probably the best we can hope for." She turned to Oraesa. "Do you know who they're sending in the delegation? Is Lead Councilman Yran coming?"

Queen Oraesa smiled slowly. "No, he couldn't be spared. They're sending Councilman Nyto in his place."

Zhafaera froze, nearly dropping the glass of water she'd just picked up. *Of all people...* she thought. She forced herself to speak. "That's lovely." Her voice sounded hollow to her own ears.

"Yes, I thought so," Oraesa said, still smiling as her eyes flashed. "Anyway, I think that's quite enough serious talk for the night. Shall we have some music?" She raised her hands, likely preparing to call the entertainment.

Zhafaera stood abruptly. "Actually, I think we'll retire for the evening," she said mechanically. "We've had quite a long journey, and I find myself in need of rest." Without waiting for the others to respond, she turned and headed back inside, Delan following closely behind.

Liara caught up with them just as they reached the inner hallway.

"Do you need help finding your way back to your rooms?" she asked anxiously.

Zhafaera forced a smile. "That would be most appreciated. I always get turned around in here."

"Yes, it's quite a way. The mages say that having more passageways that twist and turn makes it easier to keep the inside cooler."

They walked in silence for a time. "Zhafaera, I'm sorry I brought all that up," Liara finally said.

"Don't be," Zhafaera replied. She forced a smile. "It all needed to be said."

Liara relaxed somewhat and continued speaking, but Zhafaera was only half listening. Luckily, Delan held up his end of the conversation, and in no time they were back in front of the door to their rooms.

"Well, goodnight," Liara said. She reached out and pulled Zhafaera into a hug. "We'll talk more tomorrow."

"Of course," Zhafaera said, giving her friend a tight squeeze.

As soon as the door closed behind them, Delan turned to Zhafaera. "What's wrong?" he asked. "You went as white as a sheet back there." He reached for her, and she stepped into his open arms, resting her forehead on his chest. "It's something about the Laros delegation?"

Zhafaera took a breath. "Yes. I–I know Nyto."

Delan tensed. "Another one I have to beat away with a stick?"

"No," Zhafaera said, shaking her head. She looked up at Delan. "He's my grandfather."

Chapter 8

Delan followed Zhafaera through a back entrance of the palace and into the bright, warm morning still arguing.

"I really don't think this is a good idea."

"Aroha said I'm well enough to return to normal activity. *This* is normal activity for me." Zhafaera's pace made him have to lengthen his stride to keep up.

"I just don't want you to overdo."

Zhafaera sighed and turned to face him. "I feel good, Delan. Really good. And I have to build some strength back."

She stopped at the armory first. A few words to the quartermaster, and she had a bow in hand and a quiver of arrows thrown over her shoulder. Delan flashed a look behind him at Ban, hovering a respectful distance away, but within eyesight. Back outside, Delan continued.

"What if you hurt yourself, Zhafaera?" He lowered his voice. "You're pregnant, and I'm relatively sure this isn't what Aroha had in mind."

"She specifically said I could exercise, as long as I was careful. I'll be careful. I'll start with my knives and see how I feel."

Delan sighed, knowing it was absolutely no use.

Over towards the stables was a practice yard that guards used to drill early every morning. Every evening, the yard was used once again to train what seemed like all able-bodied men, and some women in the city in staff, sword, and bow. Oraesa had told them there were many such places throughout the city; she was training everyone she could to prepare them for the fight ahead. Delan had to give her credit; it's what he would have done. Not that a sword would do much against a fully grown dragon. But this time of day, the yard was deserted.

Resigned, Delan climbed over the fence after Zhafaera, leaning against it with his arms crossed as she set her bow and arrows down next to him. She gave him a smile, then turned and settled her stance, taking several deep breaths.

The first knife went flying almost faster than Delan could see. It hit with a satisfying *thunk* in one of the outer rings of the target. Delan winced. That would upset Zhafaera.

Sure enough, two more knives went flying in quick succession, these closer to the center but not quite there. She reached down to her ankles to unhook two more knives, distracting Delan momentarily. She'd barely straightened before throwing the next knife, and it hit another outside ring.

Delan could almost hear her growl. Then she took a breath, shifted her hips slightly, and flung the last knife.

It hit dead center.

"Whew," Delan called out. "I thought you'd lost your touch."

Zhafaera tossed her hair back. "Which is exactly why I needed to practice." She trotted forward and retrieved her knives, stretching her shoulder as she went.

"Sore?" Delan asked.

"Not yet."

It was nearly thirty minutes before Zhafaera was hitting the center of the target consistently enough for her to be satisfied. Slipping all her knives back into their hidden sheaths, Delan counted six in total. She paused and stretched. First her arms, rotating her shoulders, twisting and pulling them over her head. Tilting side to side, she stretched her back, then her legs, the thin flowing fabric of her cream shirt and jade green pants giving her plenty of room to move.

Satisfied, she moved to get the bow, and Delan held it out to her. She raised an eyebrow at him.

"What? Just because I don't approve doesn't mean I can't be helpful."

Zhafaera planted the end of the wood against her foot and strung the bow. The tip wobbled as she slipped the string over it. She flashed Delan a grin. "Okay, that was more difficult than I expected. He gave me a fairly light bow, too."

Delan pursed his lips, smart enough not to say, *I told you so.*

Zhafaera pulled the quiver onto her back, loosening her shoulders as she took her stance. Raising an arrow, she pulled back on the string and released. The arrow shot straight into the center of the target, and Delan grinned. She continued firing into the target, her arrows all clustering around the first one, until her quiver was empty.

"Well, at least I can still do *something*," Zhafaera said

wryly.

Slow clapping rang out across the yard, and they both jumped, spinning around. Tristain stood at one corner on the opposite side of the fence, watching.

"Very nice," he called. "I didn't know you could shoot like that."

"It's not something I show off in polite company," Zhafaera called back, moving to retrieve her arrows. Delan went to help her as Tristain hopped over the fence. Out of the corner of his eye, he saw Ban move closer.

"What about you, Delan? You any good with that sword?" Delan could hear the smirk in Tristain's voice. Delan had strapped it on before they'd left their rooms, unwilling to let Zhafaera go outside unprotected, even with Ban sticking close.

"I'm all right," he said easily.

From behind his back, Tristain pulled two practice swords – metal, but with dull edges. He tossed one to Delan, who caught it easily.

"I thought we could train together. I'm always looking for a worthy sparring partner."

Delan shrugged. "If you want," he said casually. Internally, he was ready to kick this guy's ass. Zhafaera seemed to have forgiven him, but all Delan could think about was his hands on her.

Pulling off his own sword, he rested it against the fence next to where Zhafaera had climbed to sit for the best view. He stood on his tiptoes and kissed her. "Wish me luck," he said lightly.

"Really, must you?" she asked. But her eyes crinkled

with laughter.

"Male pride," Delan said with a grin.

Delan moved forward into the center of the yard with Tristain, both of them at the ready. They were evenly matched, he estimated. Roughly the same height and build. Tristain was a couple of years younger, Zhafaera's age, but not enough to make a difference. Slowly, they started to move, circling each other, watching. Waiting.

Tristain lunged first, rushing forward and aiming for Delan's left side. Delan blocked easily, brushing away his sword and swiping under it, forcing Tristain to dance back. Delan followed, swinging in a broad stroke for Tristain's legs, ready to pull back if needed, but Tristain's sword met his before he got anywhere close.

Both men pulled back, circling again.

"Very nice," Tristain said lightly.

Delan didn't respond. Instead, he feinted left, then swung his body around and under Tristain, coming up behind him. Tristain barely dodged the blow Delan aimed for his shoulder, spinning abruptly so that his sword locked with Delan's. Both men leaned their weight in, each trying to force the other back, but they were evenly matched. Finally, they both pushed back, releasing their swords with a twist.

Then Tristain came at Delan and didn't let up. Their swords clashed and clanged in the stillness of the midmorning air, flashing in the sunlight as they twisted and turned and lunged and parried and swiped. Delan felt energized, adrenaline pumping, sweat dripping into his eyes. And then he saw it. Tristain's grip slipped just slightly on the hilt of his sword, his pinky finger bent out at an odd angle.

Delan didn't hesitate. Thrusting forward, he curved his blade up under Tristain's, catching it at the hilt and popping it from his grasp, sending it flying. With his defense gone, Delan grabbed Tristain by the shirt, swept a leg behind his ankles, and took him to the ground, kneeling next to him with the point of his sword at Tristain's throat.

"I yield," Tristain panted.

Delan released him and stood, holding out a hand to help Tristain up. He took it. "Looked like you had a bit of trouble with your grip at the end there," Delan said coolly.

Tristain grinned and shrugged. "A misunderstanding. It never did heal quite right," he said, making a fist and turning it in front of him. The pinky finger didn't bend all the way in.

"Good fight," Delan said grudgingly, holding out his hand.

"Likewise."

"Touch her again, and I'll kill you for real," Delan murmured, hearing Zhafaera coming towards them.

"Fair enough," Tristain grinned. "She's not really my type, anyway." He winked at Delan and walked off, leaving Delan blinking in the hot sun.

Chapter 9

"Are you *sure* he said it like that?" Zhafaera called from her room. Delan was in the main living area, waiting as she put the final touches on her hair. Sara had piled it up on top of her head, letting tendrils escape to curl loosely around her neck. Despite her hot bath, her upper body was sore from the exercise that morning, and her arms protested each movement. She was beginning to think having her first training session in months on the day of the ball was perhaps not her best idea.

"I'm pretty sure that's what he meant," Delan said, appearing in the doorway. She met his eyes in the mirror.

"I just don't get why he would have *groped* me if he likes men. It makes no sense."

"Maybe he likes both," Delan said with a shrug, leaning against the door frame.

"Maybe," Zhafaera said doubtfully. She'd known Tristain a long time, and she didn't particularly like the idea that Delan knew something about him that she didn't.

"Don't worry about it. If it means he's not interested in you, so much the better." Delan grinned. "It's probably for the best if I don't have to beat him senseless."

Zhafaera rolled her eyes and touched up the pale pink paint on her lips. She'd never had much use for face paint, but it was expected of her. She'd stuck to the bare minimum. Satisfied, she gave a small spin in front of the mirror, sending her deep purple gown flowing outwards. The material was a thin silk that hugged her closely around the silver-embroidered bodice, while the arms and skirt hung loosely enough to billow around her when she moved. She loved it. It made her feel a little as though she had wings.

Delan's gaze in the mirror was intense. "Do that again," he said quietly.

Zhafaera smiled, blushing as she spun again but relishing the feeling.

Coming up behind her slowly, Delan reached around her waist and placed a hand on her lower belly. Her heart jumped in her chest.

"What are you—"

"You're starting to show," he whispered almost reverently, kissing her gently on her exposed shoulder.

"What?" She squeaked, slipping out of his embrace and pushing him back. She turned to the side and smoothed her dress flat. Sure enough, there was the slightest bump, protruding slightly from her still too-thin frame. Hardly noticeable, but definitely there. "Why didn't you say something before?" she asked, her voice shooting up.

"I didn't notice before," Delan said. He couldn't seem to wipe the smile off of his face.

Zhafaera took a deep breath, trying to calm down. "It's not even worth changing," she said dully. "These dresses are all too thin to hide *anything*."

Delan rested his hands gently on her shoulders. "You don't need to change," he said. "You have to start telling people sometime – why not announce it tonight?”

“Because I’m not ready!” To her horror, Zhafaera felt tears gathering in the corners of her eyes. She blinked furiously.

“Okay, it’s okay,” Delan said soothingly. He looked confused. “Look, I’m sure no one else will notice. I only caught it because I was looking.” He rubbed her shoulders as if trying to rub away her tension.

Zhafaera took a deep breath. “I can make sure no one sees,” she said. Drawing on her magic, she wove an illusion spell. Still turned to the side, she watched in the mirror as she laid the spell over her abdomen, and the bump vanished. Putting a hand tentatively on her belly, she could still feel it there, but no one would be able to see it.

“Isn’t that a little extreme?” Delan asked quietly.

“*I* don’t think so,” Zhafaera said defiantly.

“Zhafaera, you don’t have to hide—” he stopped mid-sentence, his eyes widening. “That’s what you want, isn’t it? You want to hide it like your mother hid Alec.”

Zhafaera looked away. For once, she wished Delan didn’t make connections so quickly.

“That’s – that’s—” Delan couldn’t seem to find the words. “You can’t,” he finished lamely.

“Don’t tell me what I can and can’t do,” Zhafaera snapped, spinning abruptly to face him.

“But why? Why would you want to?” Delan paused. “Is it me?”

Zhafaera froze. “What? No, of course it’s not you. Why would you think that?”

“Because you’re a *queen*, and I’m just a minor noble

who no one has ever heard of before. You could have had your pick of anyone."

"Delan, I love you, and I'm not *ashamed* to be with you," Zhafaera said, aghast.

"Then why do you want to hide your pregnancy?"

"Because I want to keep her safe," she said quietly.

"Safe from what?" Delan asked. "Look your mother, she had somewhere to hide Alec, with my father. She knew or she thought that he'd be protected." A shadow crossed over Delan's face and he gestured angrily around them. "Tell me, where could our child go where they'd be safe in this world?"

"I don't *know*, that's why I don't want to tell anyone yet. I haven't figured it all out."

"*Nowhere* is safe from dragons, Zhafaera," Delan snapped.

"Why are you so angry?" Zhafaera said, her voice rising.

"Because you've been trying to figure out how to send our child away without even talking to me about it." Delan took a deep breath and closed his eyes.

Zhafaera's temper vanished in a wave of guilt. That was exactly what she'd been doing. "Look," she said softly. "Can we not do this now? We're going to be late."

Delan opened his eyes. "Fine," he snapped, but he held out his arm for her. She took it hesitantly, uncomfortable with the tension between them. When they reached the door, she stopped and looked up at him.

"I'm just trying to do what's best," Zhafaera said quietly.

Delan didn't respond.

***

Delan was quiet through the meal, and the voices crowding the large room grated on his nerves. They were in the main dining hall, a cavernous room with a vaulted ceiling that seemed to go up forever, and the guests filled the whole space. It seemed as though every noble in the city was present, including a few Arenthians that had arrived just after he and Zhafaera's entourage. They seemed to be sticking together – a clump of dark-haired, dark-eyed people in a sea of blonde. Esla and Elden sat at one of the lower tables, and Lady Greina of Esport was deep in conversation with a Burjan noble that Delan didn't know. But then he didn't know most of the people here. Sitting at the high table with the royals, he felt out of place. He would much rather be sitting with his father at a lower table with the rest of the advisors.

Zhafaera seemed to be faring better. She chatted amiably with Liara on her other side, hardly sparing Delan a glance. He was seated at the end of the table, for which he was grateful; he didn't think he could focus long enough to carry on a conversation.

His thoughts were still racing over Zhafaera's revelation. The thought of sending their child off into the unknown made his chest tighten and his stomach churn. Frustration roiled inside him as he tried to see things from her point of view but he just couldn't. Surely their baby would be safer with them? Zhafaera was quite possibly the most powerful mage of her time, and he would gladly give his life to protect either of them.

When Queen Oraesa stood and announced they should all move to the ballroom, Delan was surprised. The dinner had passed with him hardly tasting a thing. Standing with the others, Delan offered his arm to Zhafaera, not meeting her gaze. When she laid her hand on his arm, he could feel her apprehension bleeding through their connection. He forced a half-hearted smile and followed the others out of the dining room.

The ballroom was a beautiful room with white marble floors inlaid with gold in huge geometric patterns. One entire wall was open to the air, columns that matched the floor separating the room from a large veranda that led out into expansive gardens lit with torches. Musicians were setting up in one corner of the room, and servants moved through the space carrying trays laden with wine glasses. Delan immediately grabbed one. He needed something to dull the roaring in his ears as his heart pounded.

From there, Delan proceeded to meet what must have been every person in the room. He and Zhafaera moved around from group to group, making introductions as everyone wanted to meet the new Queen of Arenthia. Delan was usually decent with names, but tonight…it was hopeless. He did the best he could, trying to find a balance between respectful and respected as he played the part of Consort.

It wasn't until they found the delegation from Laros that his mind snapped to attention. Four men with tanned skin and dark curly hair stood before them, dressed in light, flowing tunics and thin hose. They bowed as Zhafaera approached, and one of them took a few steps forward to meet her. His gray hair flowed around his face and brushed his shoulders, and his bright blue eyes were the same color as Zhafaera's. He looked familiar, but Delan couldn't put his finger on it at first. Suddenly it came to him, he looked like an older version of Velexar, Delan realized with a jolt. This had to be Zhafaera's grandfather, Velexar's father. From the look on her face, Zhafaera seemed to have come to the same conclusion.

"Councilman Nyto, I presume?" Zhafaera asked evenly. But Delan could feel her anxiety seeping through their connection, where her hand still rested on his arm.

"Queen Zhafaera. How lovely to finally meet you, granddaughter. You're as beautiful as your mother." Nyto leaned forward, taking her hand in his and placing a kiss on it. Straightening, he turned to Delan. "And you must be the Consort."

Delan inclined his head. "I am," he said, reaching to take Nyto's outstretched hand and shaking it firmly.

"Consort Delan is son of the Lord of Crystal Point," Zhafaera interjected. Was she seeking his approval?

"I can't say I've ever visited," Nyto said.

"It's a beautiful place."

There was silence for a beat.

"I was sorry to hear about your mother. And your uncle." Delan found it odd that Nyto spoke of his children as if they were strangers.

Zhafaera must have felt the same. "It's—it's been a trying time," she stammered.

"Yes, for us all." Nyto's face clouded for a moment, and Delan relaxed somewhat. At least he seemed to feel *something* for his children's deaths. Then he smiled. "I'm sure you will pick up the reins of Arenthia easily. Or at least, what's left of it."

Delan felt Zhafaera stiffen, and he reached over, placing his hand over hers and squeezing.

"It's a shame Lead Councilman Yran couldn't come himself," Zhafaera said coolly, ignoring his jab and planting her own.

"Yes, well, he's quite busy. We all are," Nyto said smoothly, bowing again. One of his companions leaned forward and whispered in his ear. "I'm sorry, you must excuse me. I need to find Queen Oraesa."

"Of course," Zhafaera said, inclining her head. She looked to Delan. "Shall we?"

Delan bowed to Nyto, and they went their separate ways.

"That went well," Delan murmured.

Zhafaera snorted.

"How is it that you'd never met him before? If he's a Councilman, wouldn't he have been at Gatherings?"

"Not all of them are," Zhafaera said. "He tended to avoid them. And us."

"You would think he'd want to see his own children."

"You would think." They continued moving through the crowd.

"Zhafaera!" Delan recognized Liara's voice. "Over here!" She was waving them over towards a small group of Burjan nobles. Delan sighed inwardly and tried to pay attention to names.

Some time later, after what felt like hundreds of blurred faces and the same inane conversations, Delan realized Zhafaera was no longer on his arm. Looking around, he found himself in the midst of a group of nobles he'd just been introduced to but didn't know. Quickly making excuses, he left the group, looking around for Zhafaera as he fought his rising panic.

She's fine, he told himself. *She's here somewhere.*

Moving towards the veranda, he leaned against a column, sipping his wine and searching the room. He finally spotted Zhafaera on the other side, laughing with Lady Greina.

"Lover's quarrel?" a voice interrupted his reverie. Delan turned and saw Prince Tristain leaning on the other side of the marble column. He shrugged, not particularly wanting to discuss it with Tristain. He still wasn't sure how he felt about the man.

"That's okay, you'll get past it." He smiled. "Zhafaera has a temper, but it fades as quickly as it comes."

"What makes you think she's the one that's angry?" Delan asked.

"Because you look like a kicked puppy."

Delan shook himself and tried for a bland smile. "Better?"

Tristain grimaced. "Not really."

"Sorry, that's the best I've got," Delan said. He eyed Tristain. "So you and Zhafaera have been friends a long time?"

"Yes," Tristain answered. "We're the same age, so it

was natural for us to stick together at Gatherings, or when our families met periodically in between. She led me around by the nose.”

Delan quirked a smile. “She has that effect on people.”

“She does.” He eyed Delan speculatively. “You seem like a good man, Delan.”

Delan blinked at him, surprised. “I try to be.”

“I wouldn’t say that about just anyone she’d chosen as Consort. Plenty of men have been vying for the position for years, even when she was only a princess, and none of them were even halfway deserving of her.” He paused. “She’s like a sister to me, you know.”

“It seems you have a funny way of showing it,” Delan said coolly.

Tristain smiled ruefully. “Yes, well. Putting my hand where it didn’t belong was quite possibly the most idiotic thing I’ve ever done. So far.”

“Why did you do it?”

Tristain shrugged. “Why does any man do something stupid? I was confused, unsure of myself and what I wanted. Trying to please my father. He had an affair with Queen Karaena, you know. I suppose he thought I should, I don’t know, carry on the tradition. But that’s not Zhafaera’s style of diplomacy.” He stuffed his hands in the pockets of his ornate coat. “Not my finest hour.”

“She seems to have forgiven you.”

“Thank the gods. She can really hold a grudge when she wants to.”

“She cares about you,” Delan said.

"As she does for you." Tristain looked around. "Ah, finally!" he said, as the musicians started to play. "It's time for dancing! If you'll excuse me, I have to find my partner." He bowed with a flourish and moved away, slipping through the crowd with ease.

Delan found Zhafaera again and locked eyes with her. He gave her a little smile, and she smiled back. He watched as she excused herself from her group and began heading towards him. He met her halfway.

"May I have this dance?" he asked, holding out a hand.

"You may," she said formally.

Taking her hand, Delan led her into the center of the room, slipping a hand around her waist and beginning to lead them around the floor.

Are you still mad at me? Her voice in his head was quiet, almost timid.

I'm not mad, he thought back. *Just upset.*

I'm sorry I didn't say anything to you.

*It's all right. I just...*he pulled back slightly and met her steady blue gaze. *I want our child to stay with us.*

I know, she said. *And I just want her to be safe. I feel like there's a target on my back.*

You think the dragons would come after you, specifically?

I have the Sapphire, Zhafaera's eyes were wide, pleading with him to understand. *They know me. Not to mention anyone else that may have a quarrel with me.* Her eyes shot to Queen Oraesa, who was dancing with Nyto nearby.

Zhafaera, I'll protect you. I'll protect you both or die trying.

I know that. They spun sharply to avoid another couple.

You're the most powerful mage in the world, Delan thought. *Between the two of us, if we can't keep our child safe, who can?*

Zhafaera sighed. *No one.*

Delan felt a glimmer of hope. *So you won't send her away?*

No, I won't. Zhafaera gave him a small smile. *You're the father, you get a say too. And if you don't want to hide her, then I concede. I don't think I could do it anyway. Give her up.*

Delan pulled Zhafaera closer and rested his cheek against the side of her head. "Me neither," he whispered into her ear, planting a soft kiss against her hair.

I still don't want to tell anyone yet, she said.

Why not?

Because the others will see it as a weakness. Queen Oraesa, Nyto, even Tristain...they'll treat me differently. I want to avoid that for as long as possible.

I can understand that. I'll follow your lead. I won't say anything.

Zhafaera relaxed and leaned into him; their bodies practically melded together as they moved across the dance floor. Suddenly, she laughed.

"What?" Delan asked, pulling back to see her face.

"Looks like you were right," she said, nodding to the side. Delan glanced over and saw Prince Tristain twirling around the dance floor with a man about his age, with dark red hair and broad shoulders, dressed sharply in a simple navy blue coat that contrasted with Tristain's finely embroidered silk. Tristain saw them looking and waved.

"I told you," Delan said, smiling.

"I never would have guessed." She paused. "So why on *earth* did he go for me?"

"He said he was being an idiot."

"Well, he's certainly not wrong."

"All men are idiots when it comes to you."

"Now you're just trying to flatter me," Zhafaera laughed.

"Only a little."

The song finished, and another started up. Delan held Zhafaera close as he led her across the floor effortlessly. She was an excellent dancer, and he was unwilling to let her go after their disagreement.

"May I cut in?" a voice asked.

Delan turned to find his father standing close by, watching them and smiling. Reluctantly, Delan let go of Zhafaera and turned her over to his father with a flourish. "I suppose," he said. "But I'll want her back."

Delan moved off the dance floor, standing to the side and watching. It wasn't long before a Burjan noblewoman, Lady Rahaj, Delan thought her name was, came up to him and asked him to dance with her. Delan accepted, and thus began the flood of people. He and Zhafaera occasionally came back together, but more often than not, they found themselves dancing with one strange partner after another. Delan found the Burjans interesting – mostly they talked about the recent storm, and how the desert had bloomed afterwards. Apparently, deserts were very much alive under all that sand. As soon as it rained, various plants and flowers popped up and turned the barren landscape into almost-meadows.

He wasn't sure how long he danced, but finally Delan found himself back at "his" column. It had to be close to midnight, but the party was showing no signs of slowing down. In fact, as the wine kept flowing, the room seemed to get louder and louder, and the dance floor became more and more crowded as people loosened their inhibitions. Delan himself had a pleasant buzz in his head that had replaced the anxiety from earlier, and he found himself enjoying the night.

He looked around for Zhafaera and saw her dancing with Elden. His heart rate ticked up as he saw Elden's hand just a little too low on the small of Zhafaera's back, his hold just a little too intimate. But before he'd taken more than two steps forward, Prince Tristain appeared, murmuring something in Elden's ear. Elden let go immediately, and Tristain cut in. Elden did not look happy, but he moved away. Delan relaxed. Tristain's hold was much more appropriate.

He felt a change in the air behind him and turned. Councilman Nyto was coming in from the veranda, a glass of wine in his hand. From the flush on his face, it was not his first. He nodded, acknowledging Delan.

"Consort," he said.

"Councilman."

"Where's your Queen?"

"Dancing," Delan said, gesturing to where she moved across the floor with Tristain. They appeared to be deep in conversation now.

"Yes, well, I imagine she's quite popular. Like her mother." The way he said it rubbed Delan the wrong way. Nyto took a sip of his wine. "My children were always well liked."

Delan didn't think Velexar had ever been "well liked," but he kept the thought to himself. "I'm sorry for your loss," Delan said instead.

"Thank you." Another sip of wine. "I didn't know Karaena well, but Velexar…he spent quite a bit of time with me in Laros."

"You were close?" Delan tried to keep the incredulity out of his voice. Delan knew Velexar had spent much of his youth out of the country, but he hadn't thought Velexar could be close to anyone.

"Yes." He glanced at Delan. "I see that's difficult for you to believe, but he was my son," he said defensively.

"He killed his sister. And worse. He captured Zhafaera and would have—" Delan stopped abruptly. It wasn't his story to tell.

Nyto sighed and drank deeply. "I knew some of the magic he practiced was unsavory, and I suspected something was wrong after he left Laros and Karaena became…ill. But I had no idea the lengths he would go to take what he believed was his by right. He was the oldest, you know. He believed the throne should have gone to him, and I didn't disagree."

"You encouraged him," Delan accused, shocked.

"Not as such, but we discussed it at length," Nyto said. "But as you know, the Arenthian throne is passed down through the maternal line, and once Cerena had a daughter…Velexar was pushed aside. Which is why he ultimately came to me in his teens, I understood. Cerena and Karaena were inseparable; there was no room for anyone else," he finished bitterly.

"Is that why you left?"

Nyto nodded. "Once Karaena was born, that was it. Our relationship fell apart, and Cerena had no further use for me. And from what I heard, Karaena wasn't much better. She never even took a Consort, and who knows who Zhafaera's father is. My advice to you, one Consort to another—" Nyto smiled coldly. "If you want to stick around, don't get her pregnant. She'll drop you like a hot pan the second she has a daughter."

Delan's stomach clenched. *Zhafaera's not her mother. Or her grandmother,* he reminded himself.

Nyto's eyes flickered over Delan's shoulder. "Ah, your Queen returns." Delan turned to see Zhafaera breaking through the crowd, a drink in either hand. "I'll take my leave," Nyto said, and made a quick exit around the other side of the column.

***

Zhafaera watched as Nyto disappeared and Delan turned to face her. "What did he have to say?" she asked.

Delan avoided her gaze. "Not much. He said he and Velexar were close."

153

Zhafaera shrugged and handed him a glass of wine. "I'm not surprised. Velexar spent a lot of time in Laros, which suited my mother just fine."

"I'm not sure you can trust him," Delan said.

"I don't trust anyone"—Zhafaera sipped her water—"except you," she amended, seeing the look on Delan's face.

"Good," he said, taking her hand and leading her outside. It was dark, and the cool air of the desert night washed over them. Delan headed for the gardens, which were alight with torches placed strategically around the bushes. The farther they got from the main party, the quieter it got. Zhafaera took a deep breath and turned her face up to the moon, nearly full, drinking in its smooth energy.

"Finally, some peace and quiet," she said to Delan. "I forgot how exhausting these things can be. I must have talked to a hundred people tonight."

"I'd never been to a ball before," Delan said. "Is it always like this?"

"Yes," Zhafaera said, opening her eyes. "Although this one is particularly large, and dare I say, getting rowdy. For stuck-up nobles anyway."

Delan laughed. "The parties I've been to haven't been quite so civilized. If this is rowdy, I'd hate to see dull."

They fell silent, moving through the gardens and admiring the shrubbery that had been carefully trimmed into the shapes of various animals. Zhafaera was impressed. Even the gardens of the Temple District in Arenthia hadn't been this nice, and she was surprised to see so much green in the desert.

"How was Elden?" Delan finally asked.

"Ugh," Zhafaera suppressed a shudder. "Clearly not deterred, even with you as my Consort."

"I thought I was going to have to come over and fight for your honor."

"Thankfully, Tristain stepped in," Zhafaera said.

"What did he tell Elden, do you know?"

"I believe it was something along the lines of 'it'll hurt when she breaks your hand.'"

Delan laughed. "Hopefully that gave him an idea of what you're capable of. Elden is vain enough that that might make him pause and reassess his choices."

"Does it make *you* question your choices?"

"Not at all. You don't scare me," Delan said, placing an arm around her shoulders and pulling her close. "Just as long as you promise not to dump me if we have a daughter," he said quietly, more seriously.

Zhafaera looked up at him. "Of course I won't. Whatever gave you that idea?"

"Something else," the Councilman said. "He blamed your mother for being 'released' from his position. He was more than a little bitter about it, too."

"My mother has been blamed for a lot of things, but that's a new one for me," Zhafaera said lightly. "It sounds like he got jealous."

"Why would someone be jealous of a child?"

Zhafaera shrugged. "They take time and attention. Some men can't handle that."

"But it'll take my time and attention too. I don't get

it." Delan was frowning.

"That's because you're not 'some men,'" Zhafaera said with a smile. She stopped and faced him. "You're a good man."

"Funny, that's the second time tonight someone has said that."

"Who was the first?" Zhafaera said mock-indignantly.

"Tristain."

"Well, I suppose that's all right then. Besides, it's true." She stretched up onto her toes and kissed him lightly on the lips. Delan wrapped an arm around her waist, pulling her closer and deepening the kiss. When he finally pulled back, Zhafaera was slightly breathless.

"I think I've had enough of this party," he whispered, resting his forehead against Zhafaera's.

"Agreed. I think it's past time for bed."

Delan's sharp intake of breath sent a shiver down her spine, and he kissed her again. Abruptly, he released her, taking her hand and leading her back through the gardens and into the main party. They tried to make their way through the crowds unnoticed, but of course everyone wanted to talk to them again. Zhafaera did her best to make polite conversation: "Yes, this has been a spectacular ball," "No, no wine for me, thank you," but her mind was elsewhere.

Finally, they made it out of the ballroom and into the hall, where Delan pulled her into an alcove and kissed her thoroughly.

"We'll never make it back to the room if you don't stop that," Zhafaera whispered, pulling away and tugging his hand. Delan followed with a sheepish grin.

"I can't help it. Besides," he said, pointing to their left. "We're not the only ones." Looking down the hallway, Zhafaera saw more than one couple taking advantage of the darkened hallway, lit only by flickering torches that were quickly burning down. She suppressed a giggle.

Zhafaera led Delan by the hand through the twists and turns of the palace, up several floors until they reached their rooms. The second the door was closed, Delan was on her, winding his hands through her hair and kissing her forehead, her mouth, her neck.

"How was the ball?" Evey's voice interrupted.

Delan let go, and Zhafaera jumped back, startled. She bit her lip, trying not to laugh as she felt a blush creeping up her cheeks.

"You didn't miss much," Delan said in a rough voice. "Food. Dancing. Lots of people talking. Very boring." Zhafaera glanced at Evey and saw her sprawled out on the couch, her black cat form taking up more room than it should, her head tilted to the side.

I don't think you're being truthful.

"It really wasn't much, Evey," Zhafaera said. "I do believe there are probably piles of leftovers from the dinner, though. We'll be sure to get you some in the morning."

"That would be nice," Evey said eagerly. "I'm hungry."

"Well, we can't have that." Delan smiled at Evey. "We'll make sure you're well fed."

Evey's eyes glowed a brighter green in the dim light

from the fire that was stoked against the chill desert night.

"For now, though," Delan continued. "We're exhausted and heading to bed."

Evey closed her eyes and rested her head back on her paws. "Good night then."

"Good night, Evey," Zhafaera said as she turned back to Delan. His eyes twinkled in the firelight.

Taking her hand, he practically dragged her into the bedroom, closing the door firmly behind them as he bent to kiss her again.

Chapter 10

Zhafaera rubbed her temples tiredly. Three hours into the meeting with Queen Oraesa, Prince Tristain, and Councilman Nyto, and they were only just beginning to discuss what to do. She'd told her full story this time, leaving out some of the more gruesome details, and watched Nyto's face contort into a mixture of sadness and anger as she described how his children had died. She felt her own temper flare at the thought that he could be grieving for Velexar, but in the end, she couldn't blame him. He was his son after all, and he hadn't known the extent of Velexar's depravity.

"Well, for the time being," Queen Oraesa was saying. "Our best hope is to strengthen our defenses and build our armies." She looked to Zhafaera. "Arenthia lost most of their mages in the attack, but the rest of us still have enough to make a difference."

Tristain raised his hand. "That's not entirely accurate. Khichora often sent mages to train at the Cathedral in Arenthia. Not that we don't have mages left, but their numbers are less than we would like."

Nyto sniffed. "Then what is Khichora doing to prepare?"

"My father has orchestrated large-scale evacuations into the mountains. We have numerous strongholds there;

they look small on the outside and are therefore hard to spot, but they go deep underground. Most of our people are retreating there. The fortresses are easier to defend than a city."

Oraesa nodded approvingly. "We do not have anywhere to retreat to but this city. We have a large contingent of mages that are strengthening our defenses as we speak. There are towers being built around the city from which the mages will work. I do not understand the whole of it myself, but when they are finished, it will be nearly impossible for dragons to simply fall on us as they did Arenthia. Our people will retreat here. As will the Arenthians, it seems." She shot a look at Zhafaera, who was not friendly.

"And we appreciate your protection," Zhafaera said smoothly, inclining her head. "I will keep my end of our bargain and provide rainwater at regular intervals of your choosing. You need only put me in touch with whoever is in charge of provisions."

"Of course. I'll make the introduction as soon as possible," Oraesa said. She turned to Nyto. "What is Laros' plan?"

"We are furthest away from the threat," he said, waving his hand. "Our islands are not densely populated, and the jungle and volcanoes provide natural barriers. And of course, we have our own…protections."

"You have the Ruby," Zhafaera interjected.

Nyto looked at her lazily. "Perhaps."

"Now is not the time for secrecy," Zhafaera said sharply. "We need to know where the Gems are and which ones are fully accounted for. I have the Sapphire." She tapped her chest over the Sapphire. "Does Laros still have the Ruby?"

Nyto was quiet for so long that Zhafaera didn't think he would answer. "Yes, we have it," he eventually said, the words pulled from him reluctantly. "But it is hidden."

"Zhafaera's plan is to gather all four Gems and use them to go on the offensive against the dragons," Oraesa chimed in.

Nyto shook his head. "Laros will never surrender the Ruby, not to *anyone*. It is for our protection, and no one else's. With it, we should be able to keep the dragons from our islands. We'll be safe." He looked at Zhafaera. "We are, of course, willing to take in a certain number of refugees. Indeed, some Arenthians have already made their way to our shores, and they are welcome to stay with us. But space on our islands is limited, and we cannot take many more."

"And I appreciate you taking in those you have. But, Councilman, we wouldn't need Laros to *surrender* the Ruby, simply work *with* us when the time is right." Zhafaera clamped down on her irritation. Why couldn't anyone else see her plan?

"The Ruby will stay in Laros for protection and defense," Nyto said firmly.

"What about the rest of the Council?" Zhafaera asked. "This seems like the kind of thing that would require a larger discussion."

Nyto stroked his short beard. "I can bring the idea to the Council, but I doubt their answer will be any different."

"Nevertheless, I would appreciate you discussing it further with them."

Nyto inclined his head. "As you wish."

Zhafaera turned to Oraesa. "And you have no idea where the Emerald could be?"

Oraesa's mouth pressed into a thin line. "If I did, we would be using it. It vanished nearly three hundred years ago, and we've been looking for it ever since, with no luck. It's gone."

"But you wouldn't mind if I search for it myself?" Zhafaera asked. "Perhaps a fresh set of eyes will be able to shed some light on its location. And with the Sapphire, I may have an advantage."

Oraesa waved a hand. "Be my guest. But if you do find it, it belongs to Burja, for us to use as we see fit."

"And what would you use it for?"

"Protection, like Laros. Any offensive action should be left to Arenthia, since yours is the country that has been invaded."

"For now," Tristain chimed in. "You're naive if you think the dragons won't eventually crack through your defenses." He looked around the table. "Or do you really think your mages are a match for *fifty dragons*?"

Zhafaera flashed him a smile, appreciating his support. "Defeating the dragons is everyone's responsibility," she said coolly. "Whether you want it to be or not."

Oraesa had the good grace to blush, but Nyto remained impassive.

"Khichora will stand behind you, Zhafaera," Tristain

said. "We know the dragons will likely come for us next, being on the same continent. But as you know, the Diamond has been lost for even longer than the Emerald." He looked at her earnestly. "You are, of course, welcome to look, but I wouldn't know where to begin."

"The library in Zarga is the largest in the world," Zhafaera said, looking to Oraesa. "My thoughts are we start there and learn everything we can about the Gems. And dragons. Fact, fiction, or legend, I want to know. They were defeated once before, and I want to know *exactly* how it was done."

"Of course, you have free access to our library," Oraesa said smoothly. "And while you spend your time *reading,* we will continue to focus on the practical matter of defense." She paused. "In addition to providing rain for us, I would like to ask for your assistance in another matter. The Sapphire could be an invaluable tool for building our shields."

"I'm happy to help," Zhafaera said, inclining her head.

"Thank you." Oraesa sounded as if it physically pained her to say the words.

Nyto stood. "I suppose then, our way forward is clear. Queen Zhafaera, and I assume Prince Tristain, will work on finding the lost Gems. I will reach out to the Council about the Ruby, but I know they have their own plans for it." He looked to Oraesa. "And we all will prepare to defend ourselves."

***

"How did it go?" Delan asked as Zhafaera entered their rooms. She shut the door with more force than necessary. "That well?"

Zhafaera sighed and took a seat in one of the armchairs across from the couch on which Delan and Evey sat. "About as I expected," she said, leaning over and putting her face in her hands. "Oraesa wants nothing to do with fighting the dragons; she only wants to defend the city."

"Understandable, I suppose," Delan said carefully.

"Perhaps, but still." Zhafaera looked up. "Nyto confirmed that Laros has the Ruby, although he says it's hidden, and the Council intends to use it for defense. They think their islands are relatively safe, and they're probably not wrong."

"It's true, Laros will probably be the last place the dragons try to conquer."

"Yes, but it makes it difficult for us to convince them to help. Nyto said he would put the matter of the Ruby to the full Council, but I'm not convinced they'll be willing to share when the time comes." She ran her fingers through her hair in frustration. "Tristain is the only one that sees the logic of my plan. I'm not sure he thinks it's possible, but he's willing to help. Khichora is our only real ally at this point."

That makes no sense. Evey said. *The dragons will not be defeated unless all four nations stand together.*

"That's what I tried to tell them, but between Oraesa and Nyto, it was like talking to a wall."

I don't understand. Shouldn't your mother's father be

on your side?

"You would think," Zhafaera said bitterly.

"So what's our plan to find them? The Gems, I mean." Delan paused. "If they've been lost for hundreds of years, that's a pretty daunting task."

"Basically, I volunteered us to read half of the Library of Zarga looking for anything about the Gems or dragons. Or the Gems *and* dragons."

"Of course," Delan said, inwardly wincing. That library was *huge*. It was probably their best chance for finding a way to defeat the dragons, but damn, that was a daunting task.

There was a knock on the door. Zhafaera made to get up, but Delan waved her down and moved to open the door. It was Prince Tristain. Delan stepped aside for him to enter.

"Tristain!" Zhafaera said, looking surprised. "What are you doing here?"

"Sorry for the intrusion," he said with a tight grin.

"Not at all. Please, take a seat." Zhafaera waved him into a chair opposite her as Delan resumed his place on the couch. Evey watched intently.

"Who is this?" she asked, so only Delan could hear.

"Prince Tristain, of Khichora," he answered.

"He's a mage."

"Yes, an Air mage," I believe.

"I thought we could have a real talk away from the others and their unrealistic hopes," Tristain said harshly.

Zhafaera nodded and rubbed her temples. "It was about what I expected."

"How could Oraesa say that it's *Arenthia's* responsibility to defeat the dragons? Does she know *nothing*?"

"Did she really say that *again*?" Delan asked, shocked.

"She's focused on protecting her people. I can respect that," Zhafaera said. "To a point."

"Well, as I said, Khichora is with you." Tristain leaned forward intently. "I spoke with my father after our first dinner together when you mentioned it. He backs your plan but has the same concerns I do, namely, *finding* the lost Gems."

"I know it's a longshot," Zhafaera began. "But there *has* to be some clue somewhere. They didn't just vanish."

"That's exactly what they did, Zhafaera." Tristain sighed. "It's going to take no small amount of luck to find them."

"But you'll help us?"

"Of course. It's going to take more than just the two of you to sort through the Zarga Library." He looked at Delan. "I'm assuming she's already told you that you'll be helping?"

Delan laughed. "Obviously."

Tristain nodded. "I might be able to rope my own partner into it." He grinned. "He's the one you saw me dancing with the other night. He's a scholar in his own right. He'd be helpful, if you'd have him."

"I'll take all the help we can get," Zhafaera said earnestly. She grinned. "Besides, I want to meet him."

Tristain blushed.

Prince Tristain has a man as a partner? Am I understanding 'partner' correctly? Evey sounded very confused in Delan's mind.

Yes, Evey. Delan said. He was uncomfortable. *Some men like other men. Just as some women like other women. It's just something that happens.*

But that's not how mating works.

It's not about 'mating' and producing children. It's about love, Delan explained.

Oh. Evey's head was tilted to the side, and Delan prayed Tristain wouldn't notice. *Dragons don't feel love. Unless it's the love a mother feels for her children. We have friends, but I don't think that's what you would call love.*

It's hard to say, Delan said. *Friendship can be just as strong as romantic love.*

Perhaps it's better to say dragons don't have romance.

Somehow that doesn't surprise me. Delan tried to refocus on the conversation between Tristain and Zhafaera.

"I promised Oraesa I would meet with her advisors tomorrow to discuss the next rainstorm I've agreed to provide," Zhafaera was saying. "But we could meet there in the afternoon."

"That should be fine," Tristain said. He turned to Delan. "Delan, I've been helping train the new guards in the mornings. Would you be interested in joining us? They could use someone like you."

"Certainly," Delan said. "I'll need something to do

while Zhafaera is off working her magic." He shot her a grin.

Tristain slapped his knees and stood. "It's settled then. Between the four of us, I'm sure we'll find *something*."

Chapter 11

Six weeks, and they had nothing. Nothing.

Piles upon piles of books on dragon lore, Gem lore, histories, and fantasies, and they were no closer to finding the lost Gems or defeating the dragons than they had been when they started.

They had a routine. Every morning, Zhafaera went with the mages to work on building and strengthening the defenses of the city, while Delan and Tristain worked at training the people. Sometimes she and Delan would walk through the refugee tents that surrounded half the city, helping distribute food, healing, or just talking with people. Every afternoon, they met Liara at the library and read. And read, and read, and read.

Zhafeara tossed her current book aside in frustration. *The Mountains of the Dragons* was proving to be less useful than *Dragons: A Complete Analysis of Anatomy and Magical Properties*. And that one had taken her *days* to read.

She stood abruptly, startling the others that sat reading in armchairs around the low table in the space they'd claimed as their own in the library. Four pairs of eyes flicked up to her: Delan, Liara, Tristain, and Tristain's partner Ranj, all looking at her curiously.

"I'm going to find more books," she said shortly,

ignoring the stack already waiting to be read. The others nodded their understanding and went back to reading. Delan's arms stretched out over his armchair like wings; he'd recently taken to studying every map he could find. Zhafaera couldn't blame him. Reading tiny words on thousands of thick pages had nearly ruined her eyes.

Moving through the stacks, Zhafaera wandered. She just needed a break. She needed something, *anything* that would give her even the slightest hint of what had happened to the missing Gems.

Reaching out through the Sapphire, she spread her awareness through the books surrounding her, searching for any flicker of recognition. Some books had their own magic, and her idea was that perhaps Gem magic would call to Gem magic. She'd pulled most of the magical books on their first day, but it never hurt to try again…

So absorbed was she in her search; she didn't hear the footsteps behind her until someone tapped her on the shoulder.

Gasping, she spun, facing her attacker, ready to fight, until she realized it was just Tristain. Releasing a breath, she gave a faint laugh. "I nearly planted my fist in your face, Tristain."

He grinned. "I knew it was a risk sneaking up on you, but I wanted to talk to you, and I haven't had a chance to get you alone." Tristain looked over his shoulder as if expecting someone to have followed him.

Unease stirred in Zhafaera's belly. "What is it, what's wrong? Have you found something?"

Tristain shook his head. "It's not that." He shifted,

looking uncomfortable. "Look, Zhafaera, we're friends, and I respect you."

Zhafaera waited. "But…?"

He sighed. "Zhafaera, I'm an Air mage."

"I'm aware. What's your point?" Zhafaera was really confused now.

Tristain took a deep breath, and the words came tumbling out. "I can see through your illusion spell."

"You can—" Zhafaera's heart leapt into her throat, and her breathing stopped. Her hands automatically jerked in front of her to cover her belly. At more than five months, what had been a small, barely noticeable bump was now very clearly a pregnant belly.

"I thought I'd hidden it well enough…" Zhafaera could feel the blush seeping into her cheeks, and she fumbled for what to say.

"You did," Tristain said quickly. "You hid it really well. I thought it was the Sapphire at first." His eyes darted down to her abdomen and back up to meet her eyes. "I caught it out of the corner of my eye one day, and I – well, once I was *looking* for it, it was easy to see."

"Don't say anything, please," Zhafaera said quietly.

Tristain looked surprised, and leaned in closer. "But…Delan knows, doesn't he?"

Zhafaera nodded. "Of course he does."

"Zhafaera, I can only guess at why you're hiding it, but just answer me this—" His eyes flicked away nervously. "Is it – is it *his*?"

From his tone, Zhafaera knew he didn't mean Delan. She let out a breath. "No. It's Delan's."

"Then why haven't you—"

Someone cleared their throat behind Tristain, and the two sprang apart, ending their whispered conversation. Delan stood at the end of the aisle, his eyebrows pulled together in a frown.

"Did you find something?" Zhafaera asked too quickly, eager to draw attention away from her and Tristain's close-quarters discussion.

"Maybe, I'm not sure," Delan said, shaking his head slowly. "I need you to take a look and tell me if I'm going crazy."

"I know I am," Tristain said lightly, moving down the row and past Delan. Zhafaera made to follow, but Delan stopped her.

"What was that about?" he said quietly.

"Nothing," Zhafaera whispered. She shook her head when he didn't look convinced. "I'll tell you later." She swallowed her feeling of being naked, patted Delan on the arm, and moved past him. "What did you find?"

Moving back to their corner of the library, Delan grabbed the old map he'd been studying and spread it out on their table. Everyone crowded around, their heads bowed over to see.

"Okay, this map shows the major roads in Burja," Delan began. He pointed to Zarga. "We're here, and there's this road that goes straight from here to Duranja." He ran his finger along the road. "Except..." He paused, and ran his finger back, stopping in the middle of the road. "There's this bump in the road on the map." He moved his finger so the others could see.

"What is that?" Zhafaera asked.

"I'm not sure. It could just be an artifact of the map – someone with a shaky hand maybe," Delan said tentatively.

"It looks like the road curves outward," Ranj put in, turning his head for a better view.

"That's what I thought," Delan said. "But if there *is* something there, it's not on any of the maps. As far as I can tell, the only thing between Zarga and Duranja is desert."

"But that road doesn't curve," Liara said. "I've taken it before – it's a straight line from Zarga to Duranja."

"It's slight – you may not be able to feel it," Tristain said.

Zhafaera felt the beginnings of hope stir. "Delan, I think you found something!"

"It could be nothing…" Delan began.

"But it could be something!" Zhafaera looked at the others. "I think this is worth checking out."

"Absolutely," Tristain chimed in, nodding his head. "At the very least, anything is better than sitting around in this dusty old library for another six weeks finding nothing."

"How long do you think it will take to get out there?" Delan asked. "It looks like it's pretty far."

Zhafaera waved her hand. "I'm sure we can use the brick system." At Delan's confused look, she explained. "The Earth mages here have a system of rocks that they use to get across the desert. They can pack the sand into a large brick and send it gliding across the desert like a ship."

"That sounds useful," Delan said.

"It is. It would only take a few days to get there. We can go and check it out and be back within a week."

"We'll probably have to tell Queen Oraesa where we're going," Tristain said cautiously, but his eyes were sparkling with excitement.

"Who cares? She can sit around and wait for the dragons to come to her, but I'm going to do everything I can to find the Gems," Zhafaera said. She felt almost giddy at the prospect of actually *doing* something.

"There's no need for all of us to go," Tristain continued. He stared hard at Zhafaera. "It could be dangerous – we have no idea what we'd be walking into. I'm the best at spotting illusions – I should go."

Zhafaera rolled her eyes. "I'm the best at everything else, Tristain. I'm going."

Delan looked worried. "Tristain's right, Zhafaera. You're needed here—"

"I can be spared for a week," Zhafaera said, tossing her hair over her shoulders. "This was *my* plan, remember?"

"Of course I remember, it's just–"

"It's settled then," Zhafaera cut Delan off. "Let's go tell Oraesa that we'll be getting out of her hair for a bit."

"Mother will *never* let me go," Liara said morosely.

***

Delan stood in the room he shared with Zhafaera, torn between packing and planning out what he was going to say to Zhafaera. She couldn't go with them, not in her condition. The middle of the desert was no place for a pregnant woman. But he knew she wouldn't agree, and it fell to him to convince her. Or possibly die trying, depending on her mood.

Zhafaera being pregnant hadn't been easy on either of them. Delan knew he couldn't begin to understand how she felt, but so far, he'd borne the brunt of her temper. All of her frustrations with the dragons, the Burjans, and their lack of progress in the library had made her short fused and irritable. Coupled with being pregnant, Delan had learned that a combination of silence and tea was his best defense. But he knew he couldn't remain silent today, and he dreaded the confrontation that he knew was coming.

Are you packing or not? Evey asked from her spot next to his pack on the bed, startling him out of his reverie.

"I am, I am," Delan said quickly, stuffing a shirt into the bag.

Where's Zhafaera's pack?

"Zhafaera isn't going."

Evey cocked her head to the side. *But you go everywhere together.*

"Not this time, Evey. You're both staying here." Delan let out a sigh. He just had to convince Zhafaera of that.

The sound of the outer door to their rooms opening made Delan spin around, quickly trying to wipe the guilty look off of his face.

"I'm back!" Zhafaera called from the living area.

"In here!" When she appeared at the doorway to their

bedroom, Delan smiled. "How did it go with Oraesa?"

"About like I expected," Zhafaera grinned and moved over to sit on the bed. "She thinks we're crazy and there's nothing out there – she insists the road is perfectly straight – but she's happy enough to have me gone for a little while at least."

"Zhafaera, I—"

"And I have to say, I'm just as glad to be rid of her. Back on the road, just like old times." She looked up at Delan, still smiling broadly. "Except at least this time we won't be freezing our asses off as we head to confront my sadistic uncle and his pack of dragons. Win-win, I'd say."

"Zhafaera, about that." Delan took a deep breath.

"Did you find a pack for me?" Zhafaera said, looking around the room. She stood. "I should get moving if we want to be ready to leave by dawn."

"Zhafaera, you can't come with us," Delan said quickly before she could interrupt again.

Zhafaera froze, turning slowly to meet his eyes. Hers were like ice. "Excuse me?"

"Zhafaera, you can't, you know you can't. Not only does the Sapphire make you the single most important person in our fight against the dragons, but you're pregnant. The desert is too harsh, too unforgiving, too *dangerous* for you. You have to let Tristain and I do this."

For a full thirty seconds, there was no sound in the room. But as he watched, Zhafaera's eyes went from solid ice to an intense, flaming blue that looked ready to shoot sparks.

"How *dare* you tell me what I can and can't do?"

Zhafaera's voice was quiet, but it shook with rage. "This plan was *my* idea and you—"

"*I* found the curve on the map, so *I* should be the one to check it out." Delan kept his voice firm. "It's probably nothing anyway. It would be a waste of time for all of us to go out there."

"You don't believe that, or you wouldn't be preparing to go marching into the desert with a man you hardly trust."

"Zhafaera, I just want you to be safe, and if that sometimes means making sacrifices—"

"Don't talk to me about sacrifice," Zhafaera spat. "I've lost everything in this war, and we've only just begun."

Delan flinched. "I didn't mean—"

"No, you didn't *think*. You have such a hero complex that you couldn't even stop for a moment and *think* about what—"

"*I* have a hero complex?" Delan asked incredulously, his voice rising. "Zhafaera, you spend half your time looking for the next dangerous situation, and the other half beating yourself up about how all of this is your fault. If *anyone* has a hero complex, it's *you!*"

"I don't go *looking* for danger, and my *duty* requires me to—"

"To what? *Die* for your kingdom? Look around Zhafaera – you're all your people have left. Your *duty* is to *them*."

"I know my duty, Delan. Do you know yours?"

"Mine is to protect you *and* our unborn child."

Zhafaera gave a harsh laugh. "And you've done a fabulous job. You kept me from Velexar – wait, no, I was captured. But at least you got me home safely – although, now that I think of it, I almost *died* doing it your way."

Zhafaera's words cut straight through Delan, slicing through his core like a physical wound. But Zhafaera wasn't finished.

"What exactly do you think you could protect me from that I can't do myself? You're a half-trained mage with a sword that will do exactly nothing against a dragon, and you expect me to sit by the side like a good little girl and wait for the big, strong men to take care of my problems?" Zhafaera's voice shook with anger. "No, thank you; I can take care of myself and my child better than anyone else ever could. We don't need you."

Delan could feel his temper rising. "You mean the child you still haven't told anyone about? The one you were planning on hiding? The one you probably still *are* planning to abandon as soon as it's born? That child?"

"Get out," Zhafaera said quietly.

"Why did I hit too close to the truth?" Delan examined her face closely and saw through her anger that he was right. "You lied to me. You have no intention of raising our baby. You're going to give her to the first family you can find and leave her to fend for herself like your mother did with Alec. You're just like her – too selfish to see that—"

Zhafaera shoved him. Hard.

"Get out!" She screamed, pushing him out of the bedroom door.

"Fine!" Delan yelled, moving out of reach. "But my *hero complex* says you're not coming with us tomorrow, even if I have to tie you down!"

Zhafaera let out an enraged shriek just as Delan reached the main door. As he slipped into the hallway, he saw something fly through the air. Jerking the door closed, there was a loud *crash* as something shattered against the heavy wood where his head had been moments before.

Delan stood there, his heart pounding and thoughts racing, trying to decide if he wanted to go back in and continue the argument or walk away and find something to hit. Ban stood just outside the door, looking grim and avoiding Delan's gaze.

"Delan?" Delan turned to see Colin hurrying down the hall towards him, hammer in hand. "What's happening? I heard yelling."

Delan took a deep breath and tried to sound calm. He failed. "Let's just say I may not be Consort anymore," he said harshly.

Colin slowed and stopped, looking from Delan to Ban. "I'm sure it's not that bad," he said, putting a hand on Delan's shoulder. There was another scream just before something else shattered against the door. Colin looked at it warily. "Although I probably wouldn't go back in there for a while," he said hesitantly.

Delan shook off Colin's hand and turned, heading the opposite way down the hall. Colin made to follow, but Delan held up a hand.

"Stay and look after the Queen," Delan said harshly, not slowing his pace.

Delan moved through the palace, hardly noticing where he was going, his thoughts racing. He and Zhafaera had never had a fight like this before. He was still angry – really angry – but as he strode out into the palace courtyard, he could feel the first twinges of fear and guilt stirring in his belly.

If only Zhafaera would listen.

You shouldn't have told her what to do.

She still wants to hide our baby.

You lost your temper.

I do not *have a hero complex.*

You called her selfish.

Delan wasn't sure how long he'd been standing in the middle of the courtyard, pulse pounding, thoughts spinning in circles, when someone put a hand on his shoulder. Spinning suddenly, he gripped his sword and was only a half breath from drawing it when he realized who it was.

"Delan! Are you all right?" Esla said, jumping back.

"What are you doing here?" Delan asked in astonishment. "Are you following me?"

Esla bit her lip and smiled slightly. "It's hard to find you on your own now."

"This is just great," Delan said, throwing up his hands.

"Come, walk with me in the gardens. I'm sure we can find somewhere more…private to talk."

He fought to keep his temper. "Esla, I'm Consort, at least for now, and that means—"

"Just because you're Consort doesn't mean we can't be together—"

Delan grabbed Esla's shoulders and gave her a slight shake. "Don't you get it? I *love* Zhafaera. I *love* her. I've *always* loved her. I don't love you; I've never loved you, and we'll *never* be together. The sooner you accept that, the better off we'll all be." Delan let go, and Esla stumbled back.

Tears filled her eyes but didn't spill over. She opened her mouth, closed it again. Opened it. Then she spun on her heel and marched back to the palace entryway, her head held high. She didn't look back.

Hopefully, I finally got my message across, Delan thought, anger and guilt warring in his head even worse than before.

He took off towards the gardens. Esla was right – this time of the evening most everyone would be at dinner, and the gardens should be deserted.

Walking quickly, he tried to bring his thoughts into focus, but it was like trying to hold water. As he paced through the perfectly manicured hedges, past rows of flowers and sculpted trees, he concluded it came down to one thing.

Zhafaera's pregnancy.

He wanted to keep her safe, even if it meant leaving her behind.

She wanted to carry on as if nothing was different.

The reality, he realized as true dark fell around him, was probably somewhere in between. He shouldn't treat her as fragile, but she shouldn't act as though she was invincible. Two sides of the same coin.

Compromise is what's missing, Delan thought. *We*

each need to give something to get something.

So what did he really want? He wanted Zhafaera to stay home. But that was clearly a non-starter, so what came next? He wanted…he wanted Zhafaera to admit that she was pregnant. To everyone, yes, but also maybe to herself to some degree. The idea of abandoning their child, even in the name of safety, made his stomach roil. He couldn't live knowing their child was out there somewhere, and not with them.

And if she makes you choose between being with her and being with the baby?

Delan didn't want to think about that. He kept walking.

He'd walked far enough from the castle that the meticulously groomed hedges had given way to twisty paths that eventually led to the jungle oasis behind the castle. So engrossed in his own thoughts, Delan almost missed the sound of the gravel path crunching behind him. He didn't even have time to turn around before he felt a blow and a sharp pain in his back, between his ribs. As he gasped and tried to turn, another pain came, this time in his lower back, just as a shadow detached itself from the darkness ahead and ran at him.

Delan had no time to block the blow, even if he could have. But his arms didn't seem to be working, and all he could do was watch as a figure dressed in all black planted a wicked-looking knife into his chest. As he crumpled, he heard murmured voices above him and then the sound of feet on gravel as his attackers ran.

Delan could feel his blood leaking out. Already, he

was cold. All he could think was that he was going to die without having apologized to Zhafaera, without meeting his child, without saying goodbye. Sluggishly, he reached with his mind for her, spreading his awareness out like she'd taught him, trying to reach her even for just a moment, to tell her he loved her. *There.* Her presence was strong, like a beacon drawing him to her.

Zhafaera, he thought, as he *pulled* himself towards her. *Love you.*

***

Zhafaera lay on the bed, having finally cried herself out. The tears had come after the anger, and she hated herself for them.

The room was dark when she finally sat up and looked around. Evey was still on the bed by her feet, a silent but comforting presence, but Ban must have kept the servants out because no one had come in to light the candles.

Shaking her hair back from her face, Zhafaera stood and took a breath. On her exhale, all the candles lit at once. Moving slowly, feeling as tired as if she'd been ill, she moved to the washroom and washed her face, removing the evidence of her breakdown as best she could.

She wondered when Delan would come back. *If he comes back.*

Zhafaera ignored that small voice in her head. Delan would be back.

Are you all right? Evey finally asked tentatively, following as Zhafaera moved into the living area and curled up in an armchair. Calling on her magic, she lit the candles in this room as well and started a fire in the fireplace. Desert nights got cold.

"I'm fine," Zhafaera's voice shook slightly.

He just wants you to be safe, Evey said.

"I know. It's just that he and I have different definitions of what's safe."

Evey was silent for a long time. *When you were captured, he was...not himself. He was so afraid for you; we weren't sure what had happened to you, or even if you were alive or dead...it was scary. He could think of nothing but getting you back, even when he was half dead himself.*

Zhafaera swallowed the new lump in her throat. "I understand that, Evey. Really, I do. It's just... I hate being *coddled*. I can take care of myself, I have for years."

But you don't have to anymore. You have us.

"I know. But I have trouble giving up control to *anyone*. Especially after...what happened when I was taken."

Evey tilted her head and fixed her gaze on Zhafaera. *It's not just about you anymore, not now that you're with a child.*

Zhafaera placed her hands on her growing belly. "That's just it," she whispered. "I'm terrified."

Is that why you haven't told anyone?

"Partially. I also don't want to be treated differently. Like Delan – he treats me like glass."

Are you still planning to hide it once it's born, like Delan thinks?

Zhafaera shook her head. "No. I don't think I could do it, and he's so against it. It wouldn't be fair."

That's good. I'm finding I like human babies. Sara's daughter Amee is...interesting. I think she knows I'm not like other cats.

"Really? That's—"

Zhafaera...

Zhafaera sat bolt upright at the sound of Delan's voice in her head. It sounded weak, like it was far away, but he couldn't have gone too far. *Delan?*

Love you.

"Delan!" she cried out as she jumped out of her seat.

What is it? Evey asked.

"Something's happened, something's wrong..." And then she felt it. Like someone had pulled a plug, her magic was draining out of her. She tried to hold on to it, but all it did was pick up speed the longer she stood there. Running out onto the balcony with Evey close on her heels, she reached out her senses, feeling for Delan.

Where is he?

"There," she said out loud. "On the other side of the castle, in the gardens. Evey, we have to go to him!" She spun around and staggered, the loss of magic rapidly starting to affect her.

Delan stop, stop drawing from me! She thought frantically. But there was no response.

"Evey, we have to get to Delan, *now,*" Zhafaera said urgently.

Evey understood. Zhafaera stepped back as Evey transformed, slipping into her true dragon form in moments and stretching her wide, iridescent wings across the balcony. *Climb on,* she said, kneeling slightly.

For a moment, Zhafaera just stared. Evey was definitely bigger than the last time she'd seen her in dragon form. Which, granted, it had been months, but still. The young dragon was now almost the size of a carriage. Clearly, she'd had a growth spurt.

Come on, she urged, kneeling on her front legs so that Zhafaera could reach. Zhafaera shook herself and climbed up behind her wings.

"Are you sure you can carry me?" she asked.

In answer, Evey placed her front paws up on the balcony railing, spread her wings, and leapt off. Zhafaera's stomach dropped as they sank a few feet before a beat of Evey's powerful wings sent them soaring up over the river. Banking smoothly, Evey flew up and over the castle, heading for the gardens on the other side.

Zhafaera focused on finding Delan, rather than think about how high in the air she was with no saddle or handholds of any kind. Reaching out again, she found his energy, dimmer now but still drawing her power to him.

"Evey, can you sense him?" she called above the wind.

Yes.

Once they reached the gardens, Evey lowered them close to the ground, past flowers of every color, over bushes planted in geometric shapes, skimming the tops of the perfectly sculpted trees.

In the end, they almost flew over him, so well concealed was he at the edge of the path under a bush shaped like a horse. Evey landed at the last second, all four paws skidding in the gravel and sending it flying over Delan.

Zhafaera stumbled off her back and fell to her knees next to Delan. He was lying on his side, still and pale.

"Delan!" Zhafaera called as she rolled him onto his back. "Delan, wake up!"

His eyelids fluttered, his lips moving but no sound coming out. Only blood.

"Delan, stop, you've got to stop pulling power from me. Let me…"

Cupping his face in her hand, she reached out with her magic, feeling for injuries. She inhaled sharply. There were three stab wounds – one through a lung, another just nicking his heart, and a third in his right kidney. He should be dead already, but the power he was drawing…he'd done enough to slow the bleeding.

His face was lit with an eerie blue glow, one that Zhafaera dimly recognized as the Sapphire glowing from its place in her chest. Taking a deep breath, she worked quickly, pulling the blood from his lung, knitting muscle and flesh back together, healing as fast as she could. Slowly, she felt Delan begin to relax, and the pull on her magic vanished.

Alarmed, she gasped and put a hand on his throat, feeling his pulse weak but steady. She let out a breath and felt the tears gathering at the corners of her eyes. Now in full control, she sent her magic through his body, healing the last remnants of the attack. When she was done, Delan appeared to be breathing normally, the trickle of drying blood from his mouth and the tears in his coat the only signs that anything had happened.

"Delan?" Zhafaera shook his shoulder slightly, but he didn't stir.

She looked at Evey. "We need to get him back in the palace."

I don't think I can fly both of you.

Zhafaera shook her head and stood, brushing gravel off of her dress. As she straightened, her head spun. "I guess we go through the front door then. And whoever did this can just *try* me." She looked at Evey. "Although you should probably shift back into your cat form. We don't want to start a panic."

You don't think anyone saw us flying out here? Evey asked.

"I don't hear any screams, do you?"

No.

"Then probably no one saw us. It's dark, and you were fast."

Evey tilted her head, then quickly shrank into her black cat form. She moved closer to Delan, sniffing him gently.

"Come on, we need to get moving. Whoever did this could come back." Drawing power from the Sapphire, Zhafaera reached out her hand and surrounded Delan with her magic. Slowly, he rose off the ground until he hovered at Zhafaera's waist level. Then, moving Delan just ahead of her, Zhafaera made her way carefully back to the palace.

Chapter 12

Delan woke slowly, sunlight filtering in through the gauzy curtains and piercing through his eyelids. He felt stiff and tired, like he'd run for miles.

Opening his eyes, it took him a moment to realize where he was – in the room he shared with Zhafaera in the palace of Zarga. His memory came back in a rush – the fight, his walk through the gardens…getting stabbed. Reaching up, he touched his chest where the knife had pierced him but felt no pain. Was he dead?

Looking to the left, he saw Zhafaera curled up on the other side of the bed, facing away from him. Delan rolled over, ignoring his protesting muscles, and reached an arm around her, pulling her close and burying his face in her red hair. She seemed real enough. So probably not dead then.

Zhafaera stirred, snuggling closer into him, and he smiled. Gently, he moved his hand down to brush over her swollen belly, enjoying the feel of it as he relished just being alive. Zhafaera's hand moved to meet his, and he kissed the back of her neck. Then she froze.

"Delan! You're awake!" The relief in her voice was palpable as she spun to face him.

"Of course I am, it's morning," he said, smiling.

Zhafaera threw her arm around his neck and buried

her face in his chest, clinging to him as he tucked her head under his chin and held her tightly. God*s it felt good just to hold her again.* Last night, he'd been sure he never would.

"Does this mean you forgive me?" he asked tentatively.

Zhafaera pulled back, wiping her eyes. "Do *you* forgive *me*?"

"I'm sorry, Zhafaera. I'm so sorry."

"No, *I'm* sorry. I was so horrible to you, and then you almost died—"

"But I didn't," Delan said, tucking a finger under her chin. "You healed me."

She smiled slightly. "You healed yourself. At least you pulled enough power from me to keep yourself alive until I could get there."

Delan frowned. He didn't remember drawing magic from her. He studied her face carefully, and noted the dark circles under her eyes. His heart clenched. "Did I hurt you?" he asked quietly.

Zhafaera shook her head, but she looked away. "No, I'm fine." When Delan didn't speak, she finally met his gaze. "Honestly, you startled me more than anything. You pulled from a relatively long way off, and I wasn't expecting it."

"We should have Aroha look at you…" Delan began, but Zhafaera put her fingers to his lips.

"I'm fine, I swear. And Aroha will ask questions that it would be best not to answer. No one can know you're a Black mage."

"But what about the baby? What if I—"

"It's fine. Here, feel." Zhafaera took his hand and placed it on her belly. *Now follow my magic,* she said silently.

Delan opened his mind and felt her magic flow into her stomach. He followed carefully until suddenly there was something else. *There.* A flaming pulse. It shifted, and Delan jumped, snapping back into his own mind.

"It moved!" he said excitedly.

"Yes," Zhafaera said, smiling again. "She's been doing that. Not so that *you* can feel it on the outside yet, but *I* can tell. She's fine. Now stop worrying."

Delan relaxed and pulled Zhafaera close again, inhaling the scent of her hair. They were silent for a time, Delan content just to be alive and with the woman he loved.

Zhafaera broke the silence first. "I'm not going to hide my pregnancy anymore."

"Really?" Delan was surprised but tried not to sound too hopeful.

"Really. I'm ready for everyone to know. And besides, Tristain saw through my illusion yesterday, and if he can see it, the other Air mages won't be far behind."

"Tristain is probably wondering where we are. I think we missed our dawn departure."

"*Our* departure?" Zhafaera asked. "I thought you wanted me to stay behind?"

"Do I look like an idiot? I got the hint after you threw glass at my head. Although I suppose I should be thankful it wasn't knives," Delan said with a chuckle.

Zhafaera blushed. "I'm sorry."

"Don't be. I was being an ass." Delan kissed her forehead. "But really, should we be going to find Tristain?"

"No, it's fine. I ran into him in the hall last night when I was bringing you back in. Since you looked half dead, he assumed we were postponing our trip."

"How *did* you get me back to the castle?" Delan asked.

"I floated you the whole way with magic. But that's nothing compared to how we got to you so quickly…"

Zhafaera told him how Evey had flown her out into the gardens.

"And no one saw?" he asked incredulously.

"Not as far as I know. It was dark."

"That's lucky."

"I'd have done it in broad daylight if that's what it took to save you," Zhafaera said seriously.

Delan leaned down and kissed her, gently at first but quickly intensifying. When her mouth opened under his, Delan groaned, then rolled, pulling Zhafaera on top of him and making her squeak. Just as he buried both hands into her hair, a loud knock sounded from the main room. They broke apart, both more than a little breathless and grinning.

"Can we ignore it?" Delan whispered.

Zhafaera nodded and kissed him again.

The knock sounded again, insistent. "Queen Zhafaera?" someone called.

Zhafaera pulled back and rolled her eyes. "I guess not," she said, rolling off of Delan and climbing out of bed.

Delan put a hand over his eyes and breathed deep, then sat up and made to follow. He stopped when his head spun at the change in position. Sitting on the edge of the bed, he braced himself and waited for the room to stop moving.

He could hear Zhafaera greeting someone, then moving back towards the bedroom.

"Really, we're fine," she was saying as they came in the bedroom door. "There's no need to—"

"I'll judge that for myself," Aroha said firmly. Delan looked up. The older woman was leading the way into the room, followed closely by Zhafaera and Darcia. Darcia looked like she was trying to make herself very small, clearly intimidated by Zhafaera's protests.

Aroha had no such qualms. She quickly moved over to Delan and put a hand on his forehead. Instantly he felt the rush of magic through his body.

"Three stab wounds, is that right?" She murmured.

"I think so," Delan said. "How did you know?"

"The whole place is buzzing about your attack. Half the rumors say you're dead; the other half say you were attacked by a dragon that flew over the castle last night."

Delan caught Zhafaera's eye, and they both looked away before they could laugh.

Aroha was silent for a time. "Her majesty did an excellent job, there's hardly a trace left," Aroha finally said, somewhat grudgingly. Delan glanced at Zhafaera. She looked pleased.

"But you did lose a lot of blood," Aroha continued. "Are you feeling fatigued? Dizzy, even?"

Delan shrugged. "A little dizzy when I sat up."

Aroha tutted. "Not surprising. You need to *rest*." And with that, she gave his shoulder a shove and forced him to lie back in the bed.

"Now, *you*," she said, turning to Zhafaera. Zhafaera looked startled. "Tell me what happened to make you look so exhausted."

"Wh-what?" Zhafaera asked. "It's nothing—"

"Sit," Aroha ordered, pointing to the bed. Zhafaera sat. Aroha put her hand on Zhafaera's head and paused. Finally, she pulled back. "You've over-exerted yourself," she said sternly. "Not the best idea in your condition, especially since we've just gotten you healthy."

Delan felt guilt burning its way up his throat.

"I won't ask what you've been doing besides healing," Aroha continued. "But I would advise you not to do it again."

"But she's all right, isn't she?" Delan couldn't stop himself asking.

Aroha looked at him, and her gaze softened somewhat. "Yes, you're both fine; you just need rest." She eyed them both like they were about to get up and start running.

"We will, we promise," Zhafaera said, standing again.

Aroha nodded and curtsied to Zhafaera. "I'll leave you to it then. And Your Majesty…good work."

Zhafaera smiled and led them out. After seeing them at the door, she came back into the bedroom and climbed into bed. Snuggling up next to Delan, she looked up at him and smiled.

"Now, where were we?"

***

As Zhafaera marched through the palace, her deep blue gown billowing behind her, she tried to calm her mind. She wanted to talk with Queen Oraesa, but accusing her of allowing, even orchestrating, the attack on Delan wouldn't help anything. But the palace was as secure a place as any, and as Delan had said his attackers ran back towards the palace after stabbing him, Zhafaera was inclined to be suspicious. Someone *within* the walls was responsible.

Entering the throne room, where Oraesa was holding court, Zhafaera looked around. There were over a hundred nobles gathered, both Arenthian and Burjan, and all of them looked uneasy. Those closest to the door fell silent when they noticed her, nudging their neighbors and avoiding her gaze, until the whole room was quietly looking anywhere but at her.

Zhafaera moved forward through the long room, and the crowd parted, drawing back into the shadows of the huge sandstone columns lining the open space. As she passed, a buzz of whispered conversations grew behind her, and she heard the word "pregnant" more than once. She kept herself steady and refrained from wincing. Her secret was out. She'd purposefully removed her illusion spell before she'd left her room, and her belly was obviously drawing attention. She wondered how many of them would question if Velexar was the father instead of Delan. *I should have made an announcement,* she thought belatedly.

By the time she reached Oraesa, her skin was crawling

with the weight of hundreds of eyes on her. The Queen sat on her carved white marble throne, her long blonde hair pinned up in a multitude of braids. Oraesa's face was unreadable, but Liara, standing behind her, looked nervous.

"Your Majesty," Zhafaera said, inclining her head. "Your Highness. Forgive my lateness. I'm afraid I overslept after last night's trouble."

Oraesa waved a hand. "It's no matter. How is your Consort?"

Zhafaera thought she emphasized Consort but couldn't be sure. "He's resting. I healed him well enough, but he lost quite a bit of blood."

"It's lucky you were able to reach him so quickly. I shudder to think what could have happened."

"He would have died," Zhafaera said bluntly. She met Oraesa's gaze squarely. "This palace is supposed to be secure. Or do you not guarantee the safety of your guests?"

"Of course I do," Oraesa said coolly. "There is no higher priority for me or my staff. There will be a full investigation into the incident, and the would-be assassins found. Once they are, we will know how they gained entry to the gardens. They most likely came in through the oasis; as of this morning, I am increasing patrols through the area."

"Lord Delan says his attackers ran back towards the *palace*, not the jungle." There was murmuring among the gathered nobles at Zhafaera's words.

"What are you implying?" Oraesa didn't raise her voice, but her tone was icy.

"I'm implying nothing," Zhafaera said easily. "Simply stating facts that might help with your…investigation. It does, however, suggest that the attack came from within the palace." Zhafaera looked over her shoulder and raised her voice to make sure everyone could hear her. "An attack on my Consort is an attack on me. Should I find anyone here responsible, it will be considered an act of war."

"Please, Queen Zhafaera," Oraesa said dismissively. "No one here would do such a thing. Perhaps your *condition* is making you a touch paranoid." Oraesa raised her eyebrows and looked at Zhafaera's growing belly.

Zhafaera felt herself blush. "Yes, Lord Delan and I are expecting a child in the summer," she said calmly, over more murmuring behind her. "But that does not mean that I've taken leave of my senses. My Consort was nearly killed last night, and I intend to find those responsible, no matter who they may be."

Oraesa smiled. "I assure you, we're doing everything we can to do just that. You're welcome to speak with my captain of the guard if you wish. But there's no way we'll find anything linking the assassins to the palace – mark my words, they were simply street thugs from the city, unhappy with the influx of Arenthian refugees."

Zhafaera ground her teeth and bit back her desire to accuse Oraesa of the attack. "You may be right," she finally forced out.

"I'm quite sure I am," Oraesa said. "Now, please be sure to give Lord Delan our regards."

Zhafaera recognized that the conversation was over.

Giving Oraesa a small curtsy, she moved to the side, allowing the next supplicant forward as she moved through the columns and into the open air of the balcony.

Taking deep breaths of warm, dry air, Zhafaera stood and rested her arms on the railing, looking out over the city as it baked under the blazing sun. Something about Oraesa's words had made her even more certain that she was behind the attack. *No way we'll find anything, indeed,* she thought. *Because you won't be looking at your own guards.*

It *was* possible that she was being paranoid. But Geon had warned her that she'd made Oraesa her enemy, and this was possibly just the next move in their power struggle.

"Zhafaera!" Turning to face the voice, Zhafaera found Liara moving quickly towards her, smiling now. When she reached her, Liara threw her arms around Zhafaera and squeezed her in a tight hug for a moment. "Congratulations! Why didn't you tell me you were pregnant?"

"I didn't tell *anyone*," Zhafaera said as Liara let go. "Well, except Delan obviously."

"But why not?"

"Didn't you hear your mother in there? Already it's started – making me sound irrational because I'm pregnant. It was easier to hide it."

Liara frowned. "I suppose." She glanced over her shoulder towards her mother. "She *is* looking into it, you know."

"I'm sure. But is she looking in the right places?"

"You can't really think Mother had anything to do with this," Liara said, her eyebrows raising into her hair.

Zhafaera bit her lip. "I don't know what I think," she said finally. "Your mother and I aren't exactly friends these days."

"Yes, but still…" Liara looked uncomfortable. "Anyway, I'm glad Delan is all right. There were rumors that he'd been killed!"

"Thankfully, I got to him in time to prevent that," Zhafaera said with a sigh. The thought of how close she'd come to losing him still sent a chill down her spine.

"Did you hear that some people are claiming to have seen a dragon fly over the castle last night?" Liara asked nervously. "Mother says it's nonsense, but—"

"I'm sure your mother is right," Zhafaera said, though it pained her physically to say it. "If there had been a dragon in the sky last night, I'm sure they would have done more than just fly over."

"I suppose. It's just so scary, though. I mean, to think, dragons could show up here at any moment, and we'd have no warning." Liara shivered.

"We'll have *some* warning," Zhafaera said encouragingly. "What do you think all of the mages, and myself, have been working on?"

Liara looked somewhat pacified. "You mean they won't be able to sneak up on us?"

"Not completely." *Unless they're already within the shields,* she thought.

"Well, that's something, at least." Liara looked at Zhafaera, a worried frown back on her face.

"What is it?" Zhafaera asked.

Liara bit her lip. "Mother sent a group of mages out on a brick last night. After you left. She sent them to look for the curve in the road that Delan found."

Zhafaera's temper flared. "She didn't even believe me!"

"She said if anyone was going to find something, it was going to be her. No, don't!" Liara grabbed Zhafaera's arm as she turned to march back to Oraesa. "You're not supposed to know. Although I assume she'll tell you if they end up finding the Emerald."

Zhafaera took a deep breath. "I suppose we may as well wait until they come back before we go out ourselves."

Liara nodded. "And it'll give Delan time to rest."

"He's going to need it, if how he looked last night is any indication." Zhafaera jumped and turned. Tristain had come up silently behind them. "Did I scare you?" he asked with a grin.

"Only half to death," Zhafaera said, touching her racing heart.

"Sorry, I suppose I should be more careful with you in your condition." Tristain gave her a small bow. "And now that you've officially announced it, allow me to officially congratulate you."

"He knew?" Liara asked indignantly.

"Only because he could see through my illusion," Zhafaera said, wincing. "Anyway, once he found out, I knew it was only a matter of time before I had to tell everyone."

"Are you saying I can't keep a secret?" Tristain asked. Zhafaera snorted.

"I'm offended," Tristain said, frowning.

"Sorry Tristain, but she's not wrong," Liara said, grinning.

"*Anyway*," Tristain continued. "I heard you say that Oraesa sent her own scouting party out last night. I can't say I'm surprised. I'd probably do the same thing. But if we're waiting until they return to decide if we're still going to go ourselves, then what's our next move?"

"Honestly?" Zhafaera said. "I think it's back to the library."

Tristain groaned. "Somehow I knew you were going to say that."

"At least we have new material now."

"How so?"

"Well," Zhafaera smiled. "We know we're looking for something in the desert. That narrows it down."

Tristain looked at her seriously. "It's a testament to how bad the last few weeks have been that that actually makes me feel better."

***

"This one says that dragons that take human form can't change back. They're stuck as a human forever." Ranj was frowning down at the book in his lap.

Zhafaera stretched her arms above her head, cracking her neck. "That makes sense. I knew the reverse was true." Meeting Delan's eyes, she knew he was remembering Alec

201

shifting into a red and black dragon. She looked away, guilt crawling up her spine.

"Could be useful," Tristain said slowly. "I'd have to assume that they die easier in human form."

"Sure, but how on earth do you force a dragon to take human form?" Zhafaera asked wearily. It was late in the evening, more than a week after Delan was stabbed, and they were reading by candlelight now. The library matron would be along any minute to kick them out.

"I assume you'd do it like you'd transmorph any object," Tristan said lightly. "With great difficulty."

"No kidding."

Liara threw up her hands. "I'm so useless. I can barely even understand what you're saying, let alone be helpful." She slammed her book shut and tossed it to the table.

Delan reached out and put a hand on her shoulder. "Don't feel bad, I can't transmorph anything either," he said seriously.

You could if you tried, Zhafaera thought to him. His eyes flashed to hers in surprise, but he said nothing. The others didn't know he was a Black mage. *We'll practice,* she thought, smiling slightly.

"I think we've had enough for tonight," Zhafaera said out loud, standing slowly.

"Agreed." Tristain put his book on the table and ran his fingers through his already messy hair. "We need some sleep if we're going to head out into the desert tomorrow." He looked at Delan. "Try not to almost die this time, okay?"

Delan rolled his eyes. "I'll try not to let assassins

sneak up on me," he said wryly, moving to sling one arm around Zhafaera's shoulders as they all left their cubbyhole.

The mages that Queen Oraesa had sent into the desert had returned earlier this morning, reporting that yes, there was a slight curve in the road, but there was nothing to be seen for miles around the area. It appeared to be a dead end, but Zhafaera wanted to be sure. She wouldn't be until she'd been out there herself.

Since their fight, she and Delan had been better. Delan had relaxed now that she was being open about her pregnancy, and he was making a concerted effort not to hover. She knew it was hard for him. She had to admit, she felt better with it out in the open, and for the first time she was allowing herself to feel excited, imagining what it would be like to have a child. And having a goal in sight – even if it was just a pointless trip into the desert – had done wonders for her temper.

As they reached the palace, Liara broke away to the royal quarters, promising to meet them in the morning to see them off, leaving Delan, Zhafaera, Tristain, and Ranj to make their way into the guest wing. Just as Delan and Zhafaera reached their rooms, the door across the hall opened. Zhafaera turned to see her grandfather coming out of his room, wearing a thick robe.

"Zhafaera, I hoped that was you." Nyto looked at the others and nodded. "Could I have a moment?"

Tristain, a little ways ahead down the hall, glanced at Zhafaera quickly, and she shrugged. Ranj took his arm and tugged him back towards their room. Delan squeezed her hand and stepped back. Nyto stood aside and gestured into the open door of his room.

Zhafaera stepped past him and entered the room. It looked much like hers and Delan's rooms, down to the matching furnishings. She heard Nyto close the door behind her, and the hairs on the back of her neck prickled. *You're being silly,* she thought firmly. But she turned quickly to face him.

"Can I get you something to drink? Wine, perhaps?" He gestured to the pitcher on the low table in front of the couch, then stopped. "No, I suppose not, not in your condition." His eyes flickered to her belly, and he smiled, but it didn't quite reach his eyes. "I haven't had a chance to congratulate you. I'll be a great-grandfather." He didn't sound pleased.

"Thank you," Zhafaera said carefully.

Nyto hesitated, not meeting her eyes. "Can I ask you…that is to say, there have been rumors…I cannot believe that Velexar would…after all, you were his niece…"

Zhafaera let him stumble into silence. She didn't want to ease his conscience about his son, but she did want to settle the rumors. She sighed.

"The baby is my Consort's," she said firmly. "But understand this – Velexar would happily have raped me had I not already been pregnant." Nyto flinched. "Your son wasn't the man you thought he was."

"No, apparently he wasn't," Nyto said softly.

Zhafaera waited. "Was that all you wanted?"

Nyto straightened quickly. "No, no. I, um, I have

spoken with the full Council."

Zhafaera perked up. "And?" She prodded.

"Some are open to your idea," he said reluctantly, as though the words were being forced from him. "They did not deny your request for help with the Ruby outright, but they don't want to get involved unless there is some better indication of success." Nyto took a deep breath and met her gaze. "If you can find the missing Gems, we will provide the Ruby, and someone to wield it."

Zhafaera's heart soared. That was two down. Well, almost. Close enough. Surely she could find the other two Gems. "Thank you for speaking with them. I know it's not what you wanted."

"It doesn't matter what I wanted," Nyto said with a shrug. "You were right, and that's why we have a Council, not a monarch."

"For once, I'm glad of that," Zhafaera said evenly.

Nyto hesitated. "Listen, I know I haven't been around, and I haven't exactly been supportive of you, but we are family. In fact, we're all each other has left. I just want to say…good luck tomorrow. I hope you find something. Truly, I do."

Zhafaera blinked in surprise. She hadn't expected anything like that from him. "Thank you," she said again. She felt as if she should say more but couldn't quite think of anything. "I should go."

"Yes, of course, you need to rest," Nyto said hurriedly.

Zhafaera nodded quickly and turned to the door.

Once safely back in her room, she let out a breath she

hadn't realized she'd been holding.

Delan looked up from where he sat on the couch, petting Evey gently between the ears as if she were actually a cat.

"What did he want?" Delan asked, looking at her quizzically.

Zhafaera smiled. "He said the council will provide the Ruby, when the time comes."

"Really! That's great!"

"I know! We just have to find the Diamond and the Emerald first."

"Oh, is *that* all?" Delan asked.

"Pretty much." Zhafaera sighed and flopped into a chair by the fire. She wouldn't tell him the other thing Nyto had wanted to know. Thinking about it just made her angry, and there was no need for Delan to be angry too.

"Well, at least that's two out of four," Delan said helpfully.

"I thought the same thing," Zhafaera said with a grin.

The other two Gems have been missing for hundreds of years, Evey chimed in helpfully.

"Details," Zhafaera said with a wave of her hand.

Important details.

"Perhaps. But I have a feeling we're going to find one soon." Zhafaera was excited. "I think we're on the right track for something." She shook her head. "I can't explain it."

Delan stood and stretched. "I think I'm on the right track for bed." He eyed her. "Are you coming?"

Zhafaera smiled slowly, and watched Delan's eyes

darken abruptly. She stood and moved quickly to their bedroom door. "Goodnight Evey," she called over her shoulder.

Goodnight, Zhafaera and Delan.

Zhafaera turned the moment she was in the bedroom, flinging her arms around Delan's neck and pushing him back against the door until it closed with a sharp snap. Tilting her head up, she met his lips as he bent his head to kiss her thoroughly. One of his hands fisted in her hair, holding her tightly in place, while the other drifted languidly down her back. Just when she started to feel dizzy, he pulled away from her lips, kissing down her neck in the most distracting way. Mumbling something that sounded suspiciously like "mood swings," he began walking her back towards their bed.

Chapter 13

The next morning dawned hot and dry. Up north, winter snows would be beginning to melt, but here the heat was simply unrelenting. The sun was barely over the horizon, and Delan was already sweltering. Their party stood on a large covered platform as the mages prepared their brick.

Delan, Zhafaera, Evey, Colin, Ban, and Tristain waited with varying degrees of patience as three mages inspected the sandstone brick that had been waiting for them. Ranj and Liara waited with them, although they were staying behind in the city to continue the library routine.

"Tristain didn't bring guards," Zhafaera mumbled, still grumpy. This was their compromise: Delan agreed not to try to leave Zhafaera behind, as long as her guards came with them.

Delan opened his mouth, but Tristain beat him to it. "I'm *part* of your guards, darling. Get used to it." He winked at Delan and met Zhafaera's glare blandly.

"You won't even know we're here, Your Majesty," Ban said cheerfully. "We're just along to see the sights."

"You'd hurt their feelings if you sent them back now." Delan slung his arm around Zhafaera's shoulders as Zhafaera sighed.

"It was so much simpler when we could just take off

into the woods by ourselves," she muttered.

"I bet it was," Colin snorted softly from his place beside Delan. Delan elbowed him in the ribs.

At that moment, one of the mages stepped forward and bowed to Zhafaera. "If you please, Your Majesty, we're ready to set off."

"Excellent," Zhafaera said briskly, resettling her pack on her shoulders. The others did the same. Single file, they moved across the flat gangplank, connecting the platform to the brick. The brick itself was…odd. Delan had never seen anything quite like it. It *did* look like a ship, if a ship was a ten-foot by thirty-foot rectangle that stood four feet tall off the ground. A canopy covered the whole top, made of sturdy canvas that would keep the sun off of them, with thin, gauzy curtains enclosing the sides to keep the sand out while letting the wind blow through. There was a thick lip of stone surrounding the edges of the brick that could serve as benches, with a wooden railing attached to prevent anyone from falling over the side. Hopefully.

Two of the mages had followed them on to the brick, which had been packed with supplies in addition to what they carried in their packs. Water was essential in the desert, and they had planned accordingly. Even if Zhafaera could make it rain, it was best to be prepared.

As everyone settled and dropped their packs out of the way, the mages stepped up to the front of the brick, each of them taking a corner position facing outward. Looking ahead, Delan could see that the road was in fact a depression in the sand, lined with continuously smooth sandstone for as far as he could see and wide enough for two bricks to move beside each other. He couldn't begin to see how they were going to make this brick move.

As if she'd heard him, Zhafaera's voice sounded in his head. *Reach out with your magic and look at the road.*

Delan hesitated, then did as he was told, drawing just a trickle of magic from Zhafaera. Spreading out his awareness, he felt the people on the boat first, the mages popping into his mind like stars shining in the night. Zhafaera and Tristain shone the brightest in his mind, with the other two mages that would be actually piloting the brick dim by comparison. Great, now he was even *less* confident in them.

He caught Zhafaera's eyes, and she gave him a pointed look. *No, the queen didn't send her most powerful mages, but she didn't need to; it doesn't take much magic, look.* Refocusing, he turned his attention to the road itself.

And was nearly blinded.

The road glowed with power, embedded in its surface through hundreds of years of use. Now Delan watched eagerly as the two Earth mages reached out, their magic flowing out and under the brick. Smoothly, so smooth that Delan could hardly feel it, the brick began to move forward and quickly picked up speed.

Grinning, Delan released his magic and turned to look at Zhafaera. She was watching him closely. *We need to pick up your lessons again,* she said in his mind.

Delan shrugged. It wasn't something that he felt was important, not now that he could at least control it.

Zhafaera frowned. *There may come a time when you have to use magic.*

I've made it this far without it.

Please, you've saved your life with magic how many times now?

Delan thought. *Three, but —*

Evey interrupted by putting her heavy paws on Delan's leg. He looked down. *Don't be silly,* she told him firmly. *Magic is part of you, even if you don't want it anymore after what happened to your brother.* Delan flinched. *You have to keep learning.* She looked over her shoulder where the others gathered at the back of the brick, just as Tristain called over to them.

"Oi, you two lovebirds. Are you going to stand there all day, or are you going to come play cards with us?"

"That depends, are you going to cheat?" Zhafaera called back.

Tristain threw a hand over his heart in mock indignation. "I'm wounded. How could you think such a thing of me? You dare impugn my honor."

"That's because you cheat like a dockhand," Zhafaera said sternly.

"We'll keep him honest," Colin chimed in. Tristain looked at him in surprise, and Colin flushed under the scrutiny of an unfamiliar noble.

Tristain grinned. "I swear I'll be on my best behavior."

"You'd better be," Zhafaera said, heading for the group of men with Delan close behind.

"You have my word. I'm stuck on this brick with all of you for the next two days. I can't exactly run off with my ill-gotten gains, can I?"

Zhafaera eyed him appraisingly. "Fair enough. Who's dealing?"

***

"This is it," Delan said quietly, looking out over the endless sea of sand in front of them. "I can feel the road curving."

Zhafaera shaded her eyes and tried to make out anything that could indicate a change in their trajectory. There was absolutely nothing but sand in all directions reflecting the late afternoon light. "Are you sure?" she asked, keeping her voice low. The others still didn't know that Delan was a Black mage, and they intended to keep it that way.

"As sure as I can be." Delan shrugged. "I've gotten a pretty good feel for it in the last couple of days."

Zhafaera touched his arm lightly and smiled. "You're better at Earth magics than me, so I trust you." Turning, she raised her voice and called out to the others. "This is it! Stop the brick." Immediately the brick began to slow.

Tristain met her eyes and opened his mouth, but before he could speak, she felt it. A slight tug from the Sapphire, pulling her to the north. Her head snapped around, and she stared as hard as she could into the heat waves emanating from the sand. She felt like if she just looked hard enough, something large would appear on the horizon.

"What is it?" Tristain asked, coming up behind her and Delan as Colin and Ban began gathering their things

212

and making sure everything was secured in their packs.

"I–I'm not sure," Zhafaera said awkwardly. "It feels like…buzzing almost. There's definitely something out there."

As the brick came to a complete stop, Zhafaera moved away from the railing and moved to grab her pack from Colin. "Thanks," she said, slinging it over her shoulder.

"I'd offer to carry it for you if I thought you'd let me, Your Majesty," Colin said with a smile.

"Didn't I tell you two days ago to call me Zhafaera?"

"I believe you did, Your Majesty."

Zhafaera sighed. "Come on, it's into the desert for us now. Maybe you'll change your mind when you see how much I sweat."

Turning, she led the way to the wooden ladder attached to the side of the brick and made to climb down. Ban blocked her with an arm between her and the ladder. "Let a couple of us go first, Your Majesty."

Zhafaera fought the urge to roll her eyes. What *possible* danger could there be out here in the middle of nowhere? But she forced herself to step back and gesture. "Be my guest."

As Ban and Colin began the climb down, Zhafaera moved over to where Delan was speaking quietly to the two mages that had powered the brick out here.

"We can't wait for you for more than three days," one of them was saying in his high nasal voice. The mages had mostly kept themselves separate from Zhafaera and her companions, and for that she was grateful. She had the distinct feeling that anything they said would go directly back to Queen Oraesa.

"Three days may not be enough time," Delan replied slowly. "Zhafaera can provide water if it comes to that. We just need you to be here when we come back."

"And if you don't come back?" The mage asked coldly. "How long are we to wait?"

"Give us a week," Zhafaera told him firmly. "If we haven't come back in a week, we're probably not coming back."

The two mages looked at one another, and Zhafaera could guess they were communicating mind to mind. "Very well," the second mage said. "We will wait here for a week before we return to Zarga."

"Thank you," Zhafaera said, inclining her head. The mages bowed. Looking over her shoulder, Zhafaera saw that she and Delan were the only ones left on the brick. Moving back to the railing, Zhafaera turned and carefully began to climb down the ladder, wobbling a little as her feet hit the soft sand at the bottom. Delan followed quickly behind her.

The rest of the group had moved a little ways away from the brick and were standing in a half circle, waiting on Zhafaera and Delan to join them. As they took their places, Zhafaera slid her pack off and began digging through it. Finally, towards the bottom, she found what she was looking for – a wide-brimmed, lace-trimmed hat intended for wear at formal outdoor events. It may look ridiculous, but it would be better than nothing for keeping the intense sun off of her pale face. The men had similar hats, although not quite so…frilly.

"I still don't see why you had to bring your cat, Zhafaera," Tristain commented, looking at Evey strangely. "The desert is no place for a pet."

Zhafaera shrugged casually. "She doesn't like being left on her own, and she's more useful than you might think."

Tristain frowned but didn't reply.

Do you think he's getting suspicious of me? Evey asked for Zhafaera's ears alone.

He's smart, but you're well concealed. It's hard to say, Zhafaera thought back.

"So, which way?" Colin asked, looking around at the vast expanse of desert surrounding them.

Zhafaera pointed straight north. "That way." She looked around at the others and saw determined looks on all of their faces. She hoped she wasn't leading them out to their deaths in the middle of the desert. "Come on, let's get as far as we can before dark," she said as she resettled her pack and started forward.

They hadn't gone far before Zhafaera knew that they would have to do most of their traveling at night. Luckily the sun started to sink below the horizon within an hour of their leaving the brick, and they were able to pick up the pace. As the sun set, Zhafaera was amazed to see more stars appear in the sky than she'd ever seen in her life. By the time it was full dark, the air was crisp and clear, and Zhafaera was enjoying the night.

The moon was high in the sky by the time they called a stop to rest and eat. Dropping her pack, Zhafaera stretched and sat gingerly, yawning hugely. The men spread out in a circle and began opening packs, dragging out blankets and food and passing them around. Their meal was meager, as there was nothing nearby to build a fire with. More important was drinking water. Zhafaera felt like her mouth was coated in sand, even though she'd tried to keep sipping from her canteen as they walked.

"Are you all right?" Delan asked quietly. "Did you get enough to eat?"

Zhafaera took his hand and squeezed. "I'm fine, just tired." To the group, she said, "Let's rest for a couple of hours, then we'll start again and try to get a few more miles in before dawn. Tomorrow we can set up the tent and try to rest during the day."

Evey curled up next to Zhafaera, and Zhafaera slipped her an extra piece of cheese. They couldn't feed her as much as usual while traveling with the others, but since this was supposed to be a relatively short trip, they had fed her well beforehand and were hoping to take advantage of a dragon's slower metabolism to make it through.

"Zhafaera, can you still feel something?" Tristain asked as they all finished eating.

Zhafaera thought for a moment and listened to the buzzing from the Sapphire. It was almost like a tether was pulling her north towards something large and magical. She nodded and pointed north again. "There's definitely something out there, but it's faint. Can you not feel it?"

Tristain shook his head. "Nothing."

Zhafaera touched the Sapphire on her chest. "It must be this," she said slowly. She grinned. "Maybe the Gems can recognize each other. Maybe we're about to get extremely lucky."

"Don't jinx it!" Delan said quickly. "After all that time we spent in the library, I can't even begin to hope that we might actually find one."

"Fair enough, I—" Zhafaera started.

"What I don't understand is the cat," Tristain interrupted. He was frowning and squinting across the circle at Evey, barely a shadow in the darkness.

Zhafaera tensed. "What do you mean?"

"I mean, why is she here? It's been nagging at me since we left. There's almost…" He looked at Zhafaera wide-eyed. "Is that an illusion spell?"

There's no way he should be able to tell, Evey said to Zhafaera.

Zhafaera sighed and looked at Evey. "He's a *very* powerful Air mage," she said slowly.

Tristain stood up and pointed at Evey. "Reveal yourself, mage," he said sternly.

Evey looked first at Zhafaera, then at Delan. Zhafaera stood slowly and put her hands up, facing Tristain. "Listen, before you—"

But she could tell by the look on his face, it was too late. She felt Delan stand up next to her a half second before Colin and Ban stood, scrabbling for weapons as Tristain gasped and raised his hands. Zhafaera looked to her right. Where the black cat had sat, now stood a dragon, fully twelve feet long and eight feet tall. There was a great intake of breath from around the circle as Evey stretched her wings and settled them back against her body.

"Zhafaera, get *back*," Tristain called urgently.

"Listen, listen, all of you," Zhafaera said quickly. "It's perfectly safe–"

"*Safe?* That's a dragon!" Tristain hissed. Colin and Ban had drawn their weapons but seemed incapable of moving closer.

"I'm aware," Zhafaera said calmly. "Her name is Evamoria."

"We call her Evey," Delan chimed in, taking a step closer to Zhafaera.

"You call her Evey," Tristain repeated in a whisper. "How in the twelve hells…"

Zhafaera glanced at Delan. "We found her at the foot of the Angonite mountains on our way north back to Arenthia. She was starving and more than a little banged up after the fighting among the dragons – those who wanted to join Velexar against the ones who wanted to stay out of human affairs. Velexar's dragons won, and those are the ones that are attacking us now. Please, everyone just calm down. Evey has helped more than you'll ever know."

Hello, Evey said quietly, and everyone jumped. *I promise I have no intention to harm you. I want to help however I can. My…my mother was killed when Velexar came. She wanted nothing to do with his plans, and neither did I. And I had no idea that those dragons would try to take over like this.*

"Your mother…?" Tristain swallowed and looked at Zhafaera. "How *old* is she?"

Twenty-four, Evey supplied.

Tristain's eyes widened. They'd read enough dragon books in the last two months to know just how young that was for a dragon. "So you…take care of her?" he asked Zhafaera.

"We both do," Delan said. "Us and my father."

Tristain shook his head but lowered his arms. Colin and Ban did the same and lowered their weapons. "This whole time you've had a literal *dragon* right under our noses, and no one sensed it." He flinched. "A *young* dragon at that." Zhafaera thought he looked pale in the light from the moon. "And there's fifty full-grown dragons out there that could come at us anytime. They could sneak up on us tomorrow, and we wouldn't even know." He ended on a short laugh and sat heavily.

Evey returned to her black cat form as everyone else sat back on their blankets. Zhafaera noted that Colin and Ban put down their weapons but kept them nearby. The silence drew out uncomfortably.

"Look, let's all just try and get some sleep," Zhafaera said cautiously, reaching for her blanket.

Tristain laughed grimly. "Sleep? I may never sleep again."

***

They settled into a pattern over the next two days – rise in the darkest hours of the morning, after the moon had set, and before the sun even thought of peeking its rays over the horizon. Walk until the heat of the new day was too much to bear. Rest and camp under the thick canopy of the tent they had packed that was big enough for all of them to fit under, even with the others avoiding Evey. Start again

219

in the evening and walk until midnight, when they took another rest and a meal.

The further they went into the desert, the more intense the buzzing got for Zhafaera. She was beginning to doubt her earlier assertion that they might find a Gem. This felt entirely too big for that. It wasn't until nearly dawn on the third day out from the brick that she learned why.

It was Evey who stopped first. She pulled up short, her head tilted to the side. Zhafaera stopped and held up her hand to stop the men.

"What is it?" Delan asked.

"I–I'm not sure." Zhafaera took a slow step forward. Just ahead was some kind of barrier, glimmering faintly in the pre-dawn light. "Can you see that?"

I can, Evey said.

But the men were shaking their heads. "I don't see anything," Tristain said annoyedly.

"It's like a wall or something," Zhafaera said quietly, taking another step forward.

Be careful, Evey warned. *It feels…different.*

"Anyone else have a strong desire to turn around?" Ban asked quietly.

Zhafaera reached out slowly.

"Zhafaera, don't—" Delan started.

Zhafaera touched the barrier and felt a strong current run up her arm. She jerked away.

"Are you all right?" Delan was by her side in an instant, examining her arm.

"Yes, it's fine. It was more…odd than anything," Zhafaera said slowly. "It's like…it's not solid, but it doesn't want us to come in." Extending out with her magic, the barrier came into sharper focus, glowing almost green in Zhafaera's vision. Looking around, Zhafaera took a few steps back. Then a few more. Craning her neck back, she looked up.

"This extends a long way," Zhafaera said. "It goes for miles in either direction, and I can't see the top."

Tristain stepped forward and reached out a hand. "I still can't feel anything. Are you sure?"

Yes, Evey said simply. *This is very powerful magic.*

Tristain looked at Evey. "Can we break through it?"

"Absolutely not," Zhafaera said. "Even if we could, I wouldn't."

"So what do we do?" Delan asked.

Zhafaera looked at Evey. Evey shrugged and began changing, stretching into her dragon form in moments. Shaking herself, Evey moved towards the shimmering wall.

"No, Evey, don't!" Delan called, but Evey was already reaching out. They watched as slowly, very slowly, she slid through the barrier headfirst. Faint green and gold sparks appeared where Evey's body touched the barrier.

Zhafaera held her breath as Evey's long tail disappeared.

Evey, can you hear me? Zhafaera reached out with her magic and felt nothing but the smooth, buzzing wall. She looked at Delan.

"She might have made it to the other side," Zhafaera said.

"She might not have."

"We have to try it."

Delan grimaced. "Are you sure we can't listen to Ban and turn around?"

"I won't make anyone come with me." Zhafaera almost laughed at the identical expressions of indignation on the men's faces.

"Like hell, you'll go alone—"

"This is what we signed up for—"

"If the dragon can make it, so can I—" That last was from Tristain. Zhafaera raised an eyebrow at him. "Well, that is to say, I can try," he added firmly.

"Right, let's hold hands," Zhafaera said quickly, holding out her own to Delan and Tristain. As they took her hands, Ban and Colin moved to either side and grasped Delan's and Tristain's other hands, forming one long line. Taking a deep breath, Zhafaera drew power from the Sapphire and led them towards the barrier.

The closer they got, the stronger the feel of electricity. It raced across her body as she made contact, jolting her senses and making her feel more awake, alive, and vital than she'd ever felt in her life. The buzzing from the Sapphire intensified, vibrating in her bones until she thought she might explode. She was seriously reconsidering her choices when, all of a sudden, she stumbled forward, and it was over. No buzzing, no electric current, no nothing.

Before them stood an enormous city, with buildings reaching so high into the sky, Zhafaera assumed they would touch the clouds. And there must be clouds, because there must be rain, if the jungle growing up among the buildings was any indication.

Zhafaera reached out with her magic. Traveling outwards, she realized that the city extended for miles, laid out in some kind of grid, with regular intersections. Reaching deeper, she felt it – an aquifer, just like the one in Zarga, leaking up into a lake surrounded by the densest greenery, feeding the city.

Delan recovered first. Releasing her hand, he turned Zhafaera to face him, pulling her hat off to get a better look at her face. "Are you all right? Is the baby all right? Was that too much for you? Here, let's find somewhere to sit down."

Focusing her magic inward, Zhafaera relaxed. "We're fine, everything is fine." She raised her voice. "Everyone else okay?" Looking to her right, she saw Evey, her dragon form, completely still.

The others didn't appear to be listening. They were looking up. "What is it?" Zhafaera turned back around and saw a huge tan shape coming towards them from the city, flying quickly on enormous feathered wings and dropping lower and lower as it got closer.

Zhafaera drew on the Sapphire and readied herself for a fight. She heard her friends do the same as swords were drawn.

The creature landed less than twenty feet in front of them, its powerful body shaped like a lion and covered in tawny fur. At least ten feet tall, the wingspan took up another thirty. As the wings folded back, Zhafaera could see flecks of gold in them, highlighted by the light from the morning sun as it began to rise just over the horizon. But the face…Zhafaera couldn't look away. The face was that of a beautiful woman with dark wavy hair flowing down towards her powerful shoulders. And she was angry.

"A sphinx," Zhafaera said weakly. "It's a sphinx."

"Fantastic, I'm great at riddles," Tristain murmured.

"WHO *DARES* TO ENTER THE CITY OF THEBES?" The sphinx boomed. Zhafaera flinched.

"I'm sorry, Thebes?" Zhafaera asked hesitantly.

"THE CITY THAT WAS LOST AND FORGOTTEN, FOUND AND REBUILT, ONLY TO BE LOST AND FORGOTTEN AGAIN." The sphinx shook her wings out again and stepped forward. Zhafaera felt everyone tense.

"I'm Queen Zhafaera of Arenthia," she called with as much confidence as she could muster. "And you are…?"

"I AM IRIS. AND I AM NOT *A* SPHINX, I AM *THE* SPHINX."

"Yes, of course," Zhafaera said quickly. "Are you—"

"WHY HAVE YOU COME HERE?"

"We're looking for something…a Gem," Zhafaera said, quickly making the decision that honesty was the best policy.

The sphinx let out an inhuman screech and tossed her hair over her shoulders. "THERE ARE NO GEMS HERE. TURN AROUND AND—"

EVAMORIA! A new voice tore through their minds, and Zhafaera was on her knees before she knew what was happening. Looking to her right, she shaded her eyes against the rising sun and was nearly blown over as Evey took flight.

Evey, come back! Zhafaera called urgently, scanning the sky for what she knew she would find. And there it was – a huge winged shape, much larger than that sphinx, was headed towards them from between the last buildings on the edge of the city. Enormous black wings beat the air, sending the dragon hurtling towards them.

Evey ignored Zhafaera and made directly for the new dragon. Zhafaera reached out and grabbed Delan's hand. No way could Evey take on a fully grown dragon by herself. Standing shakily and pulling Delan behind her, Zhafaera drew power through the Sapphire and readied herself. She'd killed a dragon before, and she could do it again.

If the sphinx tries to stop me, block her, she thought to Delan alone.

Block... Delan's mind voice sounded weak. Then he shook his head as if to clear it. *I will certainly try.*

The men closed in around her just as Zhafaera prepared to call a bolt of lightning to at least bring the dragon down out of the sky. She felt more than saw the sphinx spread her wings. Evey was still flying at top speed towards the dragon. Now was the time to strike…and yet Zhafaera hesitated.

Her moment of hesitation was one moment too long. Evey slammed into the dragon more than forty feet in the air, but rather than dropping, they both began to rise, spiraling upwards, higher and higher, until Zhafaera was dizzy from watching them.

"A reunion between mother and child is a beautiful

thing," chimed a clear voice, and Zhafaera nearly jumped out of her skin. Looking around, her gaze fell on the sphinx. It seemed her voice was actually quite pleasant when she wasn't yelling at them.

"Mother and…" Zhafaera covered her mouth with her hands. "Are you saying that is Evey's – I mean – Evamoria's – mother? How could you possibly know that?"

"Child, I know more things than you could ever *dream* of wanting to know," Iris said coldly, still watching the two dragons. "In this case, Tarysa is my friend, and I've seen her daughter in her mind. I recognized her as soon as she came through and called for her mother." She turned back to Zhafaera, still surrounded by the men with weapons drawn. "You can put those away. I could cut through all of you before you could blink."

Zhafaera put her hand on Delan's shoulder, but he didn't relax. Neither did Ban or Colin.

Iris resettled her wings. "I apologize for my rudeness earlier. Evamoria is welcome, and I can see you have the Sapphire. But humans I have not seen for three hundred years."

Zhafaera's heart leapt in her chest. *Delan,* she thought, trying to keep a rein on her excitement. *The Emerald was lost three hundred years ago.*

He made no response, still deadly focused on the sphinx, despite her apparent change in attitude. Zhafaera squeezed his shoulder and tried to move past him. It was like trying to move a wall.

"How do you know I have the Sapphire?"

"It is obvious, child. You radiate a power that few mortals can wield. It's how you made it through the barrier without being incinerated."

Zhafaera suppressed a shudder. That was all too easy to believe. "We're looking for other Gems. Do you…have you maybe seen the Emerald?" she asked cautiously.

"ENOUGH!" The sphinx snapped. Delan, Tristain, Colin, and Ban instantly dropped their swords and hammers, gasping as though burned. Zhafaera spared a glance – they appeared unmarked, but they didn't pick their weapons back up. "I told you," Iris said, "those are unnecessary."

They stood in silence for several moments. Zhafaera looked back to where she had last seen Evey and her mother and found that they were much closer than she expected.

Evey landed with a *thwump* and skidded to a halt less than three feet from Zhafaera, spraying the humans with sand and dust. *Zhafaera, it's my* mother! Her thoughts were more excited than Zhafaera had ever felt from the young dragon. The much larger dragon landed more sedately, next to her friend, the sphinx. *Gods, this is not nearly what I expected,* Zhafaera thought to herself.

Introduce us, Delan's mind voice was tightly controlled.

Mother! Mother, come closer! Evey sounded younger than ever. Zhafaera looked up and met the huge dragon's eyes as she walked closer, reaching her head down on her long neck to be closer to eye level. Or biting level. Zhafaera took a deep breath and fought the urge to step back.

"Zhafaera, this is my mother, Tarysa," Evey said. "Mother, this is Zhafaera. And Delan, Colin, Tristain, and Ban," she continued, pointing her nose at each man in turn as they shifted slightly to pull tighter around Zhafaera.

"We–we've met," Zhafaera said. "A few years ago, when a dragon was…was killed by an Arenthian."

I remember you, Princess Zhafaera. You were quite capable. Tarysa's thoughts were smooth against Zhafaera's mind.

"Thank you, Queen Tarysa. I, too, am a Queen now," Zhafaera said.

Tarysa's head tilted in the exact same way that Evey's did. She flexed her wings, and Zhafaera realized that what she had thought were black scales were actually a deep violet. She was more than forty feet long and twenty feet tall, but her wings…her wings were at least fifty feet across from tip to tip.

You know dragons do not have queens or kings. You may call me Tarysa. Her head tilted slightly in the exact way Evey often did. *You cared for my daughter. She has told me of how you found her and healed her.* The dragon seemed to deflate slightly. *You did what I could not. I was beaten and left for dead, and when I awoke, everyone was gone. I couldn't find Evamoria.* Her mind-voice turned bitter. *I could do nothing but run and hide. So I came here to Iris, the greatest hiding place in the world. And somehow Evamoria still found me.* She leaned down and nuzzled Evey gently. Evey leaned in to her touch, and Zhafaera felt her throat tighten with tears. *I thank you.*

"Of course, Tarysa. Delan and I love Evamoria; we have been honored to care for her," Zhafaera said, inclining her head.

You make it sound like we won't see each other anymore, Evey sounded confused.

"I just assumed – I mean, of course we want to be with you, but if your mother stays here…" Zhafaera looked at Tarysa for help.

"Come, we have much to discuss," Tarysa said slowly. "Evamoria has told me some, but I need to know all IF we are to become allies."

Zhafaera smiled and was finally able to push Delan and Tristain aside.

"Zhafaera—" Delan warned.

Zhafaera turned and looked at him over her shoulder. "Dragon allies were your idea from the very beginning. Don't blame me now."

"Wait," Tristain put his hand up. "Don't we have to answer the sphinx's riddles before we can enter the city?"

Zhafaera thought that if Iris could have rolled her eyes, she would have. "My riddles were solved over eight thousand years ago. I am within my rights to allow you entry."

Tristain looked disappointed. He gestured to the city. "Lead on."

***

Delan was impressed. Outside, the buildings were covered in vines, and trees sprouted up everywhere along the roads that criss-crossed through the city. Delan could hear the sounds of any number of strange animals moving through the trees. But there was not a speck of dust anywhere inside the tall building near the center of the city that Iris guided them to. There was, however, indoor plumbing. The bathroom on the ground floor gleamed as though it had just been scrubbed fresh yesterday. The room was like no bathroom he had ever seen before – divided into half a dozen stalls, each with contraptions filled with water that Iris called toilets. And on the opposite side of the room was a line of basins, each with a tap over it that presumably poured water when activated. According to Iris, this was the small bathroom – there was a larger bathroom with actual bathing areas on the underground level, next to the exercise rooms.

The building was not the largest in the city, but at twenty stories high, it was certainly the tallest Delan had ever seen. Iris explained that, at one point, before the time of the dragons, thousands of people used to work in this building. Doing what, she was less clear on, but Delan didn't press.

They made camp in the center of the cavernous entryway, large enough to fit even the adult dragon comfortably. The only furnishings were a desk that ran the length of the back of the room, with small stools sitting behind it at regular intervals. The entire space was made of marble and glass, and they quickly spread their bedrolls and blankets to cushion the hard floor where they sat. Zhafaera and Delan took seats closest to Evey, where she sat with her mother. Both dragons had transformed into large, stunning panthers like those presumably in the jungle around them. Tristain, Colin, and Ban filled in the circle next to Iris, who had shrunk considerably to fit through the door. Delan supposed it shouldn't surprise him that she had her own magic.

"Is this where you live?" Zhafaera asked politely as they all settled down. They had been walking for hours, and it felt good to rest. Delan caught Zhafaera surreptitiously rubbing her lower back. He knew the days sleeping on the ground couldn't be easy on her now that she was six months pregnant, but she had chosen to come, so he pretended not to notice and tried not to worry.

"No," the sphinx said. "There are homes on the other side of the city that are more suitable for my long-term needs. However, the trip is impractical for a short stay, and the sky towers here are suitable for our needs for now," Iris continued.

"Where exactly are we?" Delan asked slowly.

You are in the city of Thebes, Tarysa answered. *The safest place in the world. Hidden from humans, immortals, and...others.*

"You said..." Tristain began slowly. "You said this was the city that was lost, then rebuilt, and lost again?"

"Yes. Thebes was built over ten thousand years ago, with me as its guardian," Iris explained. "Then it was lost to the sands for many years, hidden and protected. Eventually, humans came again, and it was transformed into the city you see today. But just as it was finished, the dragons overwhelmed humanity, forcing them into slavery, and this city was abandoned and forgotten again.

It remained hidden for a thousand years, until the need was very great."

"Queen Iris—" Zhafaera began.

"Just Iris, I am no Queen. I have no people to rule."

"Iris," Zhafaera tried again. "Do you have a Gem here? Is it the Emerald?"

Iris tossed her hair back. "We will get to that. But first, tell us your story, from the beginning."

Leave nothing out, Tarysa added firmly.

"We get *some* news," Iris said slowly, glancing at Tarysa. "But it's not always…clear."

Delan locked eyes with Zhafaera and nodded. Slowly, she began telling their story. How Velexar killed her mother and stole the Sapphire. Running south to get Delan's help. The only thing she left out as she told of how they made their way north to the mountains and found Evey was when Delan learned he was a Black mage.

When Zhafaera told the immortals how she was captured, Delan flinched and rubbed his chest where the thick scars from the dragon's talons marked him. First Evey, then Zhafaera healed him, so it didn't hurt, but sometimes the tight scar tissue pulled at his skin.

Tarysa appeared shocked when Zhafaera explained what Velexar planned to do to her, even the watered-down version that Zhafaera was able to share. She didn't interrupt until Zhafaera told her of Alec's transformation.

He was able to make the full change?

"Yes," Zhafaera said dully.

Didn't he know that it would kill him? No human can survive the change from mortal to immortal for long.

"I don't know what he knew or thought he knew." Zhafaera fell silent.

After a minute or so, Delan realized Zhafaera was done, and he picked up the story, telling of how they freed Zhafaera, but the dragons sacked the city.

Tarysa was less than thrilled to learn they couldn't describe any of the dragons that had attacked the city that night.

"It was completely dark, and we were running for our lives," Delan defended.

Never mind, it simply would have been helpful.

Delan continued with how they'd escaped south, first to his father, then to Zarga. "The plan is to find the missing Gems and use all four to—" he cut off and eyed Tarysa warily, changing what he was going to say. "Fight back against the dragons. Send them back to the mountains."

"And how many Gems do you have now?" Tarysa asked.

"Two," Zhafaera chimed in, roused from her own thoughts.

"Two?" Iris sounded shocked. "The Sapphire, yes, but you also have the Ruby?"

"Well, not *with* me, but the Council of Lagos has agreed to provide it when the time comes," Zhafaera said quickly.

So you have one. The Ruby will not be as easy to get as you may think, Tarysa warned.

"But you do have the Emerald? Here, in the city?" Zhafaera obviously couldn't contain her excitement.

Iris exchanged a look with Tarysa.

You do, don't you? Evey called out, earning a look from her mother. *Mother, these are my* friends! *We must help them.*

"Yes, it's here," Iris said slowly. "But it will not be easy to take it."

You do not have a suitable mage to even make a start, Tarysa added.

"Shouldn't I be able to—" Zhafaera began.

"Absolutely not." Iris' voice was firm. "No one human can wield the power of *two* Gems, and you are bonded to the Sapphire." She tilted her head to Tristain. "Your only other mage is an Air mage, but the Emerald will answer only to an Earth mage. These other three," she continued, looking over Colin and Ban and lingering on Delan, "are not mages."

Delan fought the urge to squirm under that cool golden gaze. He turned his head and found Zhafaera looking at him.

"We have to," she said quietly.

Delan took a deep breath. "I'm a Black mage," he said in a rush. "I can work Earth magic. Would the Emerald accept me?"

There was a choked sound from Delan's left. He turned to see Tristain turning slightly purple.

"You're a...you're a BLACK MAGE?" Tristain sputtered out.

Delan nodded carefully.

"This whole time, you didn't think that was important information that I needed to know?" His mouth dropped open. "Have you ever *drawn* from me?"

"No, of course not," Delan said quickly. "Zhafaera has taught me how to control it—"

"Zhafaera, you…you let him pull from you?" Tristain looked ill.

Zhafaera waved her hand at Tristain. "It really isn't that big of a deal," she said dismissively.

Tristain wasn't listening. "Wait, wait. Do you have *any* idea just how *powerful* your child is going to be?" He whisper-screamed. "The offspring of a White mage *and* a Black mage? They'll be something new. Something unheard of. Un*dreamed* of, even. Able to draw on magic from any source whatsoever?" Tristain put a hand to his head. "I need to sit down."

"You are sitting, Tristain," Delan pointed out.

"Then I need to *lie* down." And he did just that, throwing an arm over his eyes to block out the afternoon sunlight coming in from the large glass windows at the front of their building.

Delan was afraid to look at Colin and Ban, but slowly he turned to them. Colin forced a grin. "Sorry, but you're going to have to explain to me what a Black mage *is* before I get that worked up over it," Colin said.

"A Black mage is a purely human phenomenon," Iris began. "They are mages who cannot draw power from the elements, as most mages do. But they can pull power from other mages." Delan couldn't read the expression on her face. "The danger lies in the risk of pulling too much. What is right for one person may be enough to kill another." She finally blinked. "However, I do believe a Black mage could wield the Emerald."

Delan took a deep breath. "So, how do I get it?"

"I don't know," Iris said simply. "I only know where it is."

He thought on that. "So you can take me to it?"

"Yes. But you have to take it on your own. I do not know how."

Zhafaera caught his attention. "I can tell you how to bond it," she said quietly.

Tristain sat up suddenly, startling everyone in the circle. "A Gray mage, that's what she'll be," he said to no one in particular. "With each parent wielding a Gem. I might as well head back to the mountains now."

"Tristain, now is not the time for your dramatics; I shall tell Ranj on you," Zhafaera scolded. Tristain frowned but was silent.

"Can we go today?" Delan asked Iris.

Iris looked out the front windows. "We can if you wish," she said slowly. "It's not far."

"Wait, Delan, we need to plan; I need to tell you—" Zhafaera made to get up as Delan stood but couldn't seem to get the right leverage. He bent over and pulled her up as the sphinx ruffled her wings.

"Zhafaera, the mages on the brick only agreed to wait for a week, and we've already used three days. I can do this. I'm just going to run and get the Emerald. Then I'll bring it straight back here, and you can tell me how to bond it." He kissed her forehead and wrapped his arms around her. "No problem."

"You make it sound just that easy," Zhafaera's voice was muffled against his chest.

"Oh, somehow I doubt it will be easy."

Chapter 14

Iris led Delan to what he presumed was the center of the city. Leaving buildings behind, they followed a narrow path deeper into the jungle. As they passed, Delan caught glimpses of brightly colored birds flitting through the trees; orange, yellow, blue and pink feathers flashing. He thought he heard larger animals moving through the trees, but they were more stealthy than the birds and stayed out of sight.

Suddenly, the jungle broke open, and a lake spread before them. The city had clearly been built around this oasis. The water was a perfectly clear blue with a bottom that abruptly fell away like an underwater cliff. Hopefully he wouldn't have to go all the way down. He'd drawn as much power from Zhafaera as he safely could before leaving, but water wasn't his strongest element, and he wasn't sure he would make it to the bottom and back without drowning.

"Which way?" he asked Iris.

She met his gaze and resettled her wings. "I do not know. I only know that it is here," she said solemnly. "Can you not feel it?"

Delan took a deep breath and reached out magically, feeling for anything that could be as powerful as the Sapphire. He swept his consciousness out to cover the surface of the lake, then dropped down along the edges, feelings for any irregularities. Quickly, he pulled up short. There was a tunnel under the water less than fifty yards away that led to a cave that Delan *thought* contained enough air to breathe. Delan marked it in his mind and kept going, reaching the bottom of the lake and letting his mind drift across the bottom. Finding nothing but fish and sand, he pulled back.

"There's a cave over there," he eventually said to Iris. "Do you think that's it?"

But Iris was lying down, her eyes closed with her face turned up towards the fading sunlight. No help from that quarter then.

Making a decision, Delan stood abruptly and pulled off his boots. Striding forward to the water's edge, Delan dove in and began to swim along the edge until he could feel he was just above the opening to the tunnel. Taking a deep breath, he dove again and swam down until he felt the top edge of the tunnel open beneath his hand. It was too dark to see the end of the tunnel, but he could feel it. Using a tiny thread of magic, he guided himself down through the tunnel, pulling his arms through the water as his lungs began to burn.

The tunnel went on for quite some time, and more than once Delan considered turning back. But he could feel the open air ahead now, closer than the opening to the lake behind him, and he continued forward. Suddenly, his hands met rock, and he came to a sudden stop. Seeing spots, he kicked out hard, pushing himself upward until finally his head broke through the surface of the water as his starved lungs gasped for air.

Reaching out, his hands met the edge of the rock ledge that led into the cave. He held on tightly for a few moments, catching his breath, before heaving himself up onto the rock. It was pitch black. Raising his hand, he called a light and looked around.

What he had thought was a cave was actually just another tunnel, though thankfully this section was full of air instead of water. But now that he was closer and the water wasn't blocking him, he could sense something…like a flicker just on the edge of his vision. It wasn't much, but it was enough to get him moving again. Before he had gone more than three steps from the water, something on the wall caught his eye. It was a torch. Walking over, he lit the torch with a small thread of fire and let his magical light go out.

As he moved through the tunnel, the torchlight flickering over the dark walls formed erie shapes, and gave him the feeling that he was not alone. Pushing on, he eventually came to a fork in the tunnel. Reaching out with his magic, he felt a resonance coming from the right hand side and took that branch, more certain than ever that the Emerald was at the end of this tunnel.

By the time he reached what had to be the tenth fork, Delan was starting to get nervous. He could always sense the way back, but the way forward was becoming…muddy. He could feel what he assumed was the Emerald ahead, but it didn't seem to be getting any closer. And the sputtering torchlight wasn't helping.

Delan walked for another hour before finally stopping

at yet another fork. He was relatively confident he could get back to the lake, but he had to have walked for miles under the city by now. Instead of going left, where he could feel he needed to go, he sat with his back against the wall of the tunnel, in between the two forking tunnels.

"This isn't working." He sighed, rubbing his eyes. He was tired. "I think there's something off about this cave."

And now I'm talking to myself, he thought ruefully.

"Somehow it feels better," he said out loud.

Reaching out with a tiny thread of magic, trying to conserve what he had left, he felt once more for the Emerald. It was definitely there, flickering behind him as though just out of sight.

"I could use some help." He put his head between his knees. "There must be a way to reach the end. I need to find the Emerald and get back to Zhafaera."

The flickering intensified, and his head jerked up. He listened carefully but couldn't sense anything new, just stronger. "Can you hear me?" he asked, feeling silly, but trying to keep an open mind. After all, the Sapphire was sentient, it made sense that the Emerald would be too. He decided to keep going.

"We're trying to find all four of the Gems. We need them…you…to fight the dragons again. Dragons have already taken over Arenthia and are doing gods only know what to the people that are left. It won't be long before they move on to Burja, Khichora, and Laros. The whole world will be enslaved, as it once was, unless we stop them now. And the only chance we have is if we can find the Emerald and the Diamond. Zhafaera already has the Sapphire. She has bonded it, and they work together."

There was now a distinct presence in his mind, glowing green behind his eyelids. Its touch was light but insistent.

"My name is Delan," he continued. "I–I'm Consort to Queen Zhafaera of Arenthia. She's pregnant with our child. My father is Lord Geon of Crystal Point. My brother…" Delan stopped and cleared his throat. "My brother was Alec, but I lost him to the dragons." Delan fell silent, feeling raw as the Emerald's presence oozed through his mind, seeking. "I killed my brother," he said quietly, feeling the need to be completely honest. "But he was gone long before that."

"I think you and I could do a lot of good. Help a lot of people. That's all I want – for the world to be safe again. We could do it together. If you trust me."

The presence in his mind suddenly blossomed into a strong awareness, like a voice just beyond hearing. Turning, Delan looked over his shoulder and saw a strong green glow coming from the tunnel over his right shoulder – the left-hand fork had been correct after all.

Standing, he slowly resumed his walk through the tunnel, but this time he could sense the Emerald getting closer and closer. Ten yards in, the tunnel opened into a small cavern. The space was almost a perfect cylindrical room with ceilings eight feet high. At the center was a rough hewn pedestal that held the Emerald, glowing green with its own inner light. Unlike the oval Sapphire, this Gem was cut into a rectangle with the corners worn smooth.

Delan could only stare. Only the fact that he was relatively familiar with the Sapphire kept him on his feet. The stone was gorgeous. And the presence in his mind was…firm. Solid, like rock that had formed millions of years ago, but as fluid as the sand that Delan knew was above them.

"May I…may I touch you?" He finally managed. He felt it was best to be polite at the very least.

Setting down his sputtering torch, he slowly stepped towards the Emerald and reached out, brushing the tips of his fingers against the cool, smooth surface. A feeling like an electric shock went up his arm, causing Delan to jerk back on reflex, but it wasn't unpleasant. He reached out again, both with his hand and his mind this time.

The shock didn't come again. Instead, Delan almost thought he could sense the mind of the Emerald. It wasn't *thoughts* per se, only feelings, but it was enough for Delan to know that the Emerald had agreed to help.

Reaching out, he wrapped his hands firmly around the Emerald, cradling it in his hands as he lifted it from its rock pedestal.

There was no great earthquake, nor did the cavern come down around their ears. The Emerald simply sat in his palms, humming slightly. Slowly, he reached out with his mind and made to pull magic through the Emerald.

It was like riding an avalanche.

His head spun as more power flowed into him than he'd ever held before, even when drawing unconsciously from Zhafaera. He could feel every speck in every rock and piece of dirt in the cavern as if they lived and breathed as part of his own body. Delan realized that this much power could simply sweep him away, never to be heard from again. Quickly, he began to push back, fighting the oncoming rush of power until it slowed to a trickle and finally stopped.

"Thank you," Delan said somewhat breathlessly. "Thank you for sharing your power with me."

Turning, Delan resettled the Emerald into one hand, gripping it tightly and holding it aloft as his torch finally gave out and died. Using the light of the Emerald to see by, he walked back out the way he came, past the last fork where he had sat and talked to the Emerald, and straight down the tunnel towards the lake. Except…there were no other forks. Delan walked for ten minutes without seeing a single turning. And then, so suddenly that he almost fell right in, he was back at the edge of the water where he had entered this tunnel.

Delan looked at the Emerald. "I guess I have you to thank for my long walk earlier," he said wryly. "Infinite underground tunnels…excellent defense."

Taking a deep breath and holding on to the Emerald firmly, Delan jumped straight into the water and began to swim his way out. He was more than a little afraid to use his magic to guide his way out, just in case the Emerald took the opportunity to nearly overwhelm him again, but in the end, he had no choice. It was simply too dark to see. Using the barest thread of magic, he quickly found himself swimming out of the mouth of the tunnel and kicking upwards towards the cold night air.

***

Zhafaera lay silently in her bedroll, wide awake, listening to every new jungle sound that seeped in from outside. It was late, very late, and Delan had been gone for hours.

I should have gone with him, she thought for the thousandth time.

But ultimately everyone else had agreed; they couldn't risk both of them, and Zhafaera couldn't risk their child. They had no idea how the Sapphire would react to the Emerald, nor the Emerald to the Sapphire. It had made sense for Delan to go alone with Iris, but it didn't make it any easier for Zhafaera to bear.

Just as she was finally dozing off, Zhafaera jerked awake again. The Sapphire was…humming? It wasn't anything she'd felt before, but it wasn't unpleasant. Sitting up, she looked around the dark room, lit only from the moonlight filtering in through the front window panels.

As soon as she sat up, she felt more than she saw other shapes around her stir. It seemed the others hadn't been sleeping either.

"What is it?" Colin asked. "Is it them?"

"I think…" Zhafaera whispered, hardly daring to breathe.

Then she saw it – two shadows crossing the street towards them, heading for the glass doors that led into their building. Zhafaera rolled onto her knees and pushed herself up awkwardly around her growing belly. By the time she managed to get to her feet, Iris and Delan were coming through the front doors.

"Tristain, call a light," she whispered.

"Why can't you do it?" Tristain kept his voice low.

"Because I'm not sure what the Sapphire is feeling, and I don't want to blow us all up." The humming she felt was getting stronger the closer Delan got to them.

She met him halfway as a light appeared above their heads but didn't touch him.

"Did you get it?" she asked.

In answer, Delan held out his hand and opened his fist. There sat a large, perfect Emerald, glowing a deep green in the darkened room.

Zhafaera held her breath as the Sapphire sent a jolt of power through her body. Focusing, she brought it under control, but it felt...excited. From the look on Delan's face, she assumed that he felt the same thing from the Emerald.

Reaching out slowly, Zhafaera gently cupped her hand under Delan's hand that held the Emerald, being careful not to touch the Gem itself. Power surged, and she was suddenly aware of Delan's body as if they shared the same space. His thoughts passed through her mind with barely a hint that they were not her own. They both held completely still as power flowed through them, the energies of the two Gems swirling through the two of them.

Is this supposed to happen?

It's like a...a greeting.

Did you say we could blow up?

The Gems haven't been used together in a thousand years. Who knows what could happen?

Zhafaera wasn't sure how long they stood there, feeling the flow of energies, until finally the Gems began to pull back, their power separating and retreating as Zhafaera returned to her own mind.

"Okay, that was…weird," Tristain said slowly.

"What did you see?" Zhafaera asked him.

"It was like, you *blurred* a little at the edges." Tristain was staring hard at Delan. "But it seems to be gone now." He stepped closer to look at the Emerald. "So this is really it?"

"It really is," Delan said tiredly. Zhafaera looked closer at him.

"Gods, you're soaking wet," she exclaimed. "Come on, you need to change into some dry clothes." Zhafaera shooed him over to where their packs lay next to their bedrolls, only pausing to nod at Iris as she walked past them to take her spot next to Tarysa and Evey.

As soon as Delan had changed, they gathered back on their circle of bedrolls, and Zhafaera threw a blanket around Delan's shoulders. He immediately reached out and wrapped one arm around her shoulders, his other hand still holding the Emerald. The surge of power did not repeat itself, and Zhafaera let out a breath she didn't realize she had been holding.

"So how did you get it?" Tristain asked. "Did you have to complete the trials three?" He grinned.

Delan shook his head. "There was only one trial, and that was mostly just a *lot* of walking." Zhafaera listened with interest as he told them of how he had had to make his way through a maze of tunnels that never seemed to end, of sensing the Emerald but never seeming to get any closer.

"Until finally, I just sat down and started talking to myself," Delan continued. "I was truly just thinking out loud about how I needed some kind of help to find it, when I realized that the presence got stronger the more I talked." He paused and shrugged. "So I told it all about myself and why I needed its help, and suddenly it just…appeared behind me." Delan yawned and looked down at the Gem in his hand. "I was able to pick it up from there."

Zhafaera covered her own yawn. "I can't believe you actually found it," she said. "That's three Gems down!"

Two, Tarysa interjected, making Zhafaera jump. She'd been almost sure the large dragon was asleep.

"Two in our possession, yes, but Laros has promised the third."

A promise is just words. It counts for nothing until the Ruby is in your hand. Tarysa sighed. *Or more accurately, the hands of someone you trust.*

"Fair enough. I shall celebrate one victory at a time," Zhafaera relented. She turned to Delan. "Tomorrow I'll tell you everything I know about bonding a Gem. You don't have to do it," she added quickly. "You can wield the Emerald without bonding it, but…"

"If I don't bond it, Queen Oraesa will take it from us." Delan gave a humorless snort. "She'll probably try to take it even if I *do* bond it."

"We'll tell her it was necessary for you to bond it in order to take it," Zhafaera said thoughtfully. "Desperate times and all that. We can offer it back to Burja upon your *natural* death, and hopefully Oraesa will leave it at that. If not…well by then it will be much more difficult to kill you." Zhafaera slipped her arm around his waist and gave a small squeeze.

Delan yawned again. "I need to sleep if I'm going to bond a Gem tomorrow. It looked…complicated."

"It's not so bad if it likes you."

"How do I know if it likes me?" Delan asked.

"Trust me, you would know if it didn't," Zhafaera said, shaking her head.

***

Delan awoke slowly, feeling entirely too warm. With two dragons in the room and the desert heat beginning to seep through the glass, it was only to be expected. Disentangling himself from around Zhafaera, he planted a quick kiss on the back of her head and sat up.

By the time he returned from the bathroom, only Ban was awake. Delan immediately went to his pack and dug the Emerald out from the pocket he'd tucked it in before going to sleep last night. Sitting back next to a sleeping Zhafaera, he took the bread and cheese Ban handed him and ate one-handed, holding the Emerald in the other. He found that it was difficult to put it down.

"That's the biggest Emerald I've ever seen in my life," Ban said quietly, startling Delan.

Delan forced a grin. "For as much power as it draws, I should hope so."

They were silent for a time, eating as the sun rose

248

further.

"Are you sure about all this? Don't get me wrong," Ban said quickly. "I'm sure you know what you're doing. But I've known you a long time, and I just…want you to be careful." He hesitated. "You are all your father has left. He would be devastated if anything happened to you."

Delan shook his head. "I *don't* know what I'm doing. But I trust Zhafaera to be able to guide me through it. I've always managed to muddle through this magic stuff. And this is the best way to ensure it's not lost again."

"You *are* looking at it as if it might disappear," Ban joked.

"It did just that three hundred years ago, so excuse me if I'm a little cautious."

"Actually, it didn't disappear," Iris chimed in, making both men jump. "It was stolen by a mage, who brought it here."

"Well, there you have it," Ban said, standing and stretching as the others began to stir. "It's not going to disappear."

Zhafaera sat up slowly, and Delan passed her more bread and cheese. She sighed deeply. "If only we had some sausages," she said wistfully. "I could really eat a whole pile of sausages."

I don't know about sausages, but we can hunt here, Tarysa chimed in. She looked at Evey. *Will you stay here and watch, or come with me?*

Evey looked from her mother to Zhafaera. *I will stay,* she said slowly.

"I'll come with you," Colin said sleepily.

"Me too," Ban said cautiously. They had started to relax around the immortals, but it was a process.

"I'll stay here and see if I can't find a way to funnel the smoke out if we build a fire," Tristain said, looking slowly around the enormous room.

"No magic while Delan is bonding the Emerald," Zhafaera said firmly.

"Obviously," Tristain said. "I have no desire to be bonded to Delan, thank you. No offense," he added to Delan, who was staring at him in horror.

"None taken," Delan said faintly.

Zhafaera put a hand on Delan's shoulder. "It'll be fine." She at least *sounded* confident.

As soon as the humans finished eating, Tarysa stood, Ban and Colin following suit and grabbing their bows.

"Good luck!" Colin called as they headed towards the glass doors.

"What exactly are we going to be hunting?" Ban asked Tarysa quietly. Delan didn't hear her response.

The door closed behind them, and Delan found that everyone was looking at him. Tristain and Evey looked nervous. Iris showed nothing but cool interest. Zhafaera was smiling at him.

"Are you ready?" Zhafaera asked.

"As I'll ever be, I suppose," Delan said.

Zhafaera pulled herself up to her knees and kissed Delan quickly on the cheek. "I have every faith in you," she said as she sat back, cross-legged and facing Delan. "The idea is you want to merge the power of the Emerald with your own essence. The thing that makes you, you."

Delan frowned. He knew that at the center of where he stored magic, there was a core that he was never to draw on. That was his own essence, a white fire that he could sometimes see on the edge of his vision when he was drawing on magic. The thought of merging that with something else was…uncomfortable.

"How exactly do I merge them?" Delan asked slowly.

Zhafaera was silent for a moment, thinking. "Well, when I bonded the Sapphire, it was like…like I *pulled* it deep inside me until I could feel its power as my own, as a part of me instead of separate. But you also want to give some of yourself to the Emerald as well. Let some of your own essence bleed into it." She flinched. "It felt like I was fighting the ocean. But you can't let it overwhelm you. You have to blend your energies without losing yourself." She shrugged. "There's a balance."

Delan took a deep breath. "I suppose there's nothing to do but go for it," he said, trying to sound more confident than he felt.

"Half of it is simply believing that it will work," Zhafaera said earnestly. Delan caught Tristain out of the corner of his eye, scooting backwards slightly.

Delan nodded. "I can do it," he said firmly, looking down at the Emerald. He could still feel it humming softly. "Try not to kill me," he whispered to it.

Unlacing the top of his shirt, Delan lifted the Emerald to his chest. Focusing on where its cool surface touched his skin, Delan let his mind flow into the Gem. Immediately, he felt the rush of power like an avalanche bearing down on him. His mind was full of the feel of rocks grinding together, weighing him down as he struggled to bring it under control.

Gently, he thought, not knowing if it would help. Immediately the feeling of being crushed eased. As his mind recovered from the onslaught, he slipped deeper into the Emerald, underneath the waves of power, and suddenly found himself in a quiet pool of energy.

He relaxed as he felt the Emerald accept him, drawing him in. There were no words, but he could sense the Emerald searching his mind, rifling through his memories one by one, in reverse. He wasn't sure how long they sat like that, watching his life play out in flashes through his mind, but finally the images slowed and stopped. Delan took the moment of quiet to reach out to the Emerald, and slowly he began to *pull* its pure energy deep into his mind, dropping further and further through his well of magic until they reached the glaring white light that was his core self. As Delan dropped down into that white light, the Emerald's energy followed.

And suddenly his whole body was on fire. He felt his head tip back as he gasped for air, power raging through him in a way he had never felt before. His vision filled with deep green light as Delan felt another consciousness settle into his mind. He fought to find the balance Zhafaera had spoken of, receiving the energy and giving his own without being swept away. It was certainly easier said than done.

Finally, slowly, the swirling energies began to calm and the fire began to recede. Delan could still feel the Emerald in his mind, but it was a warm presence at the back. When he focused, he could see that his white core was now streaked with dark green veins, like cracks that had been filled.

Opening his eyes slowly, he looked down. The Emerald was embedded firmly in his chest, cutting right through the middle of his scars. He touched one finger to it gently and felt the presence in his mind flicker, ready to respond in an instant.

Looking up, he grinned at Zhafaera. She was somewhat pale, but she smiled back. "All good?" she asked.

Delan nodded and braced himself as Zhafaera threw herself forward, hugging him tightly. The Emerald surged at her touch, and Delan could feel its eagerness and…delight? He quickly soothed it back into quiet, but he could almost feel it observing them. It was an odd sensation.

"Seems to be fine," Delan told her, stroking her hair. As she pulled back, he stretched, finding that he was *very* stiff. "How long did that *take*?" he asked.

"Hours," Tristain said, moving closer. "You were still for a long time, but then when you started to glow…well." He shrugged.

Delan winced. "Yeah, I've seen it from the outside."

"Then you know," Tristain said. He clapped his hands. "Well, now that you're all done, I'm going to see what I can do about a fire."

Delan turned to Zhafaera as Tristain began muttering to himself. "Are you all right?" he asked. "Have you been drinking enough?"

She held up her canteen. "As much as I can stand. At least we're out of the sun." She eyed him critically. "How do *you* feel?"

"I feel fine. Energized even. Hungry," he added.

"Well, lucky for you, I think there's more bread and cheese."

***

By the time Colin and Ban returned with Tarysa an hour later, Delan was fighting not to eat the last of their stores, reminding himself that they still had to make it back *out* of the desert. Fortunately for him, hunting had been successful. Ban had an enormous dead python hanging around his neck and what looked like a chicken in one hand, while Colin had caught at least three rabbits. Most impressive was Tarysa, who was still in her panther form, dragging an actual black cow behind her. However, she swerved at the last second to drag her kill to the side of the building.

Evey jumped up and ran outside to her mother, the two dragons moving around the side of the building to devour the kill.

"There are cows in the jungle." Zhafaera asked, voicing Delan's exact thoughts.

"From the time of the last humans," Iris said simply. "There are many descendants of livestock here – cows, pigs, chickens. You just have to know where to look for them."

Delan was still starving. Standing quickly, he moved

254

around the fire Tristain had started and took the snake from Ban.

"How on earth are we going to cook this?" he asked the older man.

"Your guess is as good as mine," Ban said, shaking his head. "But Tarysa said it was good to eat, so I decided to give it a try after it dropped down on me from a tree."

"So you got it bonded, then?" Colin asked.

Delan pulled down the front of his shirt enough to show the top of the Emerald.

Colin shook his head. "This has been the weirdest couple of days of my life."

"It won't be for long if you keep hanging around with us," Delan said with a grin as they moved back towards the fire.

As they were preparing the kills to cook over the smokeless fire, Delan turned to face Iris. "Now that we'll be taking the Emerald with us when we leave tomorrow, will you come with us?" he asked.

Iris shook her head. "I do not guard the Emerald, I protect the city."

"But with the Emerald gone, won't you lose the protections around the city?" Tristain sounded concerned. "Once people know we found the Emerald, they will know something is here."

"The protections here are not tied to the Emerald," Iris said coolly. "The barrier was built by the Fae when the city was built. It will not fail anytime soon."

Delan looked at Zhafaera, but she looked just as confused as he was. "The Fae?" she asked.

Iris looked uncomfortable. "It's best not to speak of them. They don't like it."

"No wonder, I've never heard of them," Tristain put in. "And I've read at least one-third of the library of Zarga."

They are similar to humans, Tarysa said as she and Evey came back in through the front doors. *But don't ever tell them that.*

Iris was nodding as Tarysa came and took her place around the fire, just as Colin and Ban finished placing the other meats over it to cook.

"So, are they immortals?" Zhafaera asked.

"In the way that you would understand it, yes. In reality, they're more than that." She paused. "They *rule* the immortals."

Delan looked to Tarysa, expecting an objection from the dragon. She rested her head on her large paws and said nothing.

"But do they—" Zhafaera started, but Iris cut her off.

"We do not speak of them. I only told you so you would know that this city is secure no matter who comes and goes."

There was silence for a time. Suddenly, something clicked in Delan's brain. "You said this city is hidden from immortals and humans alike," he said quickly.

Iris nodded.

"But Tarysa came here."

"She came here because we are friends, and I allowed it. And she's been here before, so she knew where it was. No one can come through the barrier without my assistance. Or a Gem," she acknowledged with a tilt of her head.

"What are you thinking, Delan?" Tristain asked. At this point, everyone was looking at him.

"What if we…I mean, think about it…what if we evacuated Burja here to Thebes?" The idea was taking shape in Delan's mind. "We know how to get here now…we could get mages to extend the brick system out here…maybe even a direct line from the capital if we can be precise about the location on a map—"

"Thebes cannot be plotted on a map," Iris interrupted.

I could guide humans here from Zarga, Tarysa said. Every head in the room turned to her.

"Do you mean you'll help us?" Zhafaera asked.

My daughter says she will not leave you, and I will not leave her, Tarysa's mind voice was firm.

"It could work," Tristain said. "Queen Oraesa would have to agree to abandon Zarga and move her people here, but there's water and shelter here, and more protections than she could ever build over Zarga in a hundred years. She will see the wisdom. And if she doesn't," he shrugged. "You could always just bring the Arenthians here."

"What about you, Iris?" Zhafaera asked. "Would you allow all of Burja to come here? Is there even room for them and the Arenthian refugees?"

Iris met her gaze for several long moments before answering. "Yes, they would be welcome if that is what you wish. But—" she stopped.

"But, what?" Delan prodded.

"You would need to open the barrier," Iris said

slowly. "Not completely, just…tune it down some in one area; like a door. You shouldn't have any trouble with the Sapphire and Emerald working together."

"What's the catch?" Delan knew there had to be a catch.

"Opening the barrier may draw the attention of the Fae," Iris confessed.

"*That* is a different problem for a different day," Zhafaera said. "But my people would be safe here."

This is the safest place in the world, Tarysa said.

"Do you really think we could evacuate thousands of people across the desert before the dragons come south?" Tristain asked. "If they get caught halfway through, it will be even worse."

The others will be busy reorganizing Arenthia into slave camps for a while. We should have some time yet. Her bright eyes locked on Zhafaera. *Not much though.*

Delan felt sick but tried to clamp down on his emotions. "It's a longer term solution than hiding in Zarga, I think," he said quietly. He was thinking of the knives he took in the palace gardens. "But we'll have to get back to the capital and start the evacuation as soon as possible."

"We can help with that!" Evey chimed in. "I can carry Zhafaera, and Mother can carry the men. We can fly you back to Zarga and help explain everything."

"I'm not sure how helpful two dragons will be when trying to convince Queen Oraesa to come here," Tristain pointed out.

"Maybe we could just fly back to the brick?" Zhafaera suggested. "Then you could both transform again and travel back with us as cats. The mages hardly paid attention to you, Evey. I can make them forget an extra. Besides," she continued, "I spent the last two months working with Oraesa's mages making it nearly impossible to come at the city from the air. I wouldn't like to try flying in. They'd shoot us down."

Tarysa sneezed and flexed her claws, making Delan tense slightly. *I suppose that is something we could do. I doubt human magecraft could keep me out for long, but it's better to avoid a scene.*

Delan saw Zhafaera sit up straighter. "Actually, I killed a dragon on my own last year, before I bonded the Sapphire. It *can* be done."

Child, you are a White mage with the power of an ancient bloodline. I would not underestimate you; therefore, you would not take me by surprise.

Delan hoped Zhafaera had the good sense to let it go. He did not want to start an argument with a fully grown dragon. Thankfully, Zhafaera seemed to be thinking along the same lines. She inclined her head and moved on.

"How long do you think it will take you to get us back to the road?" she asked.

You spent nearly three days walking here? Zhafaera nodded. *Only a few hours.*

"Then we will set out at sunrise," Zhafaera said firmly. Delan glanced at the others, and from their faces he could tell they would have rather walked three days across the desert, but no one protested. They all knew time was critical.

Chapter 15

Flying on the back of a dragon was not at all what Zhafaera had imagined it to be, even with her already limited experience. Evey was big enough now to hold Zhafaera more comfortably, but the motion of her wings made Zhafaera feel as though she was going to be thrown off at any moment. Glancing to her left, she saw the four men crammed on Tarysa's back, each clinging tightly to the one in front.

Before they left, Zhafaera had decided to use the Sapphire to generate some clouds to help cover their approach to the brick. They planned to dismount and walk the last mile or so, but in the desert, there was no telling how far the mages would be able to see on a clear day. This gave them a lesser chance of being spotted flying in.

The other big decision they'd made before leaving was to wait to open the barrier until they came back with the first refugees. Ultimately, Delan and Zhafaera felt that leaving it closed for as long as possible would keep it safe and avoid potentially drawing the attention of the Fae until the last minute. Iris and Tarysa wouldn't discuss them further, and that was enough for the humans to decide they'd best avoid them if possible.

Zhafaera wasn't sure how long they'd been traveling when Tarysa began to slowly angle her flight towards the ground. Evey followed her mother, and Zhafaera suddenly realized that going down was infinitely worse than going up; she felt as though she might slide right over Evey's long neck. Thankfully they reached the ground quickly, and Zhafaera dismounted, watching the men as they hurriedly followed suit.

We are just over a mile from the road, Tarysa said as they gathered around her rapidly shrinking form. Zhafaera looked away, as the transformation tended to make her queasy these days, and when she looked back, there was a large orange cat with luxuriously long fur standing next to Delan. Evey had taken her smaller black cat form.

"We'd better get moving," Delan said, hiking his pack on his shoulders.

They set off at a quick pace, but it wasn't long before Zhafaera felt something was wrong. Surely they should have been able to see the brick by now?

Suddenly Delan, who was in the lead, threw out his arm, stopping everyone else in their tracks.

"What is it?" Zhafaera asked from behind him.

"It's the road," he said slowly.

"What do you mean, we can't be at the road yet; the brick isn't…isn't here…" Zhafaera trailed off as she stepped up and saw the smooth road clearly laid out before her.

"They left us!" Tristain exclaimed. "Those assholes left us in the middle of the desert!"

"We had at least two days left, not even counting today," Zhafaera said, trying to sound more calm than she felt.

"Okay, okay, the mages that left us here are terrible people, but we're not stranded," Delan said firmly. "We can fly to Zarga." He looked at the dragons. "Assuming the offer is still there?"

Evey and Tarysa had already readjusted into their dragon forms. *Of course,* Evey said as though this were the most obvious thing in the world.

Zhafaera met Tarysa's gaze, and the dragon inclined her head. "We'll have to be cautious approaching the city," Zhafaera said. "I'm sure you can defend yourself," she continued before Tarysa could object. "But I'd rather not take an arrow, and we want Oraesa to work *with* us. That's not going to happen if we fly in on dragons."

We can do what we did today, Evey said. *Fly as close as we can and then walk. How far do Zarga's protections extend?*

Zhafaera shrugged. "Actual *protections*? They are linked to the towers Oraesa built. But there is an early warning spell set to trigger if anything comes within five miles of the city."

"Well, five miles is better than five hundred, I suppose," Tristain sighed. "I still can't believe they left us."

"Let's all rest and eat," Delan said. "Then we can get back in the air."

"How long will it take us to reach Zarga?" Zhafaera asked Tarysa as she dropped her pack and sat gently.

A day. Tarysa glanced briefly at Evey. *Maybe more. Not including the time it will take to walk into the city.*

Zhafaera was impressed. The dragons were fast, even

going at Evey's pace.

Everyone ate quickly, anxious to keep moving even if they weren't looking forward to climbing back on the dragons. In no time, they were back in the air, soaring east over the desert. Zhafaera thought for a moment and decided to extend their cloud cover. It was difficult to drink water while flying, and that would be a problem if the sun were beating down on them all day. And they couldn't spend their time waiting for nightfall.

***

By the time they stopped to rest for the night, Delan's knees were sore from gripping tightly to the dragon's wide back. As he slid from his seat, he stumbled, catching himself with a hand on her leg, her thick hide rough against his palm. He jerked back quickly. She wasn't Evey, and he didn't want to offend her.

"Sorry," he murmured, clearing his throat and straightening his legs. Looking to his left, where Zhafaera was attempting to climb down, he flinched. She looked even worse than he felt.

Moving to help her, he put a hand to Zhafaera's elbow as she stood still, carefully holding on to Evey's shoulder. Even Evey looked worn down.

Zhafaera jumped under his hand. "Sorry," he said again. "I didn't mean to startle you."

She shook her head. "I needed it," she said. "I can hardly stay awake." The sun had disappeared behind them less than an hour before, but Delan felt the same. There

263

was nothing to make a fire with, but even if there had been, he wasn't sure he had it in him. Besides, having two dragons nearby would bring the ambient temperature of their camp up enough to keep them from freezing in the cold desert night.

The others stumbled over, and slowly everyone began setting up camp. The humans formed a circle, and the dragons settled themselves on the outside to keep in the heat. Eventually, they settled and began passing around the food.

Tristain was the first to break the silence. "Have you given any more thought to how you're going to manage Oraesa?" he asked tiredly.

No one answered at first, but Delan caught Zhafaera's wince. "She's going to throw a fit, isn't she?" Zhafaera finally answered.

"Absolutely," Tristain said.

"What do you think will be worse – the fact that Delan bonded the Emerald or us suggesting she abandon Zarga?"

"The Emerald, by a hair, in my humble opinion." Tristain sighed. "She can choose not to abandon the city, but she's not getting the Emerald any time soon." He eyed Delan cautiously. "You will need to be careful."

Delan shrugged uncomfortably. "It had to be done. Do you really think she'd try something?"

"I think she tried to kill you the *last* time," Zhafaera muttered angrily.

Tristain ignored her. "To get the Emerald? Yes," he said firmly.

"Great. Any tips for staying alive?"

"Avoid her. Don't go anywhere alone. And practice with the Emerald. But don't draw attention to it," Tristain added quickly.

"Of course," Delan said. "Easy." He touched his chest where the Emerald rested and felt a small flare of acknowledgement in his mind. He hadn't done much with it, but he was already getting used to the comforting presence.

Zhafaera reached out and took his hand. "Just stick to the story," she said quietly. "You had to bond it in order to take it from its hiding place."

"It's close enough to the truth. I had to talk it into coming to me."

"Exactly."

They fell silent for a time. Finally, Delan spoke. "You know Oraesa better than I do – do you think she will evacuate to Thebes?"

Zhafaera sighed, but it was Tristain who answered. "No," he said simply.

"She might," Zhafaera said slowly. "If she doesn't let her pride get in the way." She shook her head. "Who am I kidding? Even the Arenthians may not leave to follow me to a hidden city in the middle of the desert."

"They will if they want to survive the dragons," Delan said, squeezing her hand.

"How are we even going to *get* everyone there?" She cried. "The brick system isn't made to transport thousands of people at a time, and they'd still have to walk from where the road curves – we can't take them across untouched desert the way we've come."

"Actually, I've been thinking about that," Delan said slowly. Zhafaera's head snapped up, and he held up his hand. "I'm not entirely sure how it would work, but I think I could do it…"

"Do *what*?" Zhafaera was clearly impatient.

"Well, I think I could use the Emerald to compress a large area of sand into a makeshift brick. I got a decent look at how they work when we were traveling with the mages."

"But Delan, the bricks work *with* the road; you can't just push them over sand," Zhafaera said slowly.

"I'm not saying that the trips won't be difficult," Delan argued. "But we can't leave a trail for the dragons to follow, so we can't build a road, and the existing road isn't big enough." He paused and assessed what he wanted to say next. "I think that if we use the Sapphire *and* the Emerald together, we'll be able to cut through the sand like an ocean."

Zhafaera was silent. "That would take a *lot* of power," she said finally.

"Too much power?" Delan asked.

"I have no idea. The Gems haven't been used together in a thousand years."

Delan met her gaze. "But you've felt it. The power that they generate when brought together. And we've only felt flickers of that."

"I'm not good with earth magic…"

"Maybe not, but I am. I'm sure I can make it work. Besides," Delan pressed on firmly. "Do you have a better idea?"

Zhafaera bit her lip. "No," she admitted.

"We're going to have to learn to use the Gems together if we're going to defeat *dragons*," he continued. "Might well start now."

"He's not wrong," Tristain interjected.

"I know," Zhafaera sighed. "It just scares me."

***

It was before noon the next day when Zhafaera called a halt, sensing the spells that would alert the city to their presence coming up fast. Tarysa and Evey quickly descended to the ground, and the humans dismounted stiffly, no more graceful than the previous night. They had flown far enough away from the road to not be seen, but now they had to make up for that by cutting back over towards the road so they could enter the city through the southern gate.

They tried to keep a good pace as they walked, but the heat of the day was intense, and Zhafaera debated calling more clouds. If she provided cloud cover, it would likely alert Oraesa to her presence before they reached the city. On the other hand, heat stroke was a real concern, and they were starting to run low on water.

Ultimately, she decided that shade was more important than avoiding attention, and drew power from the Sapphire to pull moisture into the air and hold it steady. Soon after, she felt the slight waver of the alert spells surrounding the city. Evey and Tarysa, already in their respective cat forms, shivered slightly as they passed through. Zhafaera knew the spells would simply notify the mages that *someone* magical was coming towards the city on this side; they were not keyed specifically at dragons. She didn't know enough about dragons to be able to fine-tune the spells to identify only dragons, luckily for them. Even if she had known how, she wouldn't have, as Evey would have then been trapped in the city unless she wanted to out herself.

Once they passed the alert spells, it was less than half an hour before they saw dust rising in the distance, coming from the direction of the city.

"Coincidence or a welcome party?" Tristain asked suddenly.

Zhafaera shook her head. "It would be nice if we don't have to walk the rest of the way."

Within another few minutes, the brick came into view, and Zhafaera and the others stopped walking, waiting for them to either stop or pass them.

The brick stopped a few yards from their party, two mages immediately stepping to the railing. They looked vaguely familiar, but they were not the two that had left them in the desert. They seemed to pale when they saw her.

"Queen Zhafaera," one finally called out. "How wonderful to see you back from the desert. Can we offer you transport back to Zarga?" His shaking voice set Zhafaera on edge.

"You may, and we will accept gratefully," she said with as much queenly condescension as she could muster. She looked to the others, and Tristain immediately headed for the ladder on their side of the brick, intending to be the first one up just in case the mages had any surprises for them. Ban went next, followed by Delan, with Evey gripping the top of his pack. Tarysa jumped onto Zhafaera's pack as Zhafaera began to climb awkwardly, and Colin brought up the rear.

By the time Zhafaera reached the top of the ladder, she was somewhat out of breath. Between her growing belly and the heavier than she looked cat on her back, the climb was more difficult than she had expected. She was grateful when Delan reached out and helped her through the railing.

The mages bowed and lowered their eyes. "If it pleases Your Majesty," the one on the right said, "we will return immediately to the city."

"Of course," she said, moving to sit on the bench bolted to the floor off to the side. The others followed, settling themselves around her as the brick began to turn around to go up the other side of the road.

The trip back to Zarga was short. It took less than fifteen minutes for them to reach the brick's dock, where there was a carriage waiting for them. Zhafaera, Delan, and Tristain climbed into the carriage, while Ban and Colin held on to the outside in a traditional footman position that gave them a good view of the roads surrounding them. Zhafaera felt confident that they'd spot any trouble.

The ornate carriage passed through the enormous double gate, but Zhafaera felt no relief at being back in the city. In fact, no matter what Oraesa said, she intended to get as many people out as quickly as she could. As they moved through the city, Zhafaera thought it sounded quiet…subdued even. She supposed most of the defensive preparations were complete, and now people were just waiting for dragons to appear. It was terrifying.

By the time the carriage rolled to a stop in front of the place, Zhafaera was queasy; whether from nerves or just the motion, she wasn't sure. She hated the feeling – it reminded her too much of how sick she'd been early in her pregnancy. She took several deep breaths and stepped out of the carriage when the door was opened for her. The oppressive heat immediately weighed her down.

Oraesa was not there to greet them this time, but Delan's father, Lord Geon, was. He came hurrying down the steps to meet them just as Tarysa and Evey climbed out of the carriage. He slowed slightly, frowning at the extra "cat" before turning his attention back to the humans. He stopped short and bowed to them.

"My Queen. Consort," he said formally.

"Don't be silly, father," Delan scolded, moving forward and pulling him into a hug.

"Are you all right?" Zhafaera heard Geon whisper to Delan.

"Of course we are, just had a bit of trouble with our brick."

"I can't even begin to fathom how you made it back here, but it's lucky you did," Geon sounded worried. "Queen Oraesa said you were lost to the desert, and has already announced that no more Arenthian refugees will be accepted. She's even toying with the idea of making those already here leave."

"Where does she want them to go?" Tristain cut in indignantly.

"I don't think she cares, as long as they're not here."

Zhafaera took another deep breath, this time to control her temper. "Let's go and see her. I'm sure we can work this out, one way or another," she said firmly, striding towards the palace. The others scurried to catch up.

"So, did you find anything?" Geon asked quietly from behind Zhafaera.

"Delan has it." Zhafaera barely spoke above a whisper, but she knew Geon had heard her from the slight intake of breath.

Zhafaera slowed as they entered the cool shade of the palace. Hesitating briefly, she wondered if they ought to change clothes before seeking an audience, but she quickly decided she didn't care. Heading deeper into the palace, she made for the throne room.

No one stopped them as they moved through the quiet palace, and by the time they reached the throne room, Zhafaera was starting to feel unnerved at how quiet it was. The guards at the door to the throne room bowed and opened the doors, admitting their entire party without question.

There were gasps as Zhafaera entered the throne room filled with what looked like every noble in the city. The crowd parted to either side of the columned room and allowed the desert-weary group to move forward towards the front. Queen Oraesa sat on her throne, impassive, with Liara standing behind her, looking almost desperate.

Zhafaera stopped several yards from the throne and inclined her head. The others bowed.

"How nice to see you made it out of the desert. We feared you lost," Oraesa said coldly, not sounding pleased at all.

"Your mages left us there to die," Zhafaera said, keeping her tone level.

"They were running out of water and had no idea when you would be back. They had no choice but to leave." Oraesa held her head high and looked down her nose at Zhafaera. "Speaking of which, how did you make it back?"

"Crossing a desert is nothing for three mages with two Gems between them," Zhafaera said loudly enough for everyone to hear. There were gasps, then whispers. It sounded like the whole room was full of hissing.

Oraesa was on her feet in an instant. "So you found a Gem?" she asked quickly. "Which one? The Emerald legally belongs to Burja—" she cut off abruptly.

Zhafaera looked over her right shoulder to see Delan had untied the top of his shirt and was holding it open to show the Emerald nestled in his chest, reflecting the light coming in from the terrace beyond.

There was silence for several beats. "How *DARE* you?" Oraesa screeched.

"We dare because we were the only ones looking for it," Zhafaera replied loudly.

"It should have been brought to me *immediately*." Oraesa took a step forward and pointed at Delan. "The Emerald is property of Burja, and as such, you will hand it over!" She waved, and a mage stepped forward.

"It was necessary to bond the Emerald in order to take it from its hiding place," Delan chimed in.

Oraesa looked at him as if he were something disgusting on the bottom of her shoe. "You're not even a *mage*," she hissed.

"Actually, I'm a Black mage," Delan replied casually.

The silence in the room was deafening for several heartbeats. Then there was chaos.

"SEIZE HIM!" Oraesa screamed over the thunderous noise of the crowd. Immediately, the handful of guards that had been posted around the room began working their way through the crowd, hindered by the nobles that were trying to make a hasty exit. Some of the mages in the room stood still, looking absolutely horrified, while one or two had come to their senses and were making their way slowly towards Delan. The rest were among the crowd of people trying to fit out of the tall gilded doors. Liara still stood behind her mother, her hands covering her mouth.

Zhafaera drew power to her through the Sapphire and felt Delan do this same with the Emerald. Then the crowd started to scream.

Zhafaera whipped around in time to see Tarysa completing her change to dragon form, deep violet hide seeming to draw light from the room as her large body forced everyone to take multiple steps back from the center of the room. Her long silver talons dug into the marble floor as she whipped her tail dangerously close to several guards that had frozen in their tracks. Taking a single step forward, Tarysa lowered her head and made eye contact with Oraesa as she gave a low hiss.

Oraesa's eyes were wide with terror, and Zhafaera thought she might faint. Liara dropped to her knees and covered her face with her hands. Evey, also in her dragon form, stepped up to stand between Zhafaera and Delan. Everyone else was completely frozen; even the screaming had stopped now as everyone left in the room had pressed against the outer edges, with some as far as the terrace.

"Okay, everyone, it's all right. Let's just all calm down," Zhafaera said soothingly, her firm voice carrying across the silent room. "This is Tarysa and her daughter, Evamoria." She laid a hand on Evey and felt her hide ripple. "Evamoria has been with us for some time; her mother we found in the desert. They are here to help us."

Queen Oraesa tore her gaze away from the dragons and locked on Zhafaera. "*You,*" she hissed. "I should have *known* you would work with the dragons. You want to destroy us all and rule over what is left of the human race when the dragons have had their fill!" Her voice rose as she went until she was screaming again.

Evey screeched angrily and flared her wings, making Oraesa take a step back.

"Yes, I am working with dragons – *these* dragons," Zhafaera said calmly. "But I do not want to see the human race destroyed. Sometimes it seems like I'm the only one working *against* that. I'm telling you, Tarysa and Evey are *on our side.* They're going to help us hide."

"Hiding does not solve our problem." Oraesa was practically spitting.

"No, but it buys us time, and it's better than waiting

here to be crushed by dragons."

"You've already *brought* dragons here!"

The next dragons that come here will be much worse than me, Tarysa's mind-voice interrupted. She sounded calm, but there was an undertone of impatience. Oraesa's face went white, clearly able to hear her. Evey had been nervous to speak mind-to-mind with non-mages, but her mother clearly had no such trouble.

"And I suppose these *helpful* dragons have come up with a brilliant plan to protect us all?" Oraesa ignored Tarysa and addressed Zhafaera.

"Actually, no. This is Delan's plan." Zhafaera waved to indicate Delan. "Tarysa and Evey have just agreed to help where they can."

"I want nothing to do with any of *his* plans. He's just as bad as the dragons," Oraesa cried.

Zhafaera sighed, her patience waning. "Queen Oraesa, we found something besides the Emerald. A great city in the desert, named Thebes. Lost for thousands of years, it's been preserved and protected, and is impenetrable without both the permission of its guardian and quite a lot of power." She indicated herself and Delan. "*We* have the power to bring a large number of people into Thebes. There is food and fresh water, and the protections are stronger than anything I can make here. Our people would be *safe* there."

Oraesa was silent for a moment. "You want me to send *my people* blindly across the desert to some city that may or may not be open to them on *your word*?"

"Yes, that's correct," Zhafaera said coolly.

"Absolutely not," Oraesa said without hesitation. "My people will remain here in Zarga. Our defenses are strong, no matter what *you* think," she glanced briefly at Tarysa, then back to Zhafaera. "We will withstand any assault."

"Oraesa, please, be reasonable," Zhafaera began, but Oraesa cut her off.

"I have been more than reasonable for long enough. Get out of my city," she hissed. "Take your people with you." She raised her voice enough for the rest of the people in the room to hear. "Begin gathering the Arenthian refugees. Put them outside the southern gate. Any Arenthian left in the city by sunrise will be executed for treason." She locked eyes with Zhafaera. "That includes you."

White-hot rage flashed through Zhafaera but disappeared quickly as if she'd been dunked in ice. This had spiraled completely out of control, and Zhafaera couldn't see a way back on track.

"Queen, Queen Oraesa," someone called from the terrace. Zhafaera looked around to see Councilman Nyto edging forward. "Perhaps we could all discuss this further, in private?" he asked shakily, eyeing the dragons.

"I will not discuss it," Oraesa said firmly. "I want all of you out of my city immediately. Nyto, if you sympathize so much with your granddaughter, then by all means, go with her."

Nyto looked from Oraesa to Zhafaera and back. "I cannot speak for the rest of my party, but for now I will remain in Zarga."

Zhafaera's heart sank. Not even her own grandfather

took her side. Standing up straighter, she shook her head. "Fine," she snapped. "If you want to stay here and die, be my guest." Turning abruptly, she stalked towards the exit as Evey and Tarysa shrank back into their cat forms to allow room. The remaining people in the room drew back against the walls to let them pass. "Make the announcement," Zhafaera said to Lord Geon as they exited through the heavy doors. "Gather the Arenthians outside the southern gate with whatever they can carry. We leave before dawn."

***

Delan hurried to keep up with Zhafaera as she stormed back towards their rooms. Which he very much doubted were still theirs after what had just happened. But Zhafaera insisted they needed more than one change of clothes, and they needed to retrieve Sara and Amee anyway. As they reached the rooms, Ban waited outside while Colin continued down the hall to find his wife and daughter. Tristain went to his own room to repack, and Evey led her mother to the couch in front of the cold fireplace to wait.

Zhafaera moved towards her room, and Delan split off to his own. He'd barely taken three steps before Zhafaera called, "We go nowhere alone." Turning on the spot, Delan followed Zhafaera to her room.

She immediately dumped her pack on her bed, unclipping her bedroll to open the top and beginning to quickly empty her pack. At the bottom, she pulled out a worn set of pants and a light linen shirt, tossing them into a corner of the room as she moved towards the closet. Delan heard her sigh from the other side of the wall.

"What is it?" he asked quickly.

"I'm going to have to pack dresses," she said resignedly. She rubbed her belly. "These pants just aren't going to work for much longer."

"Well, I imagine these dresses will be cooler anyway," Delan said, trying to sound optimistic.

"I'm sure they will be; they're just annoying." Zhafaera sighed. "Can I give you some to hold?"

"Of course." Delan held out his arms, and Zhafaera laid a light blue gown across them.

All told, she was able to pack ten tightly rolled dresses, five shifts, two nightgowns, one pair of pants ("for later," she told Delan), and two shirts. Along with almost the entire assortment of underclothes provided. She even threw in an extra pair of soft leather boots and a pair of slippers.

Zhafaera saw Delan's look and waggled her fingers at him to indicate magic. "There's even room for food in the outer pockets," she said. "I expanded it, but it won't be any heavier." She lifted the pack with her bedroll reattached and hefted it over one shoulder.

"Maybe you can do that for mine too," Delan said, picking up his pack as they made for the door.

"I'll show you how to do it yourself," Zhafaera promised.

Once in Delan's room, Zhafaera expanded his pack as he pulled clothes from his closet. Once he had packed, with Zhafaera coaching him through the magic, they exited quickly with Tarysa and Evey close on their heels, picking up Ban from the front door. Colin and Sara came down the hallway as Tristain rose from his cross-legged position on the floor and stood next to Ranj.

Their destination was the kitchens, which they found after a number of wrong turns. The kitchen staff looked at them wide-eyed as they entered.

"We need to arrange food to be packed and taken to the southern gate by dawn," Zhafaera said imperiously.

The entire room bowed and curtsied as one. A woman stepped forward slowly. "If it please, Your Majesty—" her voice shook. "Lord Geon has already given the order for wagons to be filled with what can be bought at the market." She swallowed. "Queen Oraesa did not agree to provide any supplies from the Burjan granaries."

"That's all right, it's not surprising," Zhafaera said more gently. "How about if we pay you just for food for us…" She looked around at their party, counting. "Ten?"

The cook looked over them. "Yes, Your Majesty."

Zhafaera reached into her pack and retrieved a number of silver coins. She handed them to the woman, and immediately the kitchen exploded into a flurry of activity.

By the time they left, the sun was going down, and even Zhafaera's magicked packs were bulging, water skins hanging from every available clip. It wouldn't last them more than a week or two, but it was better than going out into the desert with nothing.

Outside of the palace, Zhafaera came to a stop. Already, Arenthian refugees were packing the square in front of the palace, to the side of the river, squeezing into the main boulevard that led to the southern gate.

"How many of them are there?" Zhafaera asked quietly.

"Before we left? My father told me nearly thirty thousand," Delan replied.

"That's almost a third of the population of Zarga." She sighed. "No wonder; she wants us gone. Do you think we'll be able to support that many people in Thebes?" she asked no one in particular.

"If Iris is correct about the food supply, yes," Ban responded. Zhafaera looked at him. "We had good hunting," he continued, "and I saw edible plants growing through the jungle as well. Even without Queen Oraesa's supplies, we should hold out for a while."

"Excellent," Zhafaera said. She looked like she was beginning to feel the strain of the day, but Delan resisted the urge to ask if she was all right. They didn't really have any options to do anything else.

As they began walking down the steps at the front of the palace, the crowd suddenly grew louder, changing directions so that they lined the bottom of the stairs as they shouted angrily.

Delan could see Zhafaera pale. She'd almost always had the support of her people, but clearly being kicked out into the desert was pushing them to their limits.

Zhafaera held up a hand for quiet, with no effect. She waited for a few moments, then touched her fingers to her throat. "ENOUGH," her voice boomed out across the square. Quiet fell slowly over the crowd, broken only by crying babies and the occasional murmur of discontent.

"Yes, it is true that Queen Oraesa has asked us to leave," she said, her voice still loud enough for everyone to hear. "And yes, I brought dragons with me to the city." The noise swelled again, but Zhafaera spoke over them. "But these dragons are *allies*. They are my *friends*, and they're here to help us. I swear to you, follow me, and no harm will come to you. We will lead you to the city of Thebes, a safe place hidden deep in the desert. There is water, food, and shelter there. But most of all, we will be protected." The crowd seemed to be listening again. They at least seemed calmer.

"I beg you," Zhafaera continued, "remain calm, and gather what things you can. Evacuate immediately through the southern gate, and meet us on the west side of the road. We will begin transporting everyone at dawn."

With that, Zhafaera began moving again, down the steps towards the crowd. Geon intercepted them just as the rest of the mass of people began to move again.

"Come, all of you," Geon said. "I've bought a covered wagon for our party, since you need a place of authority, and I didn't think flying on a dragon over a crowd of terrified people was a good idea."

"Thank you, Geon," Zhafaera sighed. "I do believe you're correct."

Chapter 16

It was three in the morning by the counting of the bells in Zarga when Zhafaera finally laid down, and only because she'd been overruled. They had structured the wagons of supplies in a loose ring about half a mile wide. With some quick math, they had determined that was as small as they could make it and still fit nearly thirty thousand people, and the wagons filled with all the food and supplies they could gather. According to Geon, he'd spent nearly half of all the coin he had left, but it was all he could buy on short notice. And the Burjans weren't exactly being helpful.

The people sat in groups, looking frightened. They gave a wide berth to the wagon that carried Zhafaera and her companions. They'd reached the front quickly, drawing the Arenthians out into the desert until they formed a teardrop shape, with their wagon at the front for Delan and Zhafaera to work from. When they first arrived at the front, they had stopped the flow of traffic for about an hour while Delan worked to build the sand into the durable rock that made a brick. She could only follow about half of what he did – Earth magic was just not her strong suit. But from what she could tell, it was a combination of compressing the sand while letting more sand fill the empty space left behind, until ultimately the camp was like its own brick that was about three feet higher than the ground around it with a wide ramp on the back for people to enter.

Once he was done, Arenthians flowed onto the brick and spread out as much as they could until the number of people entering the circle of wagons had finally slowed to a trickle. They were about ten hours into the evacuation and had about three hours left until dawn.

So Zhafaera tried to sleep. She and Sara each lay on a bench in the back of the wagon, while Delan lay on the floor with Amee's basket above his head. Even with the rest of the men circling the wagon, giving orders or trying to rest, Delan had insisted they needed protection inside the wagon. Evey and Tarysa remained in their cat forms, curled up together at Zhafaera's feet.

It wasn't easy to fall asleep, trying to find a comfortable position for her belly on the hard bench. But she must have dozed eventually, because the next thing she knew, Delan was shaking her shoulder gently as the gray light of pre-dawn bled into the wagon.

She sat up slowly, groaning softly at the aches throughout her body from sleeping on the hard surface. "Is it time?" she asked quietly. "Is everyone in place?"

"Everyone is here," Delan replied.

Zhafaera noticed Geon standing at the back opening of the wagon. He waved, and she stood, following Delan as he climbed down.

"I was able to find fourteen Arenthian mages," Geon said. "There may be more, but they're either staying hidden or lost in the crowd."

"How many are Earth mages?" Zhafaera asked.

Geon sighed. "Only three."

Zhafaera winced, but Delan put a hand on her shoulder. "It'll be fine," he said, sounding more confident than she felt. "We cut down the size to half a mile and shaped ourselves in such a way that we should be able to just slide right through the sand."

"Right, except neither of us has done anything like this before, and it's all theoretical."

"True, but we do have fourteen mages to back us up and help with the extras." Delan turned to his father. "Did you tell them what we wanted?"

"Of course," Geon answered. "Most of them are water mages; I believe they're preparing a circle right now to generate cloud cover like you did on the way here, Zhafaera. And the three Earth mages are walking the edges of the camp as we speak, building the railing you asked for. They should be done soon."

"Are there any more refugees left in the city?" Zhafaera asked worriedly.

Geon shook his head. "If there are, they've stopped coming to our camp. Anyone left now is going to stay."

"Hopefully that's nobody," Delan said. "I think Queen Oraesa meant what she said."

"So do I," Zhafaera sighed. She looked around. Their "brick" was full of people now, not crammed together uncomfortably, but definitely full. "Spread the word," she ordered. "We'll leave within the hour." Geon left them immediately.

Zhafaera sat on the back steps of the wagon and watched as a wave of activity went through the camp.

While it wasn't technically required, people seemed to be repacking their meager things and clutching them tightly. They had explained the basics of what they were going to do as they arranged people, but the refugees were understandably nervous.

When the sun began to peek over the eastern horizon, Zhafaera stood and dusted her thighs off. "It's time," she said quietly to Delan.

He nodded and took her hand, leading her to the front of the wagon and helping her up. The horses attached to the wagon stamped nervously, sensing the tension in the camp. Tristain left them, trotting off towards the back of the brick. He was going to try and minimize the dust blown up as they moved through the desert and hide their trail. Colin and Ban placed themselves on either side of the wagon, guarding the way up to Delan and Zhafaera.

Zhafaera felt Delan take a deep breath, then he turned to her and took both of her hands in his. Reaching into the Sapphire, she began drawing power. Immediately she felt the Emerald bleeding into her power, swirling and pulling the Sapphire's power through her. She tried to relax, not fighting it and letting Delan have control, but it was difficult. The Sapphire flared and Zhafaera gasped. More magic was flowing through her than she'd ever held before in her life, and she was just a conduit, riding the waves like a boat in a storm.

She looked at Delan, who was staring out into the desert. He looked calm, but a bead of sweat ran down his face as Zhafaera watched.

Suddenly, there was a grinding sound, and their brick

jerked forward, startling everyone. Delan let out a breath, and Zhafaera focused on the threads of magic she could see pouring from Delan. They flowed out from Delan to the point of the brick and out along the edges until they disappeared under the bow.

Whatever Delan was doing was working because their enormous brick was picking up speed. Zhafaera could feel Tristain and the young Air mage that had crowned Zhafaera working at the back of the brick, using the dust in the air to cover their tracks. Above them, clouds were forming as the Water mages did their work. Zhafaera was almost afraid to think it, but everything was working just as they'd hoped.

The problem was the amount of power it took to move the brick. The faster they went, the more power it took. The Gems could pull an almost infinite amount of power, and they greatly increased the amount of magic a human could hold. But humans still had a limit, and Zhafaera could feel that if they didn't slow down, they would quickly surpass theirs.

"Delan," she began.

"I know, I feel it too," he said, squeezing her hands. The brick immediately began to slow, and the pressure in Zhafaera's head eased.

After some trial and error, Delan eventually found a speed they both could tolerate, the brick gliding smoothly through the sand. The sun was directly overhead before Zhafaera spoke again.

"Should we stop for a midday rest or keep going?" she asked.

Delan seemed to shake himself. "It was harder to start than it is to keep moving," he said slowly. "I think we should keep going."

"Do you think you could eat something?"

"I think so," Delan said.

There was some scurrying behind them in the wagon, and Zhafaera jumped.

"Here," Sara said, appearing from inside and passing her some bread and two apples.

"Thank you," Zhafaera said, pulling one of her hands free to take the items one at a time and hand them out to the others. The brick slowed down slightly while Delan ate. When they finished, Sara handed them water, and they drank greedily.

The brick sped up again as soon as Delan finished, but Zhafaera had another problem.

"Delan, if I let go of your hand, will you be able to keep drawing through me now?" she asked.

"Why? What's wrong?" he said urgently, and the brick jerked.

"Nothing, I just hope the latrines have been dug. I *am* pregnant after all."

"Right," Delan said. "I think I have the hang of it if you let go."

Zhafaera unwrapped her hand from his and stretched. It was hot, but the breeze from their motion kept it from being stifling. Zhafaera climbed down and stretched again, trying to ignore her escort as Ban fell in behind her.

Zhafaera made her way through the crowd, sticking to the edges and empty spaces between groups to try and avoid notice. The people who did see her bowed quickly and looked away. Before long, her nose led her to a long area where blankets had been hung for privacy. *Better than nothing,* she thought sourly, *but a far cry from the bathrooms of Thebes.*

Finishing quickly, she returned to the wagon.

"How long do you think it will take us to get to Thebes?" Zhafaera asked as she climbed back up to her seat.

Delan was quiet for some time. "We're moving a lot slower than the dragons flew," he finally said. "It's about five hundred miles, and we're moving almost as fast as the regular bricks move, I think. So…three days? Four maybe?"

Zhafaera wasn't sure if she was disappointed or thrilled. It wasn't as fast as they might have wished, but it could certainly be worse. But three days of this power drain…she was exhausted already.

By the time the sun sank low in front of them, Zhafaera could hardly sit up straight, and the strain of keeping the flow of the Sapphire steady was starting to wear on her. Finally, she couldn't take it anymore and opened her mouth to tell Delan so.

And the brick began to slow. The flow of power through her separated so that she could feel the Emerald's tendrils leaving, and the Sapphire fell quiet.

"I have to stop," Delan said, shaking his head. "I need to rest."

The brick came to a grinding stop, and the dust settled as Delan slumped beside her.

Zhafaera stood, massaging her lower back. Looking over her shoulder, she could just see the front of the crowd behind them. "I want to talk to them," she said quietly.

Deln followed her gaze. "You want to make a speech? Now?"

"No, I just want to go sit with a few groups for a little while. Tell them a little bit about Thebes. Prepare them for Iris. I want as little chaos as possible when we get there."

Delan shrugged and climbed down, making room for Zhafaera to follow. Zhafaera started walking towards the nearest group. Delan and Geon, who had been in the back for the last hour, fell in behind her. Ban, and Colin she told to stay with their wagon. She didn't need additional protection from her own people.

As she approached the group, someone spotted her and stood quickly. The other eight or so followed suit, bowing or curtsying, while pulling their children slightly back. Zhafaera's heart clenched. They were afraid of her, or quite possibly Delan, and they needed to change that.

"May we sit with you for a while?" she asked gently as they reached the loose circle.

"Of course, Your Majesty," several adults answered at once. There was some shuffling, and an open space was indicated on a colorful, if threadbare, blanket. The three newcomers sat carefully.

"Has the trip been smooth for you today?" Delan asked into the quiet. "I did my best, but…" He trailed off, unsure what to say.

"Yes, Consort," said a woman nearby. She had dark hair and a child attached to either side. "Quite smooth. The children were even able to play." She smiled tentatively.

Zhafaera smiled back, hoping to encourage them. "That's lovely," she said. "There will be plenty of places for the children to play when we reach Thebes. Although," she added quickly, "they should probably stay out of the jungle for now."

There was quiet for a moment. "Is Thebes mostly jungle?" the woman asked.

Zhafaera shrugged. "There are quite a lot of trees in the streets, but the real jungle takes over closer to the lake. But there are plenty of safe paths." At least, that's what Iris had told her. "What's your name?" she asked.

"Danya, Your Majesty," the woman answered, ducking her head. "Will there…will there really be a place for all of us where we're going?"

"Yes, definitely," Zhafaera answered firmly. "Thebes is actually a rather…advanced city. There's running water indoors and buildings taller than I'd ever imagined. That's where most of us will live." She paused. "Iris, the guardian of the city, has assured me that there is room for everyone in the sky towers. The smaller ones are divided into individual apartments, each big enough for a family to live in with its own fireplace and water supply."

"The city has a guardian?" someone asked from across the circle.

Zhafaera nodded. "Her name is Iris. She's a sphinx," she added. "Meaning she has the body of a lion, the wings of a falcon, and the head of a human. It can be a little alarming at first, but she's perfectly nice, and she has agreed to help us as we settle into the city."

The faces around the circle looked surprised and nervous, but Zhafaera pushed on. "She has guarded the city of Thebes for the last ten thousand years," she told them. "And she helps maintain the barrier that protects the city from both mortals and immortals. It hides the city, so it's nearly impossible to find, even for dragons. We will be safe there," she finished.

"How long will it take to get there?" Danya asked.

"Another two complete days, and part of a third if we can keep up our current pace," Delan chimed in.

"So fast," Danya murmured.

"We want to be in place as soon as possible," Zhafaera said.

"Probably smart, Your Majesty," a man who hadn't spoken before said. "We were some of the last out of Arenthia a few weeks ago, and the dragons have already moved south. Any longer, and we would have been in a slave camp," he continued.

Zhafaera shuddered. She had been trying not to think of the fact that only thirty thousand Arenthians had made it to them. The capital city alone had held eighty thousand just a year ago. *Most of them are dead now,* Zhafaera thought.

Shaking herself, she said out loud, "I'm glad you were able to get out."

They chatted for a bit longer as the sun set and food was distributed from the wagons and individual packs. Zhafaera, Delan, and Geon accepted their own with thanks. Eventually, they moved on to another group and a third, repeating themselves until Zhafaera could barely keep her eyes open.

Heading back to their wagon, Zhafaera turned to Geon. "Did you know about the camps?"

"I had heard, yes." He sighed. "I didn't want to worry you when there's nothing you can do."

"Those are my people that are dying. My responsibility. I *need* to know."

"I'm sorry, Zhafaera."

"Is there anything else I should know?" she asked.

Geon hesitated. "Crystal Point was destroyed. It won't be long before they turn to Burja. A matter of weeks, maybe."

The pit in the bottom of Zhafaera's stomach that had been there since her mother died yawned open wide. "We just have to hope they can't find us," she whispered.

"What about Zarga?" Delan asked.

Zhafaera bit her lip. "I don't know."

***

The next two days passed much the same as their first in the desert, except by the end of the third day, Zhafaera and Delan were more than exhausted. Delan's head pounded, and he could barely see through the glare of the fading sun. Zhafaera didn't look much better – she didn't even insist on joining groups of people tonight. Even if she had, he doubted Aroha would have let her. The healer had been hovering all day, insisting on riding in their wagon now, and keeping both Zhafaera and Delan under her watchful eye. She didn't comment on how much they were straining themselves, but her frowns said enough.

Delan felt they had successfully turned the Arenthians back to Zhafaera's side over the last few days. Explaining the evacuation and what lay ahead for them in Thebes seemed to have calmed everyone. Zhafaera told him that even just being *seen* was enough to help, and she'd put forth a lot of effort to convince them everything would be fine.

She'd also directed Geon to take a census of everyone traveling with them. It had taken the better part of the trip and the help of every steward they could find, but they had a list of names grouped by family. When they reached the city, Iris would guide them around the lake to the north side of the city, where most of the housing was. Delan hadn't seen it, but Iris promised there were thousands of apartments available and an entire neighborhood of larger homes for Zhafaera and the handful of Arenthian nobles that had made it out.

Once the census had been completed earlier that day, Zhafaera had quietly had the Arenthian nobles brought to her. There were ten, including Esla, who avoided Delan's gaze, and her brother Elden, who just glared. Zhafaera asked for their help when they reached the city, explaining Iris' position as guardian and directing them to answer to her if they couldn't reach Zhafaera.

She also assigned them jobs, probably the first they'd ever had, but they needed help organizing a city's worth of refugees. Lady Seria was to ensure the water supply would continue to support the city; Esla and Elden were asked to oversee the distribution of food from the wagons to people's new homes, and Sir Coran was given the job of organizing hunting parties into the jungle every day to begin the long job of corralling the wild domestic animals. Lady Greina was to work with Iris to cultivate fruits and vegetables found in the jungle, while others were set to arrange the trimming of the jungle around the buildings they would be using the most.

By the time she was done, the nobles looked determined, and Zhafaera sent them to bring their things closer to the main wagon. She wanted them close when they arrived so they could help direct traffic, but she also needed them together so she could make sure they made it to their new homes.

But now Delan had pushed through until nightfall, sacrificing speed for a little extra distance to try and put them in a better position for morning.

"Can you feel the barrier yet?" Zhafaera asked as they came to a stop.

Delan shrugged. "I can't spare the power right now to reach out and check." He sighed. "I'm just too tired."

Zhafaera gave a tired laugh. "We'd better pay more attention in the morning, or we'll smack right into it," she said. "And that would *not* be good."

"We are roughly twenty-five miles from Thebes," Tarysa chimed in from her perch in the back of the wagon, making them both jump. *You need to angle slightly to the right when we start again.*

"Thank you," Delan said. "I appreciate your guidance."

I said I would lead you here, and I keep my promises.

For once, Zhafaera and Delan went straight from the front seat into the back of the wagon. They were too tired to even call a light, so Sara produced a candle from somewhere as they all ate quickly. Aroha spent the meal examining Delan and Zhafaera, taking their pulses, feeling their foreheads, and tsking at what she found.

"You're pushing too hard," she said angrily. "You cannot keep this up." She looked pointedly at Delan. "*Either* of you."

"We're almost there," Delan said tiredly as he shoveled his last bite into his mouth. He chewed mechanically, resting his forehead in his hands.

Aroha sniffed. "When we arrive, I want to see you both lie down *immediately*." She eyed them. "Including right now."

Delan and Zhafaera complied and stretched out in the back of the wagon, completely drained, and fell asleep quickly.

The next morning came with a sluggish start. Delan was still exhausted, but he knew they needed to push through to the city. Zhafaera didn't look much better, and the dark circles under her eyes worried him. He knew he was pushing too hard, but they were almost there. After today, they could rest and recuperate before they figured out their next move.

As soon as he linked with Zhafaera, drawing power through her and the Sapphire, he knew it was not going to be an easy end to the trip. The Sapphire's power kept slipping from his grasp, leaving him to compensate with the Emerald. He buckled down and focused on keeping the power flow steady as he pushed the brick forward through the desert.

He wasn't sure how much time had passed, but he could feel the sweat pouring off of him, and there was a deep rushing in his ears. It wasn't until he felt someone shaking him that he realized something was wrong. And then he felt it – a loud buzzing wove through his mind, amplified by the power of the Gems. Jerking his head up, he could almost see it – the barrier was less than a quarter mile ahead.

He immediately relaxed his grip and felt the Sapphire's power disappear, causing the brick to jerk violently as it slowed. He grabbed on to Zhafaera and wrapped his arm around the back of their seat to keep them from flying off the wagon. There were shouts and a loud crash from behind them as everyone was thrown forward; he suspected they'd lost a wagon off the side of the brick. He held onto the Emerald in his mind, barely keeping himself from being swept away, holding just enough power to keep the brick slowing without coming to a dead stop and throwing them all off.

When the brick did come to a stop, they were about ten yards from the barrier, and Delan was spent. He slumped forward and put his head in his hands as Zhafaera put a comforting hand on his back.

"That was close," she said a little breathlessly.

"I had it totally under control," Delan replied once he could speak again.

Zhafaera patted his back. "Of course you did beautifully. Are you ready to help me open the barrier now?"

Delan groaned.

"Don't worry, I can take the lead on this one." He could feel her critical gaze on him. "Assuming you can hold any power at all right now."

Delan nodded into his hands. "Just a minute."

"You need more than a minute, I think. Let's have something to eat."

***

Zhafaera didn't let Delan even think of pulling power from the Emerald until noon. They'd eaten and rested for a couple of hours, trying to generate a little more of their own energy.

Finally, they decided to climb down from the wagon and move closer to the barrier, but Delan was too exhausted to build the front ramp down, and he needed to save his strength for the barrier. Zhafaera called for the three Earth mages and explained what they wanted. In no time, there was a smooth, firm ramp of sandstone leading from the front of their brick to the ground in front of the barrier.

"It's almost like things work better if we don't try to do it all ourselves," Zhafaera said to Delan, grinning.

Delan shrugged. "I probably could have done it."

"Yes, and then you'd burn out when we tried to open the barrier, and who knows what that would do?"

"Fair enough," Delan sighed. "I'm ready to sleep for a week."

297

Moving down the ramp, they stopped in front of the barrier, listening to the faint hum it generated.

"Iris said we only need to lower a portion of it, enough for everyone to get through," Zhafaera said thoughtfully. "But she didn't say exactly *how* to lower it."

"Do we just…bore through it?" Delan suggested hesitantly.

Zhafaera was silent for some time. "I don't think it would be like that," she said finally. "Besides, I think Iris is linked to the barrier somehow, and I wouldn't want to hurt her."

"No, of course not," Delan said.

"How did Iris put it? We need to 'tune it down?'"

"Like, an instrument?" Delan suggested.

A lightbulb went off in Zhafaera's mind. She'd learned to play the harp, like most noblewomen did. She was mediocre at best. But she *did* know how to tune an instrument. "I have an idea," she said out loud.

She felt Delan draw power through the Emerald just as she drew on the Sapphire. The whole trip, she'd been stretched to her limit as the Sapphire struggled to replenish its power from the miniscule water sources in the desert. Now she could feel the strength of the aquifer beneath their feet, running deep under the barrier.

Letting the Sapphire expand in her mind, she reached out for the Emerald gently but firmly. Immediately, tendrils of power tasting of dirt, sand, and stone wrapped around her, interlocking with the Sapphire's power like pieces of a puzzle. Pure energy rushed through her, heightening every sense until she was sure she could hear every one of the thirty thousand refugees breathing. *Is this what Delan felt the whole way here?* She thought, rather giddily.

Refocusing on the task at hand, Zhafaera spread the combined magics of the Gems over the barrier, letting it rush out to cover a portion a little wider than the ramp. She let the energy of the barrier bleed into her covering, absorbing the vibrations until it felt like her very bones were humming along with the barrier. Then she let out a breath, relaxing until her own hum fell lower, taking the barrier with it. Immediately there was a wrenching sensation, like a wrong note being held. But slowly, so slowly she wasn't sure it was happening, the covered section of the barrier began to harmonize with the rest of the barrier. She kept going, listening to the chords as they came in and out of focus, passing a third and a fifth, until finally she hit a perfect octave.

Pausing, she held everything still and exact, listening. Then she opened eyes that had closed at some point and realized she could see Iris just ahead of them, on the other side of the barrier.

"Is this enough?" She called to Iris.

Iris inclined her head. "It is. You did very well." She stepped back. "I welcome you and your people to Thebes."

"Do I need to keep holding this open?" Zhafaera asked.

"No," Iris said. "It will stay like this now until I restore it."

Zhafaera relaxed and released her hold on the Gems, feeling the Emerald detach almost reluctantly. Delan sighed and slumped slightly next to her. She took his hand, hoping to offer support. "Wait a minute," she said slowly. "If you can restore the barrier, then couldn't you have just…lowered it for us?"

Iris was shaking her head before Zhafaera even finished. "Not for long enough for you to get everyone through."

"Oh well, at least we're through," Delan said.

"Are you ready to proceed? I have cleared the most direct path to the residential district. It is not far, just around this side of the lake."

"Yes, I want to get as many people into homes by nightfall as possible." *Including myself*, Zhafaera thought tiredly.

"How many did you bring?"

"Twenty-eight thousand, three hundred and twelve. Plus the two dragons," Zhafaera added. "I'd like to start with one family per apartment and then see if we need anyone to double up or if we have extra space or—"

"There will be room for everyone," Iris said calmly. "I have fifty sky towers available, each with around a hundred apartments fully furnished and preserved, ranging from one bedroom to three bedrooms. There are also smaller apartment buildings throughout the city. Altogether, the city can easily hold over a hundred and fifty thousand people if we make good use of the spaces." She paused. "And of course, that's not counting the larger homes along the northern edge of the barrier."

"Perfect." Zhafaera straightened her shoulders. "Now it's just that we have groups of all different sizes, all mingled together. I'm not sure how we're going to get them all in appropriate housing."

Light flared as Iris spread her wings to their full width, and streaks of glittering color detached from her to streak towards the city.

"The doors of each apartment will be marked – purple for three bedrooms, blue for two, and green for one," Iris said simply. "I was planning to do that before you arrived, but you returned so quickly I was…unprepared. I apologize."

"Iris, that's *perfect*," Delan said incredulously. "Thank you."

"We must start disembarking as soon as possible." Zhafaera said. "I want any family, or group that intends to live together, of eight or more, to go first and claim the purple apartments. If we run out of those, they may take a blue apartment. Groups of four to seven will go next to select blue apartments. And those with three or fewer people will take the green. Mages and nobles will settle in the houses to the north."

"This is going to be a massive undertaking," Delan mumbled.

"This was *your* idea," Zhafaera reminded him.

"I agree with Zhafaera," Iris said slowly. "Organize them by group size and let me guide the large, medium, and small separately."

"It's going to be dark in the next eight hours," Delan started. "How many do you think we can get in by then?"

"The dark need not stop us," Iris answered. "I was able to repair the solar panels for that sector, and the electricity is working. We will have light."

Zhafaera looked at Delan. "I'm sorry, 'electricity? Like lightning?'" She asked.

"Of course, you don't have it in your cities anymore." Iris shook her head. "Electricity is an energy that transfers from a power source, like the sun, to objects that can use it, like electric lights, or a cooktop. Even heating." She eyed Delan and Zhafaera critically. "I suppose we shall have to have lessons on using those things. Your fire mages may examine the solar panels if they wish. But," she added quickly, "not in the residential sector."

"Fair enough," Zhafaera said. "The point being that we can work into the night if we need to. Maybe even have everyone in a home by tomorrow?"

"Tomorrow afternoon," Iris corrected.

"Then let's get started." Zhafaera turned around and started back up the ramp towards their wagon, readying her orders.

***

Delan sat in the back of the wagon with Zhafaera, his father, Tristain, Ranj, Sara, and Amee, and the two dragons. Colin and Ban were driving the wagon. They'd left the brick with their wagon leading the way, following Iris. The two dozen mages and nobles came next, standing a little to the side since they would be following Zhafaera to the northern homes. The groups with eight or more people followed behind, and a few of the supply wagons brought up the rear.

Delan hardly noticed their surroundings as they passed through areas that were more jungle than street. He was too busy counting and rechecking their calculations regarding housing and dreading the chaos that was about to happen. They had a rough plan, sure, but how would they know when the buildings were full? What would happen if there weren't enough of the larger apartments? How would they communicate efficiently with each building? They had to all work cohesively if they were going to survive here.

"We should have each building select a leader. Even a council if they wish," Delan said, thinking out loud. Everyone looked at him strangely. "The council could determine each building's needs and deal with any minor problems, and their leader can bring anything more serious to our attention. We can also assign duties that way."

"That's…" Zhafaera started. "That's brilliant!"

"We'll need to make an announcement—" the wagon jerked to an abrupt halt, knocking everyone forward. Delan poked his head out of the front of the wagon, between Colin and Ban. Iris had stopped at the end of the road. Ahead, another street ran left and right, and Delan could see rows of sky towers. Not the giant ones like in the center of the city, but the tallest here were several stories tall.

Delan and Zhafaera climbed down to speak with Iris. "Which way?" Zhafaera asked.

"You and the other mages and nobles will go right," Iris said. "The others will go left and split up over several streets."

"Do you need us to stay and help direct them?" Delan suggested.

"No need," Iris said simply. Suddenly there was a breeze, and Iris *blurred* for just a second. When Delan refocused, there were two sphinxes. "I can be in many places at once if needed." A third sphynx split off. "This one will take you north," she said. "It is but half a mile to where you will be staying."

Zhafaera waved the band of nobles and mages closer. "We will be going right," she called to them as they scurried forward. "Follow this sphinx"—she indicated the Iris on the right—"and stay together until we get there. Then Iris will show you which homes you may choose from. I want mages grouped together by element. Except you, Alise." She pointed to the young Air mage that had been working with Tristain. "Alise, Prince Tristain has agreed that you will stay with him since there are no other Air mages at this time." The young girl looked relieved and nodded tiredly. In truth, Tristain had demanded she stay with him. Apparently, she'd mostly been left to fend for herself, and he took issue with that. Delan glanced at Tristain in the back of the wagon and saw him nod, his head resting in his hands. He looked as exhausted as Delan felt after covering their trail the whole way.

With that, Zhafaera climbed back into the wagon, Delan following close behind. They set off north, following the sphinx at a pace the others walking could maintain. Looking out of the back of the wagon, Delan could see Iris speaking to the refugees, then her other copy split off, leading the first group away towards the sky towers.

In no time at all, they reached the neighborhood, pulling up at a heavy, silvery-looking gate that stood open. Beyond the fence, Delan could tell that Iris had a very loose definition of house. Delan would call these mansions. Maybe even small castles.

Iris led the way through the gate as Delan tried to take in the beauty of the homes around him. Mostly made of stone, these were nothing like the glass and steel monstrosities that were the sky towers. These looked older, yet somehow sturdier, possibly because the jungle had not overtaken this area. Each mansion was two or three stories, with what could have been a hundred tall windows and gently sloping roofs. And the farther they got into the neighborhood, the larger and more opulent the mansions got.

"That is where I live," this version of Iris said, dropping back next to the wagon and indicating a building just ahead. It was huge, with an enormous wooden door tall enough to allow a sphinx through comfortably. Light gilting was still visible in spots, and the front was lined with sandstone, giving the building an overall golden glow. "And this," Iris continued, turning to face the house across the street, "is where I thought you could live."

Delan took in the sight of their new home with no little bit of awe. The outside was stunning – three stories, gold-like Iris' home, but carved with vines and flowers and symbols? "What are those?" He called to Iris.

"More protective spells," Iris says. "Built directly into the house, unable to be altered or erased without destroying the home, which is *quite* difficult to do. Most of the homes here have similar carvings, but they are more subtle. This one is the strongest."

"It must be like a fortress with all those carvings," Zhafaera murmured. She clapped her hands, making everyone jump. "Let's get to it then. Ban, Colin, and Sara, you're with us here," she said. "Tristain and Ranj, you can pick first—"

"We pick the one we just passed, right next to yours," Tristain broke in, waving his hand tiredly in the vague direction of his new home.

"Done. Geon, you can join us, or you can have your own—"

"I'll stay with you if it's all the same," his father said firmly.

"Of course. I prefer it that way, actually," Zhafaera said with a smile. She looked around. "Tarysa, will you and Evey stay with us, or do you have somewhere else you prefer to stay?"

Tarysa looked at Evey, and something silent passed between them. *We will stay with you for now*, Tarysa responded.

"Excellent," Zhafaera said, standing and climbing down. She went to the group of mages and nobles, all looking an odd mixture of nervous and excited. This neighborhood was certainly more to their tastes than refugee camps. She pointed out Iris' home and the two others that had been claimed. "You may make your selections now," Zhafaera began. "But stay close – I want everyone nearby in case of emergency." She didn't have to say what the emergency might be.

As the others moved off, Delan followed Zhafaera to their new home. When they reached the front door, he looked around for Iris, only to see her still in the road.

"Are you coming with us?" Delan called to her.

She smiled and vanished.

"I guess that answers that," he murmured.

Zhafaera opened the door, and they all filed in…and stopped. However beautiful the mansion was on the outside, it was nothing compared to the inside. The floors in the entrance were smooth marble with veins of green and gold flowing through. An enormous sweeping staircase rose on either side of the large open foyer, and the second floor was visible over a balcony at the top. Straight ahead, through a huge vaulted opening, Delan could see what appeared to be a kitchen, but unlike any kitchen he'd known before, with steel objects stationed between the stone countertops and white cabinets. There were rooms to the left and right, just before the staircases, with the doors open. The one on the left looked to be filled with books – probably a library – while the one on the right could only be the parlor, with a large fireplace surrounded by formal-looking couches and chairs.

"Well, this is nice," Zhafaera finally broke the silence.

"We'll find the servants' quarters." Sara sounded slightly breathless.

"You'll do no such thing," Zhafaera said firmly. "You're welcome to choose a bedroom upstairs like us."

"Perhaps the third floor will be a little less…flashy," Ban put in.

In the end, it took them nearly an hour to fully explore the mansion. There were four suites on the second floor and eight smaller guest rooms on the third floor. Delan and Zhafaera chose a suite, as did Geon. Colin and Sara, with the baby, took a room on the third floor with Ban. Evey and Tarysa left them for the parlor as they began to settle into their rooms.

As soon as Delan closed their bedroom door, Zhafaera sat on the end of their bed and put her head in her hands.

"Are you all right?" Delan asked quietly.

"Just tired," she said quietly. "And tired of packing and unpacking." She gave a humorless laugh. "Still, I suppose my clothes aren't going to unpack themselves, and we need to put what food we have left in the kitchen and figure out what we're going to eat."

Delan stretched and began emptying his pack. "If I sit down, I won't get back up until at least tomorrow," he said with a sigh.

"You *need* to rest after that journey. I know it was a strain, but you did so well."

"I *did* almost crash into the barrier," Delan objected.

"Details. We all made it here, and that's what matters," Zhafaera said, standing and hauling her pack into the closet.

"The good news is, there's a bathroom through here," Delan said, peeking his head through the door on the wall to the left of the bed. "With a tub," he added, smiling.

"Thank the gods," Zhafaera called. "I need a good soak to get the sand out of…well, everywhere." She sighed. "And then it's dresses from here on out. These pants are just too tight.”

Delan wisely kept his mouth shut.

***

Once everyone had cleaned up and changed, they gathered in the gleaming kitchen, taking an inventory of the food they had left. Which wasn’t much.

“We have running water here,” Zhafaera said. “So food is going to be our real challenge.”

“That and learning to use this kitchen,” Sara added. “Although I suppose we could cook over the fireplace in the parlor if it came down to it.” The kitchen was full of several rectangular steel and glass contraptions, none of which were self-explanatory.

“Iris said she would teach us, but it will have to wait until everyone is settled in some kind of housing. There’s only one of her and thirty thousand of us.” Zhafaera rubbed her temples against the headache that was forming. The light streaming in from the back windows wasn’t helping.

“Maybe once leaders and councils have been formed for each building, we can bring them here and have Iris teach them, then they can take it back to their buildings,” Delan suggested.

“Excellent, yes,” Zhafaera said, pointing at him for emphasis.

“As for food, for now we have enough to live off of for another week or so, but Colin and I can go out hunting again,” Ban offered. “There should be plenty of game by the lake.”

Zhafaera hesitated, worried about them going off by themselves. "Only if you go with Tarysa again," she finally said. "And be careful of the rest of the refugees coming in that way."

"I can come with you too," Delan added, getting up from his stool on the other side of the kitchen island. He swayed slightly as he stood.

Zhafaera opened her mouth, but Colin beat her to it. "No way," he laughed. "No offense, but you need a rest. You look like death, and you will definitely shoot yourself in the foot if you even manage to draw your bow."

Delan sat back down, frowning slightly.

Colin and Ban set off immediately, stopping by the parlor to ask Tarysa to join them. The dragon agreed but insisted that Evey go with them as well, much to the young dragon's surprise. Apparently, she'd never actually hunted with her mother before. Zhafaera thought back to when she and Delan found her and had to teach her to hunt. She'd come such a long way, and Zhafaera had to clear her throat to dispel the tightness.

Everyone else made themselves comfortable in the parlor, Zhafaera tucking her feet under her on one of the couches, while Delan sat opposite his father near the fireplace. Sara sat with Amee in a basket by her feet by the front window.

"Tomorrow I'd like to meet with the others in this neighborhood. I want us all to walk back to where the other refugees are being divided into the sky towers and check in on their progress," Zhafaera said to no one in particular.

"Of course," Geon responded. "I'm sure Iris has it

under control, but it never hurts to show yourself to the people. If you feel rested enough, of course."

"I'll be fine," Zhafaera said shortly. She looked over to where Delan sat and smiled. He was already asleep with his head resting against the back of the chair. "Better than some, at least."

"You both achieved something unheard of," Geon continued. "You *both* need to rest. The world will continue to turn without you for a day."

Zhafaera took a deep breath. "I know, it's just hard to let go." She settled back into the cushions of her couch.

Sara pulled out some knitting, and the faint click of her needles quickly lulled Zhafaera into a state of deep relaxation. She was very nearly asleep when there was a sharp knock on the front door, jerking her awake.

"Who on earth…" she began.

"Don't get up," Geon said, standing quickly. "I'll get it."

Zhafaera waited patiently, rubbing her eyes tiredly. She could hear low voices from the entrance hall.

She didn't have to wait long to see who it was. Aroha entered the room, quickly followed by Darcia. Zhafaera's heart fell. She liked both women, but she knew she was about to get a lecture about overdoing it.

Sure enough, Aroha tsked and hurried forward, bag in hand. "You know you've done too much," she started. "So I don't need to tell you. No, don't argue; I can tell by the purple shadows under your eyes. Nearly seven months pregnant and traipsing all over the desert. And don't get me started on *him*," she continued, pointing at Delan, who was still sound asleep. "He's lucky he didn't kill himself and us with him. Gems may be all-powerful, but your bodies are not."

When she stopped to draw breath, Zhafaera held up a hand. Aroha took it and began taking her pulse. "I know we're not invincible," she said. "But Queen Oraesa didn't give us much of a choice. We're lucky she allowed us to flee here at all, considering we're still in Burjan territory."

Aroha snorted. "Like she could have stopped you. Now hush." Zhafaera closed her mouth.

She felt the faint tendrils of Aroha's magic wash over her. Her headache eased, and her tired limbs relaxed. She sighed.

"Would you like to know what you're having?" Aroha asked quietly.

"Can you tell?" Zhafaera asked, surprised. She'd tried to check a couple of times, but she hadn't been able to tell yet if her baby was a boy or a girl. But she hadn't tried in the last few weeks; everything had just been moving too fast.

"I can tell." Aroha smiled.

Zhafaera immediately tried to draw magic and focus inward on herself, only to find she was simply too tired. She couldn't wait. "I want to know," she said excitedly.

"It's a girl."

Zhafaera let out a breath she hadn't realized she'd been holding and put her hands to her face to cover her watering eyes. "I had hoped so…" she whispered. She jerked her head up guiltily. "Not that I wouldn't have loved a boy," she said quickly. "But it does make things easier."

Aroha patted her hand. "It's all right; you don't have to explain why you're happy. Arenthia always has a queen, and after what you went through with your uncle…it's understandable. I imagine you can relax a bit now."

Zhafaera nodded and found herself smiling. "Can I wake Delan and tell him?"

"No, you may not," Aroha said firmly. "I want to examine him, but I'm going to attempt to do that without waking him. Sleep is the best thing for him right now." She left Zhafaera's side and moved quietly to Delan.

As soon as she touched his hand, he jerked awake. "What's happening?" he asked, blurry-eyed and confused.

Aroha sighed. "You're going to have a daughter, but right now I need to examine you."

"The baby's coming *now*?" He practically squealed, jerking upright and looking around for Zhafaera.

Zhafaera felt bad, but Aroha rolled her eyes. "Of course not, you silly man; now calm yourself."

Delan looked at Zhafaera, confused. "Aroha can tell the sex of the baby in the womb," Zhafaera explained. "She says it's a girl."

A look of pure relief came over Delan's face as he smiled. "Truly? That's amazing."

"Hush!" Aroha admonished.

Delan submitted quietly to the rest of Aroha's examination. "Satisfied?" he asked when she pulled away.

"I certainly am not," Aroha exclaimed. "You have worn yourself out completely. If you draw any more power in the next few days, I will not be able to answer for the consequences."

Delan looked sheepish. "At least we made it here."

Aroha softened slightly. "Yes," she said gently. "You did your best and helped a great number of people. But now you must take care of yourself if you want to meet your daughter in a couple of months."

"Understood," Delan said. He looked at Zhafaera. "What about our queen?" he asked. "What are your orders for her?"

"A queen doesn't take orders—" Zhafaera began.

"She needs to rest," Aroha spoke over her. "As do you," she told Delan.

"We'll do our best," Delan answered.

***

The Arenthian mages and nobles trickled into Zhafaera's new residence one by one in the morning, starting even before Zhafaera woke up. By the time they were all there, it was roughly ten in the morning, and they were all eager to see how much progress had been made since the previous afternoon.

They all walked together through the gate and back down the street to where they had left the *real* Iris. Even from a distance, they could see the steady stream of refugees entering at the crossroad and walking away ahead of them. When they got closer, they could see the families were being divided down three streets, each with an Iris copy directing them and giving instructions.

As they drew closer to Iris, she turned and looked at Zhafaera, smiling. "It is going well," she said before Zhafaera could even ask. "This is the last group – those with three or fewer."

314

Zhafaera stumbled and stopped, her mouth hanging open. She took another look at the line of refugees. "But I can already see the end of the line!" She exclaimed. "The medium groups – the four to sevens – they're already in?"

Iris nodded. "Yes, we moved them in overnight; most of them were in by dawn."

"That's completely amazing, Iris," Delan said, clearly as surprised as Zhafaera.

"Amazing doesn't even begin to cover it," Tristain called from behind them. "She's moved almost thirty thousand people two miles through the jungle into new homes in less than twenty-four hours!"

"Twenty-eight thousand, three hundred and thirteen," Iris corrected.

"Didn't we count three hundred and twelve?" Zhafaera asked jokingly.

"A woman gave birth yesterday on the brick," Iris clarified.

Zhafaera blanched. "Gods, and I took all the mages with me," she whispered.

"There was a midwife with her, although I am sure the conditions were not ideal." Iris resettled her wings. "They rode in on one of the supply wagons and are settled in a blue apartment with the rest of their family now." Iris looked over Zhafaera's shoulder. "I would like to meet your friends."

"Of course, how rude of me," Zhafaera said quickly. One by one, she introduced the nobles, giving their name, title, and the role she'd asked them to take on, as some of them would need to work directly with Iris. Lord Jensten in particular was eager to speak to the sphinx about clearing more paths and streets through the jungle, and Zhafaera had to cut him off tactfully. Before long, many of the nobles had set up a time to speak privately with Iris at their homes about the tasks they had been assigned. Zhafaera couldn't believe how easily they readjusted to command when given half a chance.

She allowed the mages to introduce themselves, partly because she didn't know all their names and partly because her mouth was drying out in the desert heat. All told, they had six Water mages and healers, three Earth mages, one Air mage (not including Tristain), and four Fire mages.

When everyone had finished, Iris inclined her head in a respectful bow. "I welcome all of you to Thebes," she said smoothly. "May you be safe and happy here." Her words had a certain ring to them, like what she said had no choice but to be true.

The sun was nearly directly overhead as the last of the refugees passed them and turned onto the side streets towards the entrances of the sky towers.

"It will still take some time for everyone to select their apartments," Iris began. "But my copies can handle it from here." She looked over the nobles. "Lady Greina and Sir Coran, I believe you wished to speak to me first about finding and cultivating food in the jungle. As this is a priority, I believe we can speak now."

As they all turned and walked back towards their homes to the north, Zhafaera nudged Delan.

"What?" he asked quietly.

"This was one of your better ideas," Zhafaera whispered.

Chapter 17

They had been in Thebes for more than a month when the messenger arrived from the direction of the road. It was the day after they celebrated Zhafaera's twentieth birthday, and she was just leaving a meeting with the Sky Council, as they called themselves – the leaders chosen by each building that met with Zhafaera and the other nobles at least every week. For the most part, it was a very effective system, as everyone was able to coordinate directly and communicate their needs. When Sir Coran needed men to round up the jungle cows, he had a hundred volunteers within a day. Iris had been able to quickly teach and spread the knowledge of how to use the electric kitchens found in each home. And the Sky Council had been able to advocate for the people, securing supplies for each building and bringing any issues to attention.

Zhafaera was walking with Delan back from the meeting space – an outdoor amphitheater they discovered in the center of the gated neighborhood. It was the only place nearby able to hold more than a hundred people that usually attended these meetings, including the mages. They could have met somewhere in the city center, but that was further away, and the electricity wasn't on there, so they couldn't use the elevators like they could in the refugee sky towers.

Zhafaera felt like she could use an elevator anywhere she went nowadays. At eight months pregnant, she felt heavy and hot and *hungry* all the time. So when Tarysa and Evey glided down and landed next to her, she groaned. She had been hoping to find a snack before having to deal with anything else, but they wouldn't be in their dragon forms unless it was important. Mostly, they stayed as cats to help keep the humans from being alarmed.

"What is it today?" Zhafaera asked with a false cheer.

Someone has come. Iris is at the barrier now, but if you wish to let them in, you will need to lower the barrier for a moment or walk them through. Tarysa sounded wary.

"Who is it? Can you tell?"

It is a human male.

Zhafaera sighed. So helpful sometimes. "Can you take me there?"

Of course, you both should come, Tarysa said, lowering her shoulder so Zhafaera and Delan could climb up.

In minutes they crossed the city, Zhafaera gripping Tarysa's neck spikes so tight her hands were going numb. She currently had enough trouble balancing on the ground, let alone in the air. Once on the other side of the city, Tarysa dropped quickly, aiming for what could have been the exact spot Zhafaera and her party had originally crossed the barrier when they first found the city.

From this side, she could see a figure on the other side of the barrier, though warped slightly as though looking through old glass. Dismounting with Delan's help, she moved up next to Iris, who stood directly in front of the man on the other side.

"I don't think we should lower the barrier," Delan said finally. "But I can cross over, see what he wants, and bring him back."

"I will allow it." Iris was formal.

Zhafaera nodded. "Go ahead, but be careful. The barrier packs a punch."

"I remember." Delan grimaced but moved forward. For a moment, he seemed suspended in a sea of green and gold sparks. Then he was free, and Zhafaera could see him slump forward on the other side.

Zhafaera could see the two men, but she couldn't hear them, much to her frustration. They spoke for several minutes before the new man took Delan's arm, and they both moved back through the barrier. As soon as they were through, the stranger pitched forward onto his knees, forcing Zhafaera and Iris to take several steps back. Zhafaera could sense the newcomer was an Earth mage.

"Queen Zhafaera," the man finally panted. "I have been sent by Queen Oraesa to invite you back to Zarga to discuss the future of the city of Thebes."

She sighed. "So she wants to kick us out?"

The messenger shook his head vigorously. "No, Your Majesty. She wants to join you here with as many of her people as she can transport."

Zhafaera stared at him in shock. "What changed?" She finally got out.

"We've had word…we've had word that dragons are gathering on the southern coast of Arenthia." His voice shook. "There are rumors that some have already hit

Rayen in Khichoria, but they have mostly evacuated to the mountains. The Burjans…we have nowhere else to go, and Queen Oraesa wishes to re-evaluate this option." He paused and finally looked up. "I was sent to find out what had become of you."

"We are doing quite well, thank you," Zhafaera said coolly. "There is food, and water, and shelter, as promised. And there is room for more people, if Iris agrees." She looked to the sphinx. The messenger followed her gaze for a moment before dropping his eyes again.

"I have already agreed to accept refugees," Iris said calmly and clearly. "More will be accepted."

"Thank you…um…my Lady," the mage choked out.

"Just Iris."

"Yes, of course. Thank you, Iris." He looked to Zhafaera. "Will you come back with me?"

"No, we will find our own way to Zarga, and you should stay here. Even if we delay until dawn tomorrow, we will still beat you back to the city." *Will you fly us to Zarga?* She quickly thought to Tarysa.

Yes, the large dragon replied. *But Evamoria will stay here.* Evey, who'd flown with them, immediately bristled and flared her wings. Her mother swung her long neck to look directly at her daughter, and until Evey winced and looked away. Zhafaera couldn't blame her. She didn't think she could withstand that golden gaze either.

"Are you alone?" Zhafaera asked the messenger.

He shook his head. "My partner is waiting back at the brick. Oraesa could only spare the two of us, and we thought one of us should wait…just in case."

"Fair enough." She tho

ught for a moment, but ultimately, she knew she had to try. As she opened her mouth, Delan put a hand on her arm.

"Is there any chance I can convince you to just let me go?" he asked quietly.

Zhafaera shook her head. "None at all. It will be a quick trip – there and back to coordinate with Oraesa, – and then she can be responsible for evacuating her own people. Three-day trip maximum."

Delan flinched but kept his voice low. "What if they don't *have* three days? If dragons are at Crystal Point, they could be in Zarga in a day. We could be trapped there and not rescue anyone."

"We have to try," Zhafaera insisted.

I can hide us from other dragons if they attack the city, Tarysa put in. *As long as we can get in the air, we will be able to make it out of Zarga.*

"There, that's the worst case scenario," Zhafaera said.

"Okay," Delan relented. "As long as we make it quick."

***

Delan had escorted the messenger back through the barrier to retrieve his partner and bring him to Thebes. They anticipated that they would fly to Zarga and back in less time than it would take for him to return and need to be let in again. After some quick meetings with the other nobles, it was determined that Lord Geon would be in charge in their absence, with Evey remaining by his side. They spent the evening packing a single pack for their short trip and went to bed early to be up before dawn.

The flight itself was uneventful, but it took all day. They left at dawn and arrived just outside the alarm spells right as the sun was setting behind them. Like last time, almost as soon as they passed through the spells, a brick came racing towards them.

"This is feeling uncomfortably familiar," Zhafaera murmured to Delan. Tarysa, back in her orange cat form, was riding on the pack on Delan's back.

"It'll be better this time," he said firmly.

Sure enough, when the brick reached them, they were offered a ride and taken straight to the gates, where they were met by a carriage. Except this time, once they reached the palace, they were greeted by an assortment of servants and, to Zhafaera's surprise, Liara, who immediately ran to Zhafaera and threw her arms around her neck.

"It's so good to see you," Liara whispered to Zhafaera. "The city is in a panic from some of the reports we've heard, and…well…thank you for coming back."

"I'll help however I can, of course," Zhafaera said, somewhat cautiously.

"You must be exhausted," Liara gushed, pulling back and looking at her. "And look at you! Should you even be traveling in your condition?"

Zhafaera pursed her lips, but Delan was the one who answered. "I tried to tell her that, but do you think she listens?" Zhafaera smacked him lightly on the arm, and he grinned. "This is a quick trip."

Liara faltered slightly but recovered quickly. "Come, let me take you to your rooms. Mother will see you in the morning, but tonight you can rest and recover from your journey."

"Thank you, Liara."

Liara led them to the room they used last time and left them to rest. By the time they'd washed and eaten the meal the servants brought them, it was getting late, but they curled up together by the fire, drinking one last cup of tea, something they had precious little of in Thebes.

"How many people live in Zarga?" Delan asked eventually.

"About a hundred thousand," Zhafaera said. She read Delan's next thought. "They can fill the last of the apartments, and the rest can be divided up into the sky towers at the city's center – the office buildings." She was quiet for a time. "The *real* trouble," she continued, "is what happens if they are caught out in the desert between Zarga and Thebes."

"They'd be massacred," Delan agreed. "And I don't think I can transport that many at one time. They'd have to use their own brick system."

"Exactly. We have to make sure that no matter what, they don't lead the dragons to Thebes," Zhafaera said emphatically. "Oraesa has to have her mages cover their tracks."

"She'll see sense, I'm sure," Delan reassured her.

They went to bed soon after, but Zhafaera spent most of the night tossing and turning. By morning, she was tired and irritable, a most unpleasant combination. And she had a new sense of urgency, like something just out of sight was pressing her forward.

Liara came to them after breakfast and led Delan, Zhafaera, and Tarysa directly to her mother's rooms. Queen Oraesa was dressed simply today in white linen, with minimal jewelry and her blonde hair pinned up. She looked older than Zhafaera had ever seen her, and Zhafaera's lingering anger at her faded slightly.

"Welcome, Zhafaera," Oraesa said quietly. "Would you like some tea?"

"Yes, please, thank you."

They took seats in the main living area and were quiet as tea was served. When the servants had retreated again, Oraesa began twisting her hands. She glanced nervously at Tarysa. "I'll start by saying I'm sorry. You were right, and I was wrong." She looked at Zhafaera tiredly. "Happy?"

Zhafaera shook her head. "No, of course it doesn't make me happy to see you in such a state. We need to focus on getting you and your people out of here."

"So this…Thebes…your people are living there comfortably?"

"There are challenges, as with any city, but we are making do," Zhafaera replied evenly.

"Are the protections holding?"

"They have not been truly tested, but Iris, the sphinx who guards the city, assures me no one can penetrate the barrier without her permission or the power of a Gem." Zhafaera touched her chest unconsciously.

Oraesa sighed deeply. "We've done our best here, but

I'm beginning to think it won't be enough. Our Air mages have been scrying; Rayen is in ruins like Arenthia, and there are at least a dozen dragons that have gathered at Crystal Point. I think they intend to hit us next," she ended on a whisper.

"Then it's time to go," Zhafaera said. "You need to begin the evacuation now, today."

"I started preparing supplies the same day I sent the mages to find you," Oraesa admitted. She was silent for a long time, and Zhafaera knew what she was going to ask.

"We can't transport everyone like we did the Arenthians," Zhafaera said gently.

Oraesa's head jerked up. "Why not?" she demanded.

"The amount of power that it took nearly killed us," Delan answered. All eyes turned to him, but he didn't back down. "That was only a third of the people you have here, and transporting anything bigger would require more power, which we don't have. Aside from the fact that we did this a month ago. Zhafaera can no longer put that kind of strain on her body."

Oraesa seemed to deflate. "I should have listened to you then. I can't evacuate a hundred thousand people from this city on my own before the dragons come down on us."

"Yes, you can." Zhafaera was firm. "Your mages can use the existing road and build more bricks to transport people out. Once they reach the curve in the road, it's only a three-day walk to Thebes. It may take time—"

"Time we don't have," Oraesa interrupted.

"But you will be able to evacuate," Zhafaera continued. "You say you have supplies ready – load them up with as many people as you can fit and start sending them on the bricks today. We will fly back tomorrow morning and meet them when they begin to arrive."

There was a long silence. "That is all I can ask, I suppose," Oraesa conceded. "What about housing? How big is Thebes?"

"Iris calculated that there are enough apartments to hold a hundred and fifty thousand people, and the Arenthians are occupying only a fraction of that. There are still apartments left in the larger sky towers, and numerous smaller buildings throughout the residential district. There are additional homes for the mages and nobles," Zhafaera explained. "All of Zarga can fit for sure; the rest of Burja will be a squeeze."

"Anchorsa is a ghost town already," Oraesa told them. "Almost everyone left for Laros weeks ago."

"What about Duranja and Kurja?" Zhafaera asked. Duranja was south and further from the dragons, but Kurja was on the northern border, almost directly across the sea from Southport.

"Duranja is only twenty thousand people, and they can begin coming north by brick once Zarga is evacuated. Residents of Kurja are already living in Zarga."

"Excellent," Zhafaera said. "So we're looking at maybe…a hundred and fifty thousand?"

"That would be a good estimate, yes."

Zhafaera's mind was racing, trying to think of everything they needed to do before the Burjans arrived in Thebes. Getting the electricity running in the office buildings would be a good start, but they also needed a *lot* more supplies. She told Oraesa so.

"Are there any particular supplies that are most necessary?" Oraesa asked.

"Grains," Delan said immediately. "Cotton, cloth for clothing."

"And tea," Zhafaera added with a grin.

"Any whole plants or seeds you can bring will be useful," Delan continued. "There is plenty of water, and we have been clearing some of the jungle to be used as farmland."

Oraesa was nodding. "I understand," she said. "Will you meet with my stewards to help make the arrangements? If you're not leaving until tomorrow, I could use you."

Zhafaera and Delan exchanged a look. "Of course," Zhafaera responded. "We'd be happy to help in any way we can."

Chapter 18

The rest of the day was spent in meeting with various stewards, arranging supplies to be transported to the bricks, while Oraesa began organizing her people. By noon, the first brick was full of supplies and nobles and their households heading out of the city. Apparently several houses had been planning to leave with or without Oraesa's permission, and they were more than prepared to be the first out of the city.

Even though she'd spent most of the day sitting, Zhafaera was exhausted by dusk. She'd described, in detail, the kinds of food they had access to in the jungle, starting with the variety of unusual fruits and ending with the wild chickens they'd been rounding up. She was just glad that the stewards were responsible for the calculations of what would be needed; by the end of the day, her brain felt like mush, and she was grateful that Delan was there to pick up the slack. He'd been the one to explain how they had divided up the apartments for the Arenthians – the color system would be continued for the Burjans as they arrived until all of the apartments were filled.

Tarysa stayed with them through the whole day, refusing to leave their side. Perhaps she felt the same anxiety that Zhafaera felt, as if they weren't moving fast enough. The stewards looked at her nervously but wisely said nothing.

They were walking back to their rooms, hoping to take dinner privately again, when Zhafaera heard someone calling her name. Turning, she saw Councilman Nyto walking quickly towards them from the direction of the throne room.

"Queen Zhafaera!" He was slightly out of breath as he reached them.

"Councilman Nyto," Zhafaera answered. "I'm surprised to see you – I would have thought you'd gone back to Laros by now."

"Tomorrow morning," he said, shaking his head. "I've been helping Oraesa negotiate passage for some of her people to Laros, and when she said she was inviting you back, I knew I wanted to stay until you arrived." He glanced at Delan. "I had hoped to speak to you alone."

Zhafaera shrugged. "Delan will go where I go, and nothing will change that, but perhaps we could walk through the gardens? It's such a nice evening."

"Of course, I understand." Nyto barely hesitated before sweeping his arm in the direction of the gardens and falling in beside them as they walked.

They passed through the interior passages of the palace, which were cool in the harsh heat of the day but rather chilly when the sun went down. They made small talk as they passed several corridors and until they came to the back exit, a tall set of double doors that opened onto a wide terrace. Crossing the terrace, they chose a path and began wandering through the carefully manicured garden, Tarysa stopping every so often to investigate flowers or admire a sculpted bush.

They were deep among the bushes before Nyto stopped and looked around. He looked nervous.

"I don't think anyone followed us," Zhafaera told him. "But I can set a ward if it would make you more comfortable."

Nyto shook his head. "No, that won't be necessary. I just would prefer if this didn't get out to everyone. Not that it won't eventually, but it's probably best if it's a secret…"

Zhafaera looked at Delan and saw her own confusion in his face. "It sounds serious."

"The Council has reconsidered their position on the Ruby," he said quickly. "They want to give it to you now, with the condition that they provide the person to wield it."

Zhafaera hardly dared to breathe. *Three Gems!* She took a deep breath. "Of course, that's quite reasonable," she said out loud. "May I ask what changed their minds?"

"They were impressed that you found the Emerald after three hundred years, with almost nothing to go on but a hunch and the will to walk out into uncharted desert." Nyto hesitated. "I also encouraged them to see the wisdom of your plan after we had word that Rayen had been destroyed. With the threat of dragons growing closer…they decided it was best to give it to you now, while we have the chance."

"Do you have it with you?" Zhafaera asked, shocked.

"No, no, of course not," Nyto said hurriedly. "One, or both of you, will need to come to Laros to claim it. It's hidden near the top of one of our volcanoes, and perhaps it's best if you travel there with our chosen mage so you can advise them…"

Zhafaera and Delan exchanged another glance. She knew what Delan would say before he even opened his mouth. "Don't," Zhafaera whispered.

"I will go with you," Delan said to Nyto. "Zhafaera can't travel that far right now – her healer would have an absolute conniption." He turned to Zhafaera. "We need the Ruby," he said quietly. "One of us has to go."

"Your way back could be cut off if – no *when* – the dragons attack, and you won't be able to walk across the desert." Zhafaera's voice wavered, and she shook herself firmly. "You have to take Tarysa." She held up a hand to cut off his protest. "I can get on a brick tomorrow and be back in Thebes in less than a week."

She could tell Delan was wavering. She reached out and put a hand on his arm, feeling his tension. He opened his mouth and, at that moment, an ear-splitting screech split the air. Zhafaera whipped around, scanning the sky.

"What in the twelve hells is *that*?" Nyto yelled over the noise.

"It's the alarm from the mages in the towers," Zhafaera yelled back, just as the noise stopped. "Dragons are incoming."

"Zhafaera, we have to get out of here *right now*," Delan said, grabbing her arm hard.

Her heart was racing. There was no time to get everyone out, but maybe the mages could hold the dragons off for a little while. That was the plan she'd worked out with them anyway, but it could all go to hell in the next few minutes. She made a decision. "We have to try and get

Oraesa and Liara," she said urgently. "We don't have time to argue," she told Delan and Nyto, turning and running back towards the palace. "Tarysa, can you carry all five of us?"

Yes, Tarysa answered immediately. *And I can cloak us so the dragons will not sense us, as I said before. But it will not protect us if they breathe fire down on us.*

Understood, Zhafaera responded in her mind, unwilling to use more breath to speak. Eight months pregnant was not a great shape to run in.

The first blast came when they were halfway back to the palace. She couldn't see the shields, but she could feel the amount of power being drawn by the mages to the north.

She stumbled when the next blast came from the south. Delan caught her, and together they spun around, trying to see past the jungle surrounding the palace in that direction and into the fight beyond.

Then the screams began ahead of them, from the city, and that was all the warning they had before an enormous dragon, black in the twilight of the evening, came crashing into the upper levels of the palace.

"They have us surrounded," Zhafaera whispered.

Screams rose from all directions, and there was a faint glow to the north. Zhafaera hoped the mages there were holding. The dragon ahead of them took off again, pushing an entire gilded tower over to crash down into the rest of the palace.

Zhafaera started running again, with Delan and Nyto close behind. Tarysa ran slightly ahead of her, leading the way through the maze of trails, back along the paths they'd taken. Suddenly, she stopped and spun, hissing.

Zhafaera got a shield up, bending backwards just as dragonfire rained down on them from the two dragons bearing down on them from the west. The heat from the fire pressed down on them, threatening to overwhelm her, but she held firm, pushing back against the raging flames. She felt Delan drawing power from the Emerald next to her.

The two dragons were headed directly for the palace. As the flames dissipated, a line of black fire shot out from Delan's hands and struck the closest dragon's hide. The scream that echoed from the enormous creature was like nothing that Zhafaera had ever heard. It dipped in the air just before both dragons slammed into the palace, scattering pieces like it was a child's toy.

Then they turned, hissing, angrily looking for the source of the blast.

"Delan…"

"I see them. Take my hand."

Zhafaera gripped Delan's hand tightly, and then Gems responded. They both drew power through the Gems, weaving together and building.

As the dragons pushed off of the palace walls, one flying more awkwardly than the other, Delan let go of Zhafaera and raised his arms.

"Hold a shield against the dragonfire," he murmured to her. Louder he said, "Tarysa, keep us hidden. I don't want them to see what's coming."

As the dragons grew closer, Zhafaera focused on hers.

She felt Delan's power next to her, solidifying into his hands.

Zhafaera, Tarysa's mind-voice sounded alarmed.

I see them. Hold.

They're going to breathe fire right on top of us. Again.

My shield will hold.

Tarysa was right. Just before the dragons were right on them, one split off, breathing fire somewhere just off to their right. The injured one opened its mouth, and fire came straight at Zhafaera. Her shield held, but fire surrounded them, blinding them. But Zhafaera could still *feel* the dragon as it flew above them. She could hear its enormous wings beating and feel the power of its magic echoing through the Sapphire.

She felt Delan strike, his power like a sword and shooting upwards. She wavered as it pushed through her shield, holding on for dear life. Then there was a terrible scream, and blood rained down, covering them all in the hot, sticky mess. The fire stopped, and she released her shield, turning to Delan.

He looked a little gray under his mask of dragon's blood, and she reached out to steady him.

"I'm all right," he said, sounding a little better than he looked.

There was a huge thud behind them, as the dragon he had just gutted hit the ground and skidded, taking half of the once-beautiful gardens with them.

"We need to move," Delan said. "We can't just stay out here in the open."

"Behind you!" Nyto screamed.

Delan and Zhafaera swung around to find the other dragon had returned with another friend. Two more dragons now flew at them from the east. Zhafaera took a deep breath and readied herself. She wasn't sure she wanted to be doused in dragon's blood again, but she *had* killed a dragon before even without the Sapphire.

Then the dragons split up, flanking them.

You've pulled too much power – they can sense the Gems, Tarysa sounded resigned.

Any ideas? Delan asked.

Yes, and it should go better than it did when I fought Evamoria's father, Targan.

Zhafaera felt her shield drop as Tarysa transformed and took flight. There was no time to watch – a huge red and gold dragon was coming straight for Zhafaera. Raising her arms again, she drew power until the air began to crackle and pop around her. Then she waited.

And waited.

Finally, when she could swear that her dragon made eye contact with her and opened his mouth a mere fifty yards away, she released the Sapphire's power.

Lightning rained down on the injured dragon from all directions, some strikes missing as he tried to weave and doge, but most of them hitting all over his body, his wings, passing through his belly to the ground until he slumped and began to fall.

Zhafaera realized at the last second that he was falling right at them. "MOVE!" she screamed to Delan and Nyto, giving them each a small shove. They all dodged right just as the dead dragon passed just over their heads, hitting the ground hard and skidding to a stop right behind where they had been standing.

Another screaming hiss ripped through the air that cut off abruptly. Zhafaera turned in time to see Tarysa banking sharply south, away from the dragon that was dropping like a stone. They watched as it hit the ground and *shattered* into a million pieces. They ducked, covering their eyes as Zhafaera felt tiny shards of stone slicing into her arms.

"Did she just—" Zhafaera heard the shock and awe in Delan's voice next to her, and she peeked out from behind her arm to see him staring. "I think she turned that one to stone."

"Maybe she'll teach you how, but later."

Looking up at the sky, Zhafaera saw that while they had downed three dragons, the damage had been done. The city surrounding them was on fire, with a deep golden glow rising from the other side of the palace. She took a deep breath.

"How many dragons were sent to take the city?" she asked out loud.

I am not sure, Tarysa replied. *No more than ten.*

Just then there was another screech and an enormous crash. They all flinched and jerked towards the palace just in time to see the body of another dragon come flying into the palace, taking down an entire tower as it fell. More screams rose nearby.

"It looks like Zarga's own mages were able to take at least one," Delan said, sounding impressed.

"We have to help them – almost half of the dragons

are down. If we can take more, we might be able to save the city." Zhafaera looked back at the orange glow rising around them. "Or at least, the people. Long enough to get them to Thebes."

Delan gripped her hand tightly. "Zhafaera...I'm not sure I can take another dragon."

Zhafaera stiffened her spine. "There are at least four that have been killed. Hopefully half of what they sent. If we can take down another, we may drive them off." She turned to watch Tarysa land behind them, bracing herself as the ground shook slightly.

Tarysa met her gaze for barely a second before she lowered her shoulder. *Get on,* she thought quickly. *You'll be more mobile from the air.*

Zhafaera, Delan, and Nyto scrambled onto Tarysa's back. They were barely settled when Tarysa flexed and took off, her giant wings propelling them high into the air before Zhafaera had hardly taken a breath. Tarysa rose higher and higher, until Zhafaera could see the whole city laid out beneath her.

And what she saw was nothing but chaos and destruction. There were fires all over the city, from the fragmented palace to the half-demolished sphynx statues at the river entrance. Zhafaera counted an additional four dragons throughout the city. One seemed to be engaged with a small band of mages on the north tower, dodging fireballs and increasingly feeble lightning. As Zhafaera watched, the dragon made a complicated motion through the air, and the tower simply...fell. As she watched, the other towers surrounding the city just melted away, moving like a trail of dominoes that had been knocked over.

There go the mages, she thought glumly.

Delan nudged her and pointed. "Over there," he called over the rushing wind.

Zhafaera followed his hand and saw two other dragons simply flying circles through the city, raining fire down on the dwellings below.

"We need to bring them down!" An idea popped into her head, and she turned to look behind her. The oasis behind the palace, where the aquifer pumped water into the lake, was still untouched. *Get their attention,* she added to Tarysa, sending an image of the lake and hoping Tarysa understood.

Tarysa immediately dove and headed towards the pair. As they came closer to the nearest dragon, looking down on them from above, Tarysa banked, breathing fire towards them as she banked and turned. The dragon she hit roared, and Zhafaera almost lost her balance as she tried to look behind them. Delan tightened his grip as they raced towards the lake.

They're following, he thought to her. *Now what?*

A net, Zhafaera replied. *Force them down into the water.*

Zhafaera, dragons can swim.

Yes, but they still need to breathe.

She felt Delan shrug behind her. *Too late now,* he thought as he grabbed her hand.

Together they drew power through their Gems, feeling the buzz as the Gems reacted to each other. *Like smoothing the sand?* Delan asked?

"Just like it," Zhafaera said. "Drop it into the water, but keep hold of it. We'll use it like seaweed to drag them down."

Tarysa dove again until she skimmed over the top of the palace, flying over the gardens in moments until they reached the lake, dipping so low that her legs were nearly touching the pristine surface of the water.

As they flew, Zhafaera and Delan let the net they were building fall from their hands and into the water on either side, filling the water with their trap lingering just under the surface.

"Nyto, tell me when the dragons have crossed into the water," Zhafaera called behind her, trying to balance and focus at the same time.

She felt him shift behind them. "Not yet!" he called.

"Zhafaera, you are going to have to hold them firmly and deeply in order for this idea to work," Tarysa chimed in.

But it can *work.*

Maybe.

Well, it's a bit late to change the plan now, so you better hope it works, Zhafaera couldn't decide if she was annoyed, scared, or just plain angry at the level of destruction around them. *It's going to work.* "Nyto?" she said out loud.

"Almost…they've crossed into the water!"

Zhafaera risked a glance behind them just as Tarysa said, *We are going to run out of lake very soon.*

"NOW, DELAN!" she yelled.

Zhafaera let the last of the net fall into the water below just as Tarysa began to bank right. Reaching out, Zhafaera let her power flood into the net and felt Delan do the same. As the dragons passed over the deepest part of the lake, Zhafaera released her power upwards. Tendrils of light shot out of the water, wrapping around the two large dragons following them like the tentacles of a kraken devouring a ship.

The dragons screamed as their motion halted and they were pulled directly into the lake, water splashing in all directions. Zhafaera didn't flinch as the warm water sprayed over them, merely shaking the blood and water out of her eyes and focusing on her hold on the dragons. She could feel both of them as Delan's power merged with hers, pulling the dragons down into the depths of the lake as Tarysa pulled up slightly and circled back the way they had come. She began a slow drift around the edges of the lake, flying just under tree height to avoid notice of the other two dragons still demolishing the city.

Zhafaera could feel the struggles of the two dragons underwater growing more and more frantic. The water in the lake began to bubble, and she realized it was boiling as the dragons tried to breathe fire underwater. Her heart sank as she realized she had probably just ruined the lake's ecosystem, but she continued to hold the dragons beneath the surface.

Delan's hand was tight around hers, almost to the point of pain. His hand was slick with blood and water and sweat, but she held on just as tight. She could feel her energy waning, the power of the Sapphire keeping her upright while she fought to maintain enough control and focus to keep the dragons underwater.

Tarysa was on her fourth pass around the lake when the dragon's struggles finally grew slow and then quiet. Zhafaera glanced at Delan. He was pale and sweating, still covered in blood from the dragon he had gutted earlier, so that his face was striped. Zhafaera imagined she wasn't much better.

It took another two passes before Zhafaera felt confident that the dragons were dead underwater.

"Let it go," she croaked to Delan.

She finally let her power drain away, the tentacles and net fading as one. She and Delan slumped against each other, and she felt another hand on her shoulder. Turning her head slowly, she saw Nyto holding his arms around Delan and gripping her tightly. She smiled and took a deep breath.

"Thank you," she said quietly. She wasn't convinced he could hear her over the wind. And the sound of fire. And somewhere, stone was crunching. It was like all the sounds she had put out of her mind while she was focused on drowning the dragons came flooding back in.

Tarysa, get us up high again, she thought, trying to sit up straighter.

Tarysa gave a deep sigh, which was quite loud coming from a dragon. *Promise you will not fall off.*

None of us will fall.

You cannot handle another dragon, and I cannot fight with you on my back.

We need to see.

As they rose in the air above the trees, Zhafaera gasped. The palace was in ruins, the city on fire…but there were no dragons nearby. She sat up and looked around, squinting through the dark and smoke, looking for a sign.

They have moved north, Tarysa said, turning slightly in that direction. *The last two have gone.*

Zhafaera shook her head. "We needed to get all of them. They will tell the others what happened here and come back. With friends."

Yes, but you now have time to move the remaining people to Thebes.

Zhafaera paused. "That number is going to be a lot smaller than it was this morning."

"You told Oraesa weeks ago to leave. It's not your fault that she didn't listen," Delan sounded tired. "Tarysa, land where you can."

Try to land near the palace, Zhafaera interjected. *We need to try to find Oraesa and Liara.*

Tarysa circled back around, slowing and drifting down as she came back to the gardens behind the palace. Zhafaera gripped her back tightly, preparing for the jolt as they touched down so that she wouldn't just bounce off of Tarysa's back.

As soon as they landed, Tarysa dropped her shoulder slowly, letting Zhafaera adjust to the change in position.

"Let me down first," Delan said quietly. "Then I'll help you."

Zhafaera nodded tiredly. In the end, it took both Delan and Nyto's help to get her down. She felt like her belly weighed a thousand pounds, and all she wanted to do was sleep. But they'd killed dragons and driven off the rest. Looking around at the smoke rising in the sky and the rubble that used to be the palace, it didn't feel like a win.

There was no way they could get in the palace to look for Oraesa and Liara. It didn't even look stable enough to search through, but she did see a few people emerging from a crevice where a tower was leaning over a door.

She was just looking around to see where to start when she heard someone screaming her name.

Zhafaera jerked her head up in time to see Liara running towards her at full speed. She opened her arms just in time to catch her younger friend as she threw her arms around her neck.

"Where's your mother?" Zhafaera asked her urgently.

"I don't know, I was in the kitchens, ordering your dinner, when something slammed into the palace and everyone started running and—"

"It's all right," Zhafaera cut her off. But she knew this wouldn't be easy.

The glow to the north had spread all around them. Fire was still engulfing Zarga, and she wasn't sure she had the strength to get it under control.

That was enough for Zhafaera. "Liara," she began gently. "We have to leave. Tarysa can carry us out of here and back to Thebes."

"Of course, but we have to find my mother!" Tears ran down Liara's face, and Zhafaera thought she might be near hysterics.

"Liara, the palace is gone. You can't go back in there." Liara opened her mouth to protest again, but

Zhafaera stopped her. "Ring the bells. We have to get everyone out to safety."

"We're supposed to go to Thebes," Liara said shakily. "But the bricks…"

"They're made of rock," Delan said quickly. "But dragonfire…hopefully they're not melted yet."

"There's not as much fire to the south…" Zhafaera drifted off, thinking. Then she shook her head. "Spread the word. Get everyone onto bricks. Any mages that are left, gather there. We're going to Thebes with *everyone* left in the city. Right now." Nyto ran towards the nearest group of people standing outside of the palace. They scattered soon after he reached them, running south.

Liara jerked away angrily. "You go then! I'm going back in there to look for my mother!"

Zhafaera didn't spare a glance for Delan; he was already in position. Zhafaera reached out and touched Liara's temple before she could pull away. And immediately the younger girl fainted.

Delan caught her and eased her gently to the ground. Zhafaera looked at Tarysa. "There's an easier way to do this."

Tarysa nodded and bent for them to climb back on just as Nyto returned to them. Between the three of them, they got Liara settled on Tarysa's back, holding her up between the men with Zhafaera in front again.

Zhafaera raised her face to the sky and touched her fingers to her throat, taking a deep breath and drawing on the last of her power as Tarysa rose slowly into the sky, keeping as low as they dared. Zhafaera opened her mouth.

"People of Zarga," she called, her voice booming loudly across the city, "the dragons have left. Grab whatever you can and make for the closest brick. You will be led to a safe place."

She could see people below her begin to scurry south. She could only hope they weren't just running away from Tarysa in the sky, and that they would actually reach the brick system. She took a deep breath as they continued their flight over the city. "People of Zarga, the dragons have left. Grab whatever you can…"

***

It took nearly two days to return to Thebes. None of them had spoken a word since leaving Zarga near sunset the day after the dragons razed the city, once Zhafaera was satisfied that the remaining Zargans were on their way to Thebes. She had wanted to stay longer, but Delan and Nyto had insisted she and Liara needed to get quickly to safety, just in case the dragons came back faster than they anticipated.

They couldn't see Thebes ahead of them, but Zhafaera could sense the barrier coming closer. When Tarysa began to slowly lose altitude around noon, Zhafaera tried to pull herself together. They were home and safe, and the people of Zarga would arrive in a few days. They needed to prepare.

Once they had landed and dismounted, Zhafaera reached out for everyone to hold hands to cross the barrier. Liara put herself between Delan and Nyto, avoiding

345

Zhafaera altogether. It hurt, but Zhafaera couldn't blame her. She couldn't have let Liara back in the palace, but hopefully Liara would forgive her in time. Surely Oraesa would have wanted Zhafaera to save her daughter.

Iris was waiting for them on the other side of the barrier. Zhafaera didn't know how she knew when and where they would appear, but she always did. Zhafaera introduced her to Liara.

"Welcome, Princess Liara," Iris said solemnly. Liara's lip trembled as she curtsied to the sphinx, but her back was straight.

"And this is my grandfather, Councilman Nyto of Laros," Zhafaera said as Nyto stepped forward and bowed. "This is Iris," she continued, indicating the sphinx. "She has guarded the city of Thebes for ten thousand years."

"And will for ten thousand more," Iris predicted. "Tell me what happened."

"It was the dragons," Zhafaera explained shortly. "They made it to the city last night, before the evacuation could really start." She sighed. "We fought them off the best we could, but the city has been destroyed. There are bricks of people and a few supplies on the way. Assuming they're not overtaken by dragons, they should be here in the next four or five days."

"We will be ready for them." Iris eyed Zhafaera critically. "Come, let me lead you home. Will Princess Liara be staying with you or setting up her own home?"

"My own home," Liara interjected quickly.

Zhafaera winced. "Liara," she began, "there's no reason you have to—"

"You left my mother there to die. I have *every* reason," Liara hissed.

"She saved you." Delan was calm but firm.

"Saved me for what? My people are dead, my country in ruins, and I'm alone."

Delan shook his head. "That's what Zhafaera thought after she lost her mother, but it wasn't true for her then, and it's not true for you now. There are people who left last night on bricks," Delan reminded her. "They will be here before the end of the week, and they will need you."

Liara slumped and closed her eyes. Zhafaera sighed. "What if you stayed with Tristain?" she asked gently.

The blonde head snapped up, and Liara's eyes were wide. "Could I?"

"I'm sure Tristain won't mind," Zhafaera told her. She knew Tristain well enough to know that.

Iris led them around the lake to the gated neighborhood. Liara paid no attention to the opulent homes; her eyes focused on the ground in front of her. Nyto, on the other hand, looked amazed.

"I can't believe this entire city was in the middle of the desert, and no one knew," he said quietly to Zhafaera.

"It was pure luck that we found it," Zhafaera admitted. "If not for an old map showing a curve in the road…"

"And you found the Emerald."

"Technically, Delan found it."

"I meant what I said about the Ruby." Nyto shook his head. "We're going to have to find a way to get to Laros, and soon."

Zhafaera took a deep breath. And another. "I can't

worry about that right now, with new people coming in. We have so much to manage here. But Delan can go with you, just like we said." She reached out and found Delan's hand, gripping tightly. "You can both ride Tarysa, if she agrees, and once things are more settled here. I may need you to help me lower the barrier for larger groups to come through," she defended.

Delan nodded. "We probably need to let things settle over Zarga for a while anyway. I'd rather not run into dragons again if we can help it."

"Exactly," Zhafaera breathed, relaxing some. They had reached Tristain and Ranj's mansion, and Zhafaera and Liara walked up to knock on the door. When Tristain opened the door a few minutes later, bleary-eyed, Liara threw herself into his arms. As he patted her back soothingly, he met Zhafaera's gaze, his own eyes widening in shock.

Zhafaera drew herself up, pulling herself together. "I'm going to sleep for a few hours," she told him firmly. "And then I want to see the Sky Council. We have work to do."

Epilogue

Evamoria peeked carefully over the edge of the roof she perched on, her long talons curling around the gutter. Out of the corner of her eye, she caught sight of Iris, the sphinx of Thebes, disappearing around a corner ahead. There was an amphitheater nearby where the Sky Council met every week, but somehow Evey didn't think Iris was headed there in the middle of the night.

Pushing off silently from the roof of the home she perched on, Evey rose above the street and made to follow.

Cutting diagonally across from the direction Iris had gone, Evey started looking for her next perch. They were still in the section of the city where the nobles were currently living, but they were quickly coming up on the cultured garden that sat at the very northern tip of the city, near the barrier. Evey could feel the barrier's magic – like a constant hum moving over her sensitive skin, getting firmer as she got closer.

Just as she was starting to wonder if she had lost Iris, the sphinx appeared from under a tree just ahead. Evey pulled up short and dropped a few feet as Iris looked directly at her. Well. Her hunting skills still weren't perfect. And the sphinx *was* thousands of years old. She decided to land as gracefully as she could a few yards away from Iris.

Iris started at her long enough that Evey had to try not to squirm. "I had intended to do this alone, but they will know you are here. They do not like being spied on," Iris finally said.

Who? Evey asked. *Are you meeting someone?*

"The Fae have called me," Iris said simply. Evey's blood ran cold. She had heard of the Fae, both briefly from Iris and from the elder dragons in her mountain home. They were not spoken of often, and when they were, even the dragons hesitated.

"You may come with me, or turn back now," Iris continued. "But if you continue to try to hide and spy, they will kill you when they see you."

Evey suppressed a shiver, stretching her neck to cover it. She took a deep breath and looked around. Delan and Zhafaera needed to know what was happening, and she wasn't sure she entirely trusted Iris to tell them. *I will come with you,* Evey said.

"Very well." Iris turned and cut across the lawn of the last home to follow the road into the gardens. Evey quickly followed.

Iris followed the central path, moving quickly and ignoring the statues and trees around them until the path split off in five spokes at the center. Choosing the bricked path to the north west, Iris moved into a darker, shadier part of the garden that Evey had never explored before.

Ferns and vines lined the bricks and encroached on the path as they moved deeper and deeper into shadow.

Iris turned a corner and came to a sudden stop, and Evey jumped. The barrier's hum was almost unbearable to her; Evey assumed it was just beyond the stand of trees to the left. Ahead was a wooden archway covered so heavily in flowering vines that it looked alive. Iris stepped to the side and tilted her head, indicating the archway. "This is it," she said simply.

Evey tilted her head. She could feel the power coming off the archway, even as still and silent as it appeared. Iris sat directly in front of the arch and waited.

Ten minutes passed, and Evey was struggling to stay focused on the arch when a small, white-blue light appeared in the center of the arch. The light grew rapidly until it filled the entire archway, rippling slightly but giving off no heat. A dark shadow appeared in the middle, quickly growing into the shape of a human as it grew larger. But as they stepped out of the arch, Evey could immediately tell they were not, in fact, human at all. A cold shiver ran down her spine as the Fae's eyes slipped over Iris and immediately locked her gaze with theirs. She reflexively tried to draw on her magic, but there was a flicker of icy power, and the next thing she knew, she was sprawled out on her side on the brick path. She flinched at the pressure on her wing and tried to jump up and towards the Fae, but found that she couldn't.

"Do not resist. You are not the one we need," the Fae said flatly as the pressure around Evey intensified. Their head turned to face Iris. "We called you, not your guests. We allowed Tarysa and her daughter as a matter of course, but the humans…these *refugees* you have taken in…Thebes is not a place for stray animals."

Evey felt her scales flash in anger. She struggled

again, preparing to defend her friends, but before she could move, the Fae met her eyes again, and she found she couldn't form words.

"Evamoria, you would do well to remain silent." She felt their gaze flow over her skin, and she felt as though she was being examined inside and out. The Fae blinked, and the feeling lifted, along with the pressure holding her in place. "You are very young, and the loss of a kit would be unfortunate."

The moonlight shimmered off of the Fae's pale skin as they turned back to face the sphinx. Evey scrambled to her feet, quickly trying to recover her dignity. Evey stretched her wings and refolded them, but the Fae ignored her. She focused on Iris, who gave a slight twitch of her wing. Evey took the hint and moved closer to the sphinx.

"I am surprised you waited so long to object to the humans," Iris was saying. "The barrier was compromised for almost two months—"

"We have no objection to the humans remaining here, Iris, no matter how distasteful," the pale visitor interrupted. They didn't seem impatient, exactly. But there was a certain urgency under the Fae's calm exterior. "The barrier was not permanently damaged, and the city can hold many more humans than this."

Iris inclined her head and Evey belatedly followed suit. When she looked back at the Fae, they were directly in front of Iris. Evey took an involuntary step back, startled by how quietly they moved.

"We want the girl," the Fae whispered.

Evey leapt forward and ran face first into Iris' outstretched feathered wing. She screeched in frustration.

Suddenly Evey's mouth clamped shut as cold fingers wrapped around her muzzle. Iris retracted her wing, and Evey came face to face with the Fae. They blinked slowly, and Evey relaxed, dropping her head. The hand did not let go.

"Zhafaera is needed here," Iris said slowly from somewhere above Evey's head.

"When we call you here next, you will bring her to us. Alone." They spoke as if Iris' cooperation were a foregone conclusion.

"She is pregnant. She will be giving birth very soon."

"Precisely."

Evey tried to shake the hand off of her face, but the grip tightened, and she whimpered.

There was silence for some time, and none of the three immortals moved. "You would make a trade?" Iris finally asked.

Evey whimpered again. Trade Zhafaera for *what*? What could possibly be so important to consider losing Zhafaera?

"A trade is what she needs and will be for everyone's benefit. She has a plan. Bring her."

Iris shifted next to her. "I will."

Evey struggled fiercely against the hand on her muzzle. The Fae jerked her head up by the nose and held her firmly. Their eyes were nearly black in the low light, and they bored into Evey's brain.

"I have had enough of you. You will return home and forget. Now."

Evey's world went black.

www.ingramcontent.com/pod-product-compliance
Lightning Source LLC
Chambersburg PA
CBHW032148190726
48290CB00005BB/1465